A Woman Scorned

by

Marilee Brothers

This is a work of fiction. Names, characters, places, and incidents are either the product of the author's imagination or are used fictitiously, and any resemblance to actual persons living or dead, business establishments, events, or locales, is entirely coincidental.

A Woman Scorned

Contact Information: info@thewildrosepress.com

Cover Art by *Debbie Taylor*

The Wild Rose Press, Inc.
PO Box 708
Adams Basin, NY 14410-0708
Visit us at www.thewildrosepress.com

Publishing History
First Crimson Rose Edition, 2020
Trade Paperback ISBN 978-1-5092-3347-2
Digital ISBN 978-1-5092-3349-6

Published in the United States of America

I frowned at the computer. "Play hasn't started yet."

"Mickey Warren's out there," Rita said. "He always sneaks out early to get tuned up before his tee time."

I clucked my tongue in disapproval. "Totally against the rules, but if his foursome doesn't mind, who am I to—" I turned and gazed out the window. "Oh, this isn't good. Two blasts are the rule for a birdy. One long blast means there's an emergency."

Rita wiped her hands on her apron and joined me at the window. "Oh my God, is that Sofia?"

Behind the wheel of a golf cart, my daughter tore down the middle of the eighteenth fairway. The back tires spit up chunks of wet grass. A second cart, driven by head greenskeeper, Sammy Espinosa, raced along the cart path. Before I could respond, my cell phone burst to life.

"Mom! Mom! It's Mickey Warren. He's facedown on the eighth fairway. I think he's dead. I called 911."

Rita and I raced to the door, reaching it at the same time. We bounced off each other, regained our balance and stumbled through. Sirens wailed in the distance.

Sofia's golf cart shuddered to a stop. She bailed out and ran over to me, her olive complexion tinged yellow. Her brown eyes were wide with shock. "He looks dead, Mom. I think he's dead."

Praise for Marilee Brothers

1st Place - Booksellers Best

Finalist in the following:

Emerald City Opener
Phoenix Desert Rose Golden Quill
Write Touch Readers' Award - Wisconsin RWA
Beacon Contest - First Coast Romance Writers
River City Romance Writers - Duel on the Delta
Heart of Denver - Molly Award

Dedication

To my sweet, wonderful, goofy golf girlfriends.
You know who you are.
Thank you for your encouragement
and steadfast support.
Keep your head down and hit 'em long and straight.

Chapter One

The alarm on my phone pinged. 6:58 p.m. My two-minute warning.

Late again.

I punched the accelerator, checking the rear view mirror for flashing lights. The monthly board meeting for the Fairway to Heaven golf course commences precisely at seven, chaired by Mickey Warren, filthy rich owner of a car dealership and lousy golfer.

For the McKenna family, Fairway to Heaven is a vital part of the air we breathe. It's a four-generational thing. My grandfather, Victor McKenna, was one of the founders. Ed McKenna, my dad, appointed himself treasurer in perpetuity. My daughter Sofia's summer job is toiling on the groundskeeping crew, specifically keeping the greens in pristine condition.

I'm Libby McKenna and—not to brag—a highly skilled multi-tasker. I have multiple jobs at the golf course. I also supervise the groundskeeping crew. Answer phone calls. Set tee times. And field complaints about the condition of the golf course. Because complaints usually follow a bad round of golf, I don't take them to heart. I file them in my imaginary Cause and Effect file.

Finally at my destination, I followed a Harley Davidson Electric Glide into the parking lot. The bike carried two leather-clad riders. The driver was big and bulky, obviously male. His passenger was diminutive and wrapped around the guy's back like a baby chimp clinging to mama. Daddy and son? Daughter? Color me intrigued. Despite being late, I pulled in next to them and parked.

As they dismounted and removed their helmets, I stepped out of my jeep. The two advanced toward me. First impression: The guy was all bushy black hair, huge smile filled with sparkling white teeth adorned with a flash of gold. His slate gray eyes were punctuated with coal-black pupils. Despite the smile, the overall effect was a bit intimidating. His female rider wasn't a child, but possibly the tiniest woman I'd ever seen. Dyed auburn curls cascaded down her back. Upon closer inspection, her childlike appearance was deceiving. Tiny lines around pale blue eyes told me she would never see forty again.

The man extended a hand and boomed, "Hi there, I'm Reverend Farley Faraday and this is my wife, Faith."

"Oh, um," I stammered as he gripped my hand in a paw the size of a catcher's mitt. "You're him. Right? Farley on a Harley. I've seen your billboard."

I received a benevolent smile. "That's me all right. I hang out at the Last Bus Stop to Salvation Church where we kick Satan to the curb every damn day."

"Nice to meet you both." I freed my hand and stepped back.

"And you are?"

"Oh, sorry. I'm Libby McKenna. I'm here for the board meeting."

Faith Faraday linked arms with her husband and gave me a brief, mirthless smile. "What a coincidence.

So are we."

The meeting was underway when we entered the conference room. Actually, entering is too weak a word. As we approached the door, the Faradays stepped around me and pushed the door open. They stood, framed in the open doorway as if expecting a round of applause or a photo shoot.

Janice Pomeroy, the recording secretary who'd been reading the minutes of last month's meeting, stopped mid-sentence, apparently mesmerized by our entrance.

Due to my tardiness, I tried to be invisible. I slipped around them and plopped down on the chair next to my dad. The Faradays remained standing.

"You know them?" Dad murmured.

I shook my head.

"They're bad news."

Knowing my dad, his comment could be a multiple-choice question on a test titled, What's Wrong With the Faradays? I ticked off the possibilities. Were the Faradays… behind in their golf dues? Not picking up their dog poop? Neglecting their lawn? Or playing their music too loud after ten p.m.? The answer? Soon to be revealed.

Mickey Warren, a frown puckering his forehead, stood. "Glad you could make it, Libby."

His tone was slightly sarcastic, my punishment for being late. I nodded and slunk lower in my chair.

"Would you like to introduce your friends?'

My friends?

I bolted upward. "Oh, they're not my friends. I mean, maybe they could be, but we just met in the parking lot for the first time and happened to walk in together. Total coincidence."

An uncomfortable silence followed. Was Mickey actually expecting me to introduce these people? Faraday stood next to the wall, a veritable mountain of a man. Faith had both hands wrapped around his massive forearm. Faraday's dark gaze swept over the board members, lingering over each one as if trying to read secret thoughts. He didn't speak.

The lengthy silence filled me with dread. What if he had an ax to grind? Pulled out a handgun and started firing? I squirmed in my chair, unsure what to do. As usual, Dad sensed my discomfort.

He rose. "I'm Ed McKenna. You're Faraday, right?"

Faraday flashed his megawatt smile. "Yes, I'm Reverend Farley Faraday and this is my wife, Faith. We're here as leaders of our church, The Last Bus Stop to Salvation."

"This is a private board meeting, Reverend, and you're not on the agenda, but if you have something to say regarding our golf course, we'll accommodate you."

"Actually, Ed, we've quite a full slate tonight. How about next month?" Mickey Warren said.

Faraday reached inside his leather jacket and pulled out a large envelope. "This won't take long, Chairman Warren. I was hoping to deliver it to Bruce Hargraves, the actual owner of the golf course, but I heard he's out of the country."

"Isn't he always?" Dad said.

Faraday strode to the head of the table. Faith, still clinging to his arm, had to take teensy, tiny baby steps to keep up. I bit back an inappropriate snicker.

Faraday handed Mickey the envelope. “This document is signed by the members of our church, a veritable multitude I might add. The name of your golf course offends us. We want you to change it. Correct me if I’m wrong, but I believe your front nine is called Hell and the back nine Heaven.” He paused until Mickey nodded. “You even have blasphemous names for individual holes, like Purgatory Pit, Serpent’s Tail, God’s Little Acre and Pearly Gates. Ignore us at your own risk. God has a way of punishing sinners. We plan to picket your property, our legal right according to the constitution of this great country. We’ll be leaving now. Goodbye and God bless. If you don’t have a church home, please consider joining us and we’ll help you kick Satan to the curb.”

Mickey’s mouth fell open in surprise. He stared at the envelope without replying. My dad was not similarly afflicted.

As the two headed for the door, Dad, my hero, yelled, “In your dreams. Farley on a Harley, my ass!”

Chapter Two

After the Faradays left, the room was eerily silent except for my father who muttered a string of obscenities. Finally, Janice Pomeroy raised her hand like she was in algebra class and couldn't figure out what X equaled.

"For God's sake, Janice, you don't have to raise your hand," Mickey barked. "Speak up!"

Chastised, she squeaked, "About the Faradays. Shall I put their request in the minutes?"

Mickey shrugged. "Beats me.'

Dad slammed a fist onto the table. "You think you can sweep this under the rug? They'll be out in full force tomorrow with picket signs. I vote to put it in the minutes."

A loud discussion followed. Bottom line: The board of directors will not cave to Faraday's demand. The name of the golf course is Fairway to Heaven and will remain as such.

"Faraday mentioned individual holes. Maybe we should list each one by name and state we no intention of changing them," I suggested.

"Excellent idea, Libby." Mickey rewarded me with a lascivious wink for my brilliance.

Because I needed my job, I fought an eye roll and the urge to utter, Save it for some airhead bimbo.

After we finalized our plan regarding the Faradays,

Janice finished reading last month's minutes. Time for new business.

Stella Roy, president of the ladies' division, was first on the agenda. She stood and, I swear, snorted like an angry bull.

"Damn it, Mickey, the guys are still peeing in the bushes behind the number twelve tee box. This has to stop. I told you about it last month. You said you'd take care of it. You didn't."

I glanced at my dad. He was trying to disguise a guffaw as a coughing fit. Unsuccessfully. Dad had a special name for Stella. B-Four. Big. Blonde. Busty. Broad.

"Behave yourself," I whispered.

Mickey waved a hand toward his best buddy Earl Tomlinson, member at large. "I delegated it to Earl. So, Earl, you got a pee-pee report?"

"Nope."

Stella puffed up in righteous indignation. Her angry glare darted back and forth between the two men. "Of course not, since you two are the biggest perpetrators. And let me make this crystal clear. When I say biggest, I'm not talking about your talleywhackers."

Nervous chuckles rippled through the gathering.

Stella was not amused. She whirled and pointed at Janice Pomeroy who hunched over her notebook, pen frozen in hand. "I want this recorded in the minutes. Everyone in the ladies' division will get a copy."

Janice nodded and began scribbling furiously.

Mick sighed. "Oh, for God's sake, Stella. Is it really such a big deal?"

Stella settled her ample butt back in the chair. "I've had complaints. There's a simple solution. Post a sign that says no urinating in the bushes."

"Oh, yeah, that'll work," Dad said.

Stella narrowed her eyes at him, but held her tongue.

"Libby will take care of it. Okay, Libby?" Mickey said,

"Yes, I'll take care of it."

Dad patted my knee. "I'll make the sign, kiddo."

I nodded my thanks.

Mickey checked his agenda. "Ed, treasurer's report?"

Before the meeting started, Dad had handed out a financial report for each board member. He didn't bother to stand. "We're solvent. Check the report."

Mick chuckled. "Excellent. Man of few words. Still doing the bee thing?"

Dad had an active bee colony and sold his honey under the label, Nun of Your Beeswax. It featured the image of a scowling nun with a ruler clutched in her hand.

"Yep."

"That special honey of yours is something else."

Alarm shot through my body. I inhaled sharply. Oh, crap, don't mention the special honey.

"Damn straight," Earl chimed in.

"Special honey?" Stella asked.

Mick chuckled. "You could use some, sweetie. Do you a world of good."

Time to change the subject. I shot out of my chair. "Tristan has a special coming up. Right, Tristan?"

"Relax," Dad whispered.

Tristan Kensington the Third, Fairway to Heaven's golf pro, sprawled in his chair. At the sound of his name, he catapulted upward. "Yes, indeedy. Seventy-five dollars an hour for private lessons, fifty dollars for group."

With an obsequious grin, he tilted his head toward Mickey. "Don't judge me by Mickey's slice, though. It's still a work in progress."

"Tristan the Turd still has his nose up Mickey's behind. That slice will never be fixed. Ever. Cash cow," Dad murmured.

"Hush," I said.

Tristan the Turd was named for his father, Harold Tristan Kensington Junior. He chose the moniker Tristan to distinguish himself from his father who preferred to be called Harold T.

"Looks like it's time for the handicap report. We'll find out who's been naughty and who's been nice. Herb?" Mickey said.

Tristan and Earl chuckled. Janice kept her gaze fixed on her notebook. Stella checked her cell phone. Anticipating another zinger from Dad, I shot him a warning glance. Having completed his report, he slouched in his chair, eyes at half-mast.

Herb Talcott shuffled papers and cleared his throat, his gimlet gaze fixed on Warren. "Unfortunately, we still have members who flaunt the rules. As you know, it's my job to make sure the playing field is level which requires people to honestly record every round of golf they play."

Mickey tilted his head toward his buddy, Earl, who then realized it was his turn to speak. "And you do a hell of a job, Herb."

Momentarily taken aback by the compliment, Talcott blinked rapidly and stammered, "Well, um, thank you, Earl. However," he continued, "there are those among us who still ignore the basic rules. Like sneaking out on the course and practicing before starting the day's play."

Warren averted his gaze and shrugged. "Anything else, Herb?"

Before Talcott could reply, the door to the conference room flew open with such force, it banged against the wall with a resounding thud. Two women stood in the doorway, their fiery gazes darting around the room before zeroing in on Mickey Warren.

Dad was now fully awake. "Uh-oh. Wife and girlfriend alert."

Nostrils flaring ominously, Mickey's wife, Heather, advanced toward her husband. Fairway to Heaven's cocktail waitress, Tammy Witherspoon, was close on her heels. Tammy's fists clenched, her eyes blazing with fury.

Dad straightened in his chair, a broad smile blooming on his face. He winked at me. "Mickey is so screwed. Let the games begin."

Chapter Three

I was on my way home, trying to process the weirdness of the evening when my cell phone rang. I checked the screen. Juliana Russo, my best friend since kindergarten. "Hey, girl! Any good news to share about the book?"

I pulled over to the curb and hit answer.

"Hey, yourself. Sadly, the rejections are still pouring in."

The master plan for my life did not include toiling behind the counter of the local golf course until I shriveled with age and became increasingly bitter with regret. I'm a decent writer with some published short stories and poetry to prove it. My first attempt at finding a publisher was akin to keeping my eye on the rainbow while bumping down a road lined with potholes.

"Do I have a deal for you! Wherever you are, stop, turn around and come to my house. You won't regret it."

Intrigued, I felt compelled to offer something in return. "I have news for you too. You won't believe what just happened at the board meeting."

As I drove to Jules's house, I filled her in on the bizarre evening, saving the best for last, Mickey Warren's domestic crisis. I paused for breath after describing the two women marching in, hatred in their eyes and violence on their minds.

"Oh my God, then what happened? Details, I need details."

"Remember, this goes no further. We were behind closed doors. At least we were until those two busted in."

"Any blood spilled?"

"Not while we were there," I said. "We all froze in our chairs. Heather was spitting mad and Tammy was screaming at Mickey. 'You bastard, you said you were leaving your wife!' Mickey's face turned bright red. He ordered everybody but Earl out of the room. Not sure what happened after that."

"No worries, your secret's safe with me. But trust me, it'll be all over town by morning. Stella Roy is a huge gossip. Herb Talcott too."

"Not to mention my dad. He probably can't wait to spread the news. He's not a big fan of Mickey Warren."

I pulled into the driveway of Jules's two-story house where she lived with her two teenage kids. Her ex-husband, a commercial pilot, cheated on her one too many times and was history. In Jules's words, Larry gave the term "layover" a whole new meaning.

Jules's art was recently featured in a one-woman show at a local gallery. A talented artist, her landscapes depicting the unique steppe shrub terrain of eastern Washington State were a hot item.

Jules stood in the open doorway, a glass of wine in each hand. "Get your butt in here, 'cause I can't wait to tell you the news."

Jules was loyal as hell. She knew how much I loved writing and would not let me give up on my dream. Because of her, we'd started our own custom greeting card business. Words by Libby. Art by Juliana. Our logo was on the back of each card. The image featured two little girls with their arms slung around each other's shoulders. Our names, Lib&Jules, were written in flowery cursive beneath the picture.

I took a slurp of wine and headed for my favorite chair. Jules settled onto the couch and picked up the sketchpad never far from her reach. She extracted the pencil tucked behind her ear and drew as her words spilled out.

"Do you know the Cavendishs? Willard and Abigail Meacham Cavendish to be exact? Old money, my sweet. Abigail inherited a fortune from her lumber baron father before the business went south."

"Don't think I run in their circle."

She shot me a look, punctuated with a series of significant eyebrow rises. "They love my landscapes, which is a good thing. As you know, our greeting card business isn't exactly raking in the dough."

"Is that secret code for we're going broke?"

"No, no, dear friend, but I have something better for you." Upping the drama, she paused, her eyebrows still doing their up-and-down dance.

"So are you going to tell me?"

"It seems Abigail Bingham has always wanted to write a sexy romance novel. Turns out she can't write worth a damn, but she'll pay big bucks if somebody writes it for her."

I stared at her, trying to process the information. "She's looking for a ghost writer?"

"Exactly. I told her you're a talented writer, which you are. She wants to meet you."

"And if I choose to write this book, my name won't

be on it?"

Jules nodded. "She'll require you to sign a non-disclosure agreement."

"And by big bucks you mean…?"

"How does twenty-five thousand sound?"

Incredulous, I squeaked, "Dollars?"

"Trust me, it's a drop in the bucket for sweet little Abigail. Need time to think it over?"

I blinked rapidly, trying to calm my racing mind. Could I write a full-length book? A sexy romance? Damn straight I could. I tried not to appear too eager. "Well, I could meet with her, see what she has in mind."

Jules grinned. "Good news since I made an appointment for you to meet Abigail on Friday. Want me to tag along?"

"Yes, please." I drew a shaky breath. "Oh, Jules, you have no idea how much the money will help us. I've always hated the thought of Sofia being saddled with debt when she graduates from college." I wiped away a few tears.

Jules set her sketchpad down, stood and held out her arms. "Anything for my best buddy."

We hugged and both cried a little.

As I headed for the door, Jules said, "Almost forgot. I need a verse for Cheryl Abbot's anniversary card. ASAP."

I sighed. "Here's the problem. She wants me to include the word Chevy. Apparently the first time they did it was in a Chevy Malibu. What rhymes with Chevy? And, don't say heavy because Cheryl weighs about three hundred pounds."

"Fleshy?"

I snickered. “You’re a big help.”

“What about free verse?”

“She wants it to rhyme. I’ll work it out. Text you soon.”

Jules returned to her sketchbook.

I paused, one hand on the doorknob. “Can I see what you’re drawing?

Jules was very private about her art. She didn’t like to share until it was perfect. Not this time. With a mischievous grin, she held up her sketch.

“Idea for a new greeting card. For that special occasion when your wife finds out about your girlfriend.”

With a few strokes of her pencil, Jules had captured the moment perfectly. Two angry women chased a man toting a golf bag. One of the women wielded a rolling pin, the other, an upraised beer mug.

“All it needs is a caption. If you’re gonna cheat, ya better beat feet.”

Jules lifted a hand in farewell. “Love ya, girlfriend.”

“Love ya back.”

Chapter Four

Though it was only a short drive home, I fought to keep my eyes open. After a full workday and the emotionally charged board meeting, all I wanted was a bubble bath and bed. Dad's truck wasn't in its usual spot when I pulled into the driveway. Probably with his longtime girlfriend, Suzy Reynolds, spreading the news. Daughter Sofia was also missing. Right on cue, my phone pinged with an incoming text from her.

—Hi Momser. Ran into some friends from school. Be home soon. Don't wait up. Love ya. No worries, I'll be at work on time. We're sanding the greens tomorrow so get ready for a lot of bitching.—

Dad's ill-tempered attack cat Clawdius guarded the back door of the house. I stepped around him.

"Am I the only one in this household without a social life?"

Clawdius snarled his agreement and half-heartedly swiped at my ankles, claws extended. I darted out of the way.

"So, Clawdius, you're a fully intact tomcat. Why aren't you out tomcatting around?"

The cat hunched his back and hissed, before stalking away in a huff.

"The truth hurts, huh?"

Though weary to the bone, sleep eluded me. After tossing, turning, and pounding the pillow, I gave up and went to my writing spot in the breakfast nook, determined to finalize Cheryl Abbot's anniversary verse. After a couple of false starts, I texted the words to Jules.

—I know it's cheesy, but, trust me, she'll love it.—
—From a bevy of beauties, she was his pick.
Inside the Chevy down by the crick.
Their spark of love became a flame.
Across the years, they've shared a name.
The flame still burns as hot as ever.
When will it die? Never!—

—Oh, my, if you say so. Now go to sleep. No bad dreams. Okay?—

—No guarantee, but I'll try.—

Trying didn't work. After several hours of fitful slumber, the familiar nightmare returned. Panicky and gasping for air, I tried to claw my way to consciousness. The drumming of my heart provided a rhythmic background to the desperate struggle. The damp, dark walls of the cave moved inward.

Within seconds, my escape route would be blocked. My gaze fixed on the shrinking glimmer of daylight. Run, Libby, run! But running was impossible. My feet were leaden, stuck to the slimy floor of the cave. I opened my mouth to scream for help.

I awoke, shaky and dry-mouthed then rose from my bed. I walked to the window and searched the night sky for the brightest star.

"Mama, miss you."

Claustrophobia invaded my soul when my mother died. My twelve-year-old mind fixated on the image of her casket as it was lowered into a dark, gaping hole. Searching the night sky for the brightest star and picturing my mother's beautiful face always had a calming effect. When my heartbeat slowed to its normal rhythm, I returned to bed.

"Mom." Sofia tiptoed into the room. "Are you okay? The cave dream again?"

"Yeah." My voice was hoarse, as if I'd been screaming in real time.

Sofia climbed in next to me and snuggled close. I drew in deep, calming breaths, willing myself to enjoy the comfort of my daughter's warm presence. A year of college under her belt, nineteen-year-old Sofia considered herself an adult. Therefore, mother-daughter cuddle moments were rare and to be cherished.

"It's funny," Sofia murmured. "When I was little and had a nightmare, you always came to me. Guess it's my turn now."

"Tables turned."

"The McKenna girls and their hang-ups, huh? You and tight places. Me and gory stuff."

I chuckled. "Guess it's a good thing we're perfect in every other way."

We fell silent. Sofia turned onto her side. Her breathing became rhythmic and regular. Finally drowsy, I closed my eyes,

Sofia's clear voice startled me into wakefulness. "Tell me more about the dream. All you ever say is you're stuck in a cave."

I turned and snuggled against my daughter's back, spooning like we did when Sofia had her night terrors years ago. "Not much to tell."

Not exactly the truth. But how do you tell your

daughter that had it not been for my claustrophobic tendencies, a midnight trek into a narrow cave with a handsome Italian spelunker, and subsequent panic attack, Sofia would not have been conceived? No, some things are better left unsaid.

Sofia persisted. "It has to do with him, doesn't it? Antonio Carone. Just saying his name makes Pop's eyes bug out."

I gave her a squeeze and diverted the conversation. "Have you changed your mind? Do you want to meet your father?"

Sofia flipped over and pressed her forehead against mine. "Hell, no. Pops raised me. I don't give two hoots about the sperm donor. Got it?"

"Got it."

"Good enough for me."

Smiling in the dark, I murmured, "Me too."

Chapter Five

The next morning, I stood behind the pro shop counter staring at the computer screen and list of upcoming foursomes. My concentration was so intense, the sound of Gabriel's Horn barely registered in my consciousness.

"Sounds like some old fart got a birdie. Maybe he'll tip more than fifty cents on his next brewski," called Rita, manager of the adjoining bar and grill.

I frowned at the computer. "Play hasn't started yet."

"Mickey Warren's out there," Rita said. "He always sneaks out early to get tuned up before his tee time."

I clucked my tongue in disapproval. "Totally against the rules, but if his foursome doesn't mind, who am I to—" I turned and gazed out the window. "Oh, this isn't good. Two blasts are the rule for a birdy. One long blast means there's an emergency."

Rita wiped her hands on her apron and joined me at the window. "Oh my God, is that Sofia?"

Behind the wheel of a golf cart, my daughter tore down the middle of the eighteenth fairway. The back tires spit up chunks of wet grass. A second cart, driven by head greenskeeper, Sammy Espinosa, raced along the cart path. Before I could respond, my cell phone burst to life.

"Mom! Mom! It's Mickey Warren. He's facedown on the eighth fairway. I think he's dead. I called 911."

Rita and I raced to the door, reaching it at the same time. We bounced off each other, regained our balance and stumbled through. Sirens wailed in the distance.

Sofia's golf cart shuddered to a stop. She bailed out and ran over to me, her olive complexion tinged yellow. Her brown eyes were wide with shock. "He looks dead, Mom. I think he's dead."

Sammy approached. "He's dead all right." He used his finger to make a slashing motion across his throat. "*Muerto*."

Rita gasped. "You mean someone cut his throat? Oh, sweet Jesus, all that blood."

"No, no, no," Sammy muttered. "My gesture was but a symbol used to indicate death. No throat slashing."

"Thank God," Rita replied.

I shot Rita a disapproving look. "Why are you thanking God, Rita? The man is still dead."

Rita shrugged.

Sofia's brow furrowed. "Or is he? Dead, I mean. Doesn't somebody official have to determine that?"

Sammy held up a hand. "I checked, *chica*. Turned him over to see if he needed resuscitation. Like I said before. The man is *muerto*."

Rita inhaled sharply. "You touched him? Isn't that against the rules?"

"For Pete's sake, Rita, he was trying to help." I turned to Sammy. "Did you put him back like you found him?"

Sammy flapped a hand at me. "Yes, yes, of course. I did not tamper with the death scene. I know better."

Sirens screaming, an aid car followed by a fire truck pulled into the parking lot, squeezing by clusters of newly arrived golfers ready to hit the links.

"Sofia, go tell the golfers to wait in their cars. I'll take care of the rest," I barked.

Sofia, still looking wan, rolled her eyes. "Yeah, right, like they'll listen to me." Sofia was petite and looked younger than her age. She'd grown up on the golf course. The members still called her Libby's kid.

I turned her around and gave her a little push. "Give it a try. Be assertive."

I went out to meet the aid cars. Sammy trotted beside me, talking non-stop.

"Remember, absolutely no vehicles on my course. I do not wish to see the grass torn up and destroyed by tire marks."

"Sammy," I warned. "Be reasonable. You can't toss poor, *muerto* Mickey into a golf cart and drive him to the funeral home. Show some respect for the dead."

Sammy's eyes narrowed. He waved a cautionary finger in my face. "Ha! Then they better drive slow or they will hear from me, Sammy Espinosa, golf course superintendent."

He picked up the pace and marched toward the emergency vehicles. "I will inform them of my decision."

Sammy on a mission was a force to be reckoned with. Despite his impassioned pleas to the first responders, an aid car was dispatched to the eighth fairway, led by Sammy and me in a golf cart. Sammy proceeded at a snail's pace, frequently glancing over his shoulder to make sure their vehicle had one set of wheels on the cart path.

"You might want to go a little faster. They're crawling up our bumper."

Sammy threw his hands in the air. "Why? The man is dead. What's the hurry?"

"Think about it, Sammy. People are waiting to tee off. I know this sounds insensitive, but I've got a business to run. Mickey probably had a heart attack. It's not the first time somebody died on the golf course. Remember Hugh Simmons?"

Sammy nodded. "*Si*, I remember. His buddies put him in their golf cart and drove him in. So much better than this. People said they played a few holes along the way, but I don't believe it."

He turned and glared at the aid car. "Back then, we had none of this nonsense with large, heavy vehicles making ruts in my beautiful grass."

I patted his arm. "If you need help to fix it, bring your boys in. I'll make sure they're on the payroll." Sammy's sons, Henry and Gabe, were hard workers and often helped their dad.

Slightly mollified, Sammy punched the accelerator. I gripped the seat brace as we sped down the path to the fairway of A Woman Scorned, named because it lacked a ladies' tee box. Peering ahead, I spotted the crumpled form of Mickey Warren a few yards from the wooded area on the right. His bright red shirt seemed incongruously cheery considering the circumstances.

As we pulled up next to the body, Sammy said, "Every day, the same thing. The man cannot hit a straight drive. He hits many balls off the tee box, but has a *malvado* slice. Wicked." He paused and pointed down the fairway. "Big dogleg right. *Si*?"

"*Si*," I agreed.

We watched the EMTs unload equipment and approach the body.

"So when he slices the ball, it goes into the woods. He parks here to look for the balls he's lost. That is my theory. I know it is correct so I will go tell the authorities," Sammy said.

I caught hold of his arm. "Maybe we should hold off on the theories. Let them do their job."

Sammy snorted his disapproval, and we edged closer.

"Stay back," a woman EMT barked.

Sammy stiffened but stopped and remained silent. I peered through the huddle of first responders. Mickey was turned face-up and given a thorough examination before a heart monitor was attached to his chest.

"He's gone. Let's load him up," said one of the EMTs.

"Told you," Sammy muttered.

As the group parted, I got a good look at Mickey's face and bit back a gasp of horror. His face was blue. Foam trickled from the corner of his mouth. His wide-eyed sightless gaze was fixed on the sky above. His eyes bulged ominously from their sockets.

"Is that normal?" I whispered to Sammy.

He lifted his hands and shrugged. "The man is dead, so, yes, I'd say it is normal."

My only point of reference, dead body-wise, was Herb Simmons whose color had been ashy-gray. He had looked peaceful, unlike Mickey who appeared anything but.

I approached the woman EMT. "Excuse me, when you, um, remove the body, may we open the golf course for play? This isn't a crime scene, is it?"

The woman frowned at me, held up a finger and joined her colleagues. When she returned, she said, "The medical examiner will determine the exact cause of death. However, considering his age, he has all the classic signs of a massive heart attack."

Her eyes narrowed in suspicion. "Any particular reason you might think this is a crime scene? Was he by himself?"

"He was alone," Sammy said.

Using flowery phrases and dramatic gestures, Sammy launched into a blow-by-blow description of Mickey Warren's early morning practice of hitting balls from the A Woman Scorned tee box. He was still talking as the body was loaded into the aid car. The female EMT squirmed with impatience.

"Wrap it up, Sammy," I said.

Sammy pointed at the woods. "I will prove my theory is correct by searching the underbrush where I will find at least four Bridgestone golf balls. I know exactly what brand he used…" He whirled and marched into the woods.

"Is he always like this?" asked the woman.

I nodded.

"But it has nothing to do with this being a crime scene, right?"

"Right," I said. "He's trying to be helpful by doing a re-enactment of the death scene. I've found it best to humor him. Otherwise he might show up at your workplace. Now would be a good time to make a run for it."

Too late. Sammy popped out from behind a massive pine. His right hand was extended and clutched four golf balls.

"Just like I said," he hollered.

"Thanks," the EMT muttered, then sprinted to the aid car.

Chapter Six

Because of Mickey Warren's untimely demise, regular tee times were delayed. Hours later, the buzz died down and the last of the regular foursomes happily hacked away. Play moved briskly through Hell, the front nine, but the back nine, Heaven, was a different story. Heaven featured two par threes in a row. Angel Crossing—named for the small creek running through it—was followed by the aforementioned Gabriel's Horn. Consequently, each group had to wait to tee off until the foursome ahead of them finished playing the hole.

If a golfer was lucky enough to birdy Gabriel's Horn, he—or she—was allowed two toots on the horn affixed by a chain to a metal post. If adult beverages were involved, this practice became problematic, as each person in the group clamored for a turn. Adding to the delay was a health and safety issue. Each horn blower was required to disinfect the horn with sanitary wipes thoughtfully provided by management.

Just last month, I'd had voiced my concerns at the board meeting that Gabriel's Horn was a huge pain in the ass. Foursomes piled up and I had to send Sammy out to confront the tooters. I was greeted with a chorus of boos when I suggested getting rid of the noise maker. In retrospect, not surprising since many of them were perpetrators of the delay.

As if we didn't already have enough drama, Farley and Faith Faraday, along with a loud, obnoxious gaggle of church members, set up camp on the sidewalk adjoining our parking lot. Golfers entering or exiting their cars were greeted with waving picket signs and shouts of Sinner! Repent! Fairway to Heaven is a blasphemous stain on our fair city.

Hence, I was on the receiving end of phone calls from irate golfers attempting to exit the parking lot, not to mention the verbal abuse I got from the newly arrived.

I sent Sammy out to shepherd golfers to and from the clubhouse. His large presence calmed the waters. When the phone remained silent for five consecutive minutes, I heaved a sigh of relief. My tummy emitted ominous sounds, reminding me hours had passed since my meager breakfast of toast and honey. It was time for a long overdue lunch. As I devoured the tuna melt daily special, my cell phone burst into "Stairway to Heaven", my signature ring.

It was Dad. "Hey Libby, you know that pocket park at the corner of Tenth and Spruce?"

Uh, oh, I knew what was coming. "Yes," I replied cautiously.

"Suze just called. She spotted a swarm in a spruce tree. I'm going after it and I need somebody to man the smoker. You busy?"

Dad's passion was honeybees. When he spotted a swarm, he felt it was his civic duty to retrieve it. Although Suzy supported his hobby, she was rarely available when it came down to the nitty-gritty of actually retrieving the swarms.

Suzy Rentz, her thriving rental business, and her

boutique bakery, Suzy's Booty Bunz, could always be counted on for emergencies requiring her immediate attention. It was then Dad relied on his live-in helpers, Sofia and me.

I couldn't hold back a groan. "It's been crazy around here, Dad. Did you hear about Mick Warren?"

"Yeah, I heard," he replied. "Never liked the guy. Cheated at golf. Anyway, dead is dead. You might as well help me move some bees."

"Farley on a Harley and his sorry gang also showed up today. Wish I could help but I can't leave right now. What about Donny or Ronny? Are they home?"

Dad snorted. "Oh, please. I'm not in the mood to hear grown men scream like little girls."

"I'll track Sofia down."

"Fine, Tenth and Spruce. ASAP."

"It might take a few minutes to locate—"

Waste of breath. Dead air. From past experience, I knew Dad's flip phone was now in his back pocket and he was trotting to his battered but trusty Ford pick-up, fully loaded with the beekeeping equipment needed for this emergency. When it came to bee rescue missions, Ed McKenna was on the job.

Sofia's cell went to voicemail. What the hell? Did she have ESP that kicked in when a bee capturing enterprise was afoot?

"Hey, Rita, I need to chase Sofia down. Can you take care of the phone for a sec? Did Tiffany ever show up?"

Rita stomped into the pro shop. "Yeah, she's here. Showed up two hours after the lunch rush was over. Typical."

Tiffany Hanson was the airhead daughter of a

board member who thought she needed a job. Tiffany didn't agree and did everything in her power to get fired.

I promised to hurry and dashed out the door, hopped into a golf cart and headed for the maintenance shed where Sofia liked to hang out. I screeched to a halt when I spotted her cart parked against the side of the building. Indistinct baritone murmurs and a familiar giggle emanated from the building.

Oh, crap. I banged a fist against the shed. "Sofia, it's your mother. Come out, come out, wherever you are."

After a moment of silence, the unmistakable sound of zippers being zipped wafted through cracks in the metal siding.

I held my ground and tried to look non-judgmental.

The door slid ajar. Sofia's flushed face appeared in the opening. "Oh, hi, Mom. Gabe came in to help his dad fix the grass. I was showing him where all the stuff is. You know, the stuff he needs to help his dad."

I bit back a sarcastic reply. "Your grandfather has a swarm to capture at Tenth and Spruce. He needs your help."

Sofia stepped out of the shed.

"Gabe, I know you're in there."

With an ingratiating smile, Gabriel Espinosa popped into view. Movie star handsome with melting brown eyes and a sculpted torso worthy of a body builder, Gabe was a babe magnet and Sofia was not immune. Unfortunately, I had been equally susceptible to swarthy charms when I was Sofia's age.

I totally understood. Understood, but didn't approve.

"Okay, you two," I said. "You're on the job here, so whatever you were up to, do it on your own time."

I whirled, stomped to the golf cart and tore back to the pro shop, mumbling to myself.

And I thought Tiffany an airhead.

Chapter Seven

As the five o'clock hour approached, the din from the cocktail lounge adjoining the pro shop grew in volume. One voice in particular grated on my nerves. Tristan Kensington the Third took over my duties until closing time at twilight. Every afternoon it was the same story. Tristan the Turd scheduled a couple of afternoon golf lessons and then hung out with his golf buddies—and ladies—in the bar. He considered it beneath his station to answer phones and set up tee times. Consequently, my first priority in the morning was to un-muddle Tristan's messes.

I strode to the archway leading to the lounge and shot a steely-eyed glare in his direction. He smirked and murmured something to the pretty little blonde seated next to him.

When he rose from his chair, I retrieved my purse and phone. Another five minutes elapsed before Tristan sauntered into the pro shop and greeted me in his usual fashion.

"Hey, sweet cheeks, how's it hangin'?"

At one point in our relationship, I had tried to point out the obvious error in his greeting. "That particular phrase is more appropriate for your male buddies who have downward drooping organs. The only part of a woman's body capable of hanging down are her boobs. In which case the greeting makes her feel insecure."

Tristan tried mightily to understand the concept. His smooth forehead wrinkled in concentration as he pondered my comment. Fingers raked through his dyed blond locks. Yes, I thought. He got it.

Then he'd responded, "Oh, yeah? Well, her buns could sag too."

Now I just rolled with it.

"Hangin' in there, Tris. How about you?"

He pulled a fake frown-y face. "Too bad about Mick. Shitty golfer, though. Terrible slice."

I gave him my sweetest smile. "Gee, one would think after all his private lessons with you, his slice would be history."

Tristan's eyes widened. "Do you think people blame me for not fixing his slice? I heard he was out in the woods picking up balls when he had a heart attack."

I almost felt guilty. Almost. It was far too easy to mess with Tristan's head, kind of like teasing a dog, which I would never do. Tristan was a different story. He usually deserved it.

I stroked my chin like I was thinking it over. "Probably not. How many lessons did you give him?"

"Once a week for the last year."

I headed for the door. "You're probably off the hook. Unless, of course, the horrific slice caused his heart attack."

Tristan's face paled a little.

"No worries, Tris. That would be hard to prove. Try not to mess up the tee times for tomorrow. Okay?" I called before I exited the pro shop.

I glanced over my shoulder and saw him staring after me. Deer in the headlights. My work here was done.

When I pulled into the long, narrow driveway leading to Dad's detached garage, I noticed Sofia's car was gone. Dad's truck was parked beneath the enormous walnut tree next to the garage. With three vehicles, a tight work schedule and a narrow driveway, parking order was crucial. Since I was usually the first to leave in the morning, I steered around the truck and parked beneath the apricot tree bordering the drive. Hopefully Sofia would get the message and pull in next to the garage, leaving the driveway free. The plan should work, barring the possibility my daughter's blood supply had vacated her brain and migrated southward.

"Hey, Libs! I've got a nice glass of chardonnay with your name on it."

Next-door neighbor Ronny, half of the Ronny-and-Donny couple, leaned over the hedge, a wide smile on his way-too-pretty face.

He added, "You look like you need it. I heard some old fart croaked on the golf course this morning."

"I absolutely need it. First, I need to see what's up with Dad and Sofia."

"No worries. I'll bring the bottle."

Clawdius napped on the ledge outside the back door. He opened one eye and growled a warning. I stayed out of range and made my way into the house I'd grown up in.

Once through the back door, concrete stairs plunged downward into the darkened basement, my dad's domain. If one chose to go there—I didn't—the bottom of the stairs terminated in a long narrow room strung with a clothesline. Wooden cupboards containing remnants of my childhood lined the back wall. Three doors led to separate rooms. An abrupt right turn led to Dad's bedroom. The laundry room/second bathroom was conveniently located a few steps across from the bedroom. An ancient washer and dryer huddled against one wall. A showerhead was situated over a sunken drain. A small enclosure concealed the toilet. A dank and dreary second bedroom was located a few steps past the makeshift bathroom and served as a storage place for Dad's many hobbies, including bits and pieces of bee-related items and ancient photography equipment.

At one point in his life, he'd developed his own photographs, using the spare bedroom as a dark room. The upstairs bookcase contained albums filled with embarrassing pictures of my awkward childhood.

The remaining room in the basement was my least favorite, one I refused to enter. Euphemistically dubbed The Fruit Room, it once held gleaming rows of canned peaches, raspberries, and cherries lovingly harvested and preserved by my mother Rebecca, before she died at the indecently young age of thirty-five, felled by ovarian cancer. Now the room contained only dusty jars, spider webs, and memories of the past.

Instead of descending to the basement, I turned right and climbed three stairs, entering the kitchen of our home built in the 1940s.

Rhythmic snores emanated from behind swinging doors leading to the living room. As was his custom, Dad napped in his recliner, the TV tuned to his favorite news channel. It never failed to induce slumber.

I paused and examined the glistening jars of honey lined up on the counter top. Jules had designed the label. The brand name Nun of Your Beeswax with its scowling nun was followed by the words, It's the Bees' Knees.

Tucked behind the pint jars were ten smaller jars, containing what Dad called his old age pension. At first glance, the labels looked identical. Same scowling nun with upraised ruler ready to strike. Same golden honey, but with a slightly darker cast. The words at the bottom of the label told a different story. In tasteful script letters, it said Ed's Special Dark. The Bees' Knees honey sold for $5.95 a jar, Ed's Special Dark for $15.00.

Dad had no problem justifying the high-priced product including the following: It's labor intensive. The plants need enough sun to grow properly, hidden like they are in the raspberry patch. Then they're dried, buds harvested, ground, and infused with honey. He had a growing list of folks who needed the stuff. Dad thinks of it as an act of mercy.

I pushed the taller jars back in position, concealing the fruits of my father's illegal enterprise, which never failed to induce high anxiety. A note from Sofia was attached to the refrigerator by the moose magnet from Dad's trip to Yellowstone Park.

Mom, sorry about earlier. You're right. I was supposed to be working, not acting like an irresponsible dip wad. That's why I told Gabe I'd hang out with him tonight when we're off the clock. No worries. I'm on the pill so won't be dropping out of college to marry Gabe and pop out a bunch of cute little half-Mexican babies. More importantly, you won't become a grandma at age thirty-nine. Ha ha.

Followed with a hand-drawn smiley face. I massaged my suddenly throbbing temples.

BTW, I helped Mr. B & B capture the swarm, yay, me! See you sometime tomorrow or maybe later tonight.

Hugs and kisses, Sofia.

As I stuffed the note into my pocket, Dad's recliner returned to its upright position with a resounding snap.

He pushed through the swinging door, rubbing the sleep from his eyes. "Hi there, Chickadee. Rough day? Did you get the note?"

There was an excellent reason Sofia and I referred to Dad as Mr. B and B, fascinated as he was with birds and bees. Despite our protestations, I would always be Chickadee; Sofia, Baby Bird.

I nodded and gestured at the rows of honey. "I see you've got another batch ready to go."

He beamed. "Yep. Sure glad pot is legal now. Life is good."

"We've been over this a bunch of times, Dad. You have to be licensed in the state of Washington to grow and distribute marijuana. You're not."

Dad scowled. "Bunch of bullshit. I'd have to raise my prices."

I clucked my tongue. "I'll consider visiting you in prison."

"At least I'll have free health care." He chuckled.

Before I could dish out a snarky reply, a patrol car with the Vista Valley Sheriff's logo emblazoned on the door rumbled into the driveway.

Chapter Eight

A scant moment later, Ronny and Donny, each clutching a bottle of wine, burst through the back door and entered the kitchen, both feverish with excitement.

I parted the living room curtains and watched through the window as Sheriff Riley O'Connor stepped out of the car. Donny and Ronny closed in behind me.

"Oh my God, it is him! Sheriff Sweet Cheeks. Swear to God, Libby, we didn't call him this time." He paused to fan himself with an open hand. "What's happening, girl? I bet it has something to do with *the dead body found on golf course case,*" Donny exclaimed.

Ronny and Donny were devoted to each other, but both had mad crushes on the local sheriff and invented the flimsiest of excuses to summon him. Unfortunately for the pair, Riley was straight as an arrow.

Dad pushed through the swinging door from the kitchen. "What the hell's going on?"

I hoped he'd ditched his special dark honey since Mr. Law Enforcement, large and in charge, now climbed the stairs leading to the covered front porch.

Donny sidled toward the front door, closely followed by Ronny. "Sheriff Hardbody is here. That's what's going on."

Beaming, he flung the door open. "Welcome, Sheriff, come right in."

"You two again?" Riley muttered. and peered around them. "Lady of the house home?"

I pushed my way through the pair. "Yes, she is. What can I do for you, Riley?"

The corner of his mouth twitched in amusement, like he prioritized a list of things I might be willing to do for him. His warm brown gaze drifted south of my chin for brief moment before looking into my eyes.

"How you been?"

Dad nudged the boys aside and shook hands with the sheriff. "Good to see you, Riley. Have a seat."

As he settled on the couch, Ronny and Donny closed in. "Would you like a nice glass of wine? It's from our private stock."

Donny and Ronny grew their own grapes and owned Druid's Glen, a successful winery in the rich agricultural valley south of town. Even though the area was known for red wines, the boys specialized in white. Their best seller was a sparkling wine called "Light in the Loafers". The label featured a single brown shoe and included the phrase, 'Wine With a Fruity Touch'. Apparently fine wine and quirkiness were a good combination. Their tasting room was jammed every weekend.

The sheriff waved them away. "I'm on the job. Another time." He stabbed a finger in my direction. "Actually, I need a few minutes to talk to Libby. Privately."

"You heard the man. Let's go." Dad herded Donny and Ronny into the kitchen.

I waited until they settled into the breakfast nook and the wine glasses clinked. "What's going on, Riley?"

He leaned forward, bracing his elbow on his knees. “It’s possible Mick Warren didn’t die of a heart attack. Clark Rafferty at the funeral home called me. Said I needed to contact the coroner.”

“Did he say why?”

“Apparently he found an injection mark on Warren’s body.”

“Maybe he’s diabetic.”

“He’s not. Plus, diabetics don’t inject themselves in the right butt cheek.”

I caught my breath. “Oh, my.”

“Rafferty said the foaming at the mouth, in addition to other signs, led him to believe poison might be involved.”

I processed the information for a long moment. “Which would mean he was—”

“Murdered.”

I stood and stared down at the sheriff. “Why are you telling me this?”

He rose and stepped toward me, taking care not to invade my space. “I need your help. I’m relatively new to the area. Fairway to Heaven is like a village. You know these people. You know their families. You and your dad have been around a long time. Maybe you even know their secrets. Keep your ears open and let me know if you hear anything suspicious. In the meantime, I’ll be checking things out.”

“Have you heard about last night’s board meeting?”

“Yeah, sounds like the wife and girlfriend were both ready to kill him on the spot. I’ll be talking to both of them.”

“A lot of folks don’t, I mean, didn’t care much for

Mickey Warren."

"So I've heard."

I thought it over for a moment. "So I'm like an undercover agent?"

Riley grinned and extended his right hand. "We got a deal?"

I slipped my hand in his, surprised by the little tingle spiraling through my body, reaching parts I assumed were dead from lack of use. "Yeah, we got a deal."

Still holding my hand, he leaned close. "When are you going to say yes?"

I frowned and tugged my hand from his. "To what?"

He flashed a smile. "Dinner. Just dinner. What did you think I meant?"

Heat flooded my cheeks and I looked away from his intense gaze. "I was just trying to understand your intent."

His grin grew larger. "My intent? Let's just start with dinner."

"Sure, as long as you clarify one little thing for me."

I pointed at his left hand. "I think you know what I'm referring to. It's the reason I turned you down before. It's gold, circular and on the ring finger of your left hand. Normally, this particular piece of jewelry suggests the man already has a wife. Maybe I'm wrong. If so, please enlighten me."

Riley's grin vanished. He heaved a sigh. "Okay, here's God's honest truth. I was married when I worked in southern California. We split, but I kept my ring. When I came to Vista Valley, one of the commissioners said, 'Boy, you're fresh meat for the single ladies in Vista Valley. If I were you, I'd keep the ring. Sure, a man has needs and you want to date. Make up a good story. Tell 'em your wife's been in in a coma for five years and will probably never recover. Or that she ran off and joined a commune. Use your imagination!' So I took his advice. That's it. End of story."

I fought a grin. "I guess it worked since I've heard both of those stories. Not that I believe you."

He sobered quickly. "Damn, girl, you're a tough one."

"Best you should keep that in mind."

"I will."

With a little twinge of guilt I glanced down at my own left hand and its naked ring finger.

It was probably a good thing he didn't know my secret.

Chapter Nine

Two days after Riley's visit, I had to face the facts. I sucked at the undercover game. When Sofia was a little girl and got mad at one of her friends, she'd yell, "You don't just suck, you suck dirty dishwater!"

Yeah, when it comes to spying, I suck dirty dishwater.

In spite of being on high alert for clues, the only comments I overheard were the usual sentiments surrounding the death of a member. At first I was super-organized. I bought a special notebook and kept it close at hand, in case I overheard something juicy. Atop the first page and printed in block letters were the words, POSSIBLE SUSPECTS. The page contained only one name, written tentatively in pencil and punctuated with a question mark. I had Sofia's love of gossip to thank for it.

Sofia gleaned information from hanging out with the greens-keeping crew. Just last night, she'd told me that Herb Talcott and Mickey Warren hated each other. Talcott's condo overlooks the sixteenth green so he sits on his deck and watches who goes by. Then he checks the computer to see if the scores are recorded. Apparently, Mickey was selective about the scores he posted, plus he sneaked out on the course every morning before play began. Talcott accused him of being a sandbagger and they got into a big fuss. Warren called him a fat bastard. Talcott took a swing at him, missed and fell on his butt. Talcott yelled to Mickey he'd be sorry. Therefore, Herb Talcott was the only name faintly inscribed in my notebook.

On high alert for clues, I eagerly awaited the arrival of the Mahjong Mavens who played in the clubhouse every Wednesday at precisely one p.m. In between games—which seemed to demand absolute silence—the women indulged in juicy gossip. Maybe I'd hear something I could pass along to the sheriff.

As luck would have it, each time a game ended and gossip began, the phone rang or someone needed a bucket of balls. I finally lucked out when the call of nature was too urgent to ignore. With Rita covering for me, I hurried into the ladies' locker room and entered a stall positioned around the corner from the sink, vanity and mirror. Perched on the toilet, I heard the door open and the sound of female voices I recognized. Carolyn Talcott and Ginny Baker were both part of the Mahjong Mavens.

I resisted the urge to flush and pressed my ear against the door, straining to hear their conversation.

"I heard Mickey's death might not have been a heart attack," said Ginny.

"I heard that, too. What else could it be though?"

"No clue, Carolyn."

"He wasn't a nice man."

"Tell me about it. He hit on me at the New Year's Eve party. Must have been desperate. Right?" Ginny chuckled.

"No way, you look great, girl. Besides, he hit on me, too."

Hearty laughter ensued. I imagined the two

exchanging high fives, a tribute to their ability to attract an over-the-hill older man.

"I heard his second wife—what the hell's her name—had to sign a prenup before they got married and that she left him," Ginny said.

"Heather. Her name is Heather. So if she leaves him she'd get nothing?"

"My source said if they got divorced, she scored an agreed-upon amount. But if he died, she could contest the will and get more."

Finally, the juicy stuff. I slid the door open a crack and strained to hear more of their conversation.

"Are you thinking what I'm thinking?"

"Yeah, probably, but how would she do it?"

"Not that I've made a habit of studying up on it, but people our age take a lot of pills. Maybe he had allergies or took heart meds. Easy to tamper with. And she could always say poor Mickey got confused and took too much, or not enough, or even the wrong pills. Something along those lines."

Ginny made a clucking sound. "Oh my God, she'd have to be one cold-hearted bitch to do something so evil."

"I've never liked her. She has fake boobs and her eyes are set too close together. It's a well-known fact you can't trust people with eyes like that."

The door opened.

"For heaven's sakes, Carolyn, close-set eyes and fake boobs don't make her a murderer," Ginny said.

I waited a full minute before leaving the locker room. Although I heartily agreed with Ginny's last comment, I'd seen fury in Heather Warren's eyes. She looked mad enough to kill, but so did Tammy. I decided to add both women to my suspect list.

Back in the pro shop, I strolled by the table where the Mavens were deeply engrossed in their game.

"Libby, dear," Carolyn called. "There's an extremely handsome man at the counter talking to Rita. He's asking about you." She fluttered her eyelashes and smirked. "New boyfriend?"

Mahjong game forgotten, all four women stared at me, breathlessly awaiting my answer.

Ginny snickered. "Rita looks like she's about to have a stroke."

My gaze swung to Rita. Her mouth was agape, her eyes fixed on the well-built, dark-haired man on the other side of the counter.

The denial I was about to deliver died in my throat. Clad in a white polo shirt and pressed slacks that emphasized his muscular build, the man looked vaguely familiar. Familiar in a way that zinged a tingle of alarm through my body.

No way. It couldn't be him. But then he swept a hand through his dark wavy hair and I knew.

Swamped with a tsunami of emotions, equal portions of shock, anger, and outrage, I stood paralyzed, unable to move or speak.

"What is it, dear?" one of the women asked. "You've gone white as a ghost. Do you know him?"

The man turned, spotted me, and flashed a gleaming smile. Arms outstretched, he covered the distance between us in long strides. He cupped my face in his hands. "*Cara mia*, it's me, Antonio. I'm back."

I pushed him away and gripped the back of a chair to hold myself upright. Conversations swirled around me. The words were muffled, echoing and bouncing like I was at the bottom of a well. Bits and pieces floated through my consciousness like flotsam on the incoming tide.

“Oh, my!”

“Do you think…?”

“Maybe she should sit.”

“Is she going to faint?”

The last comment brought me back to my senses. I pushed away from the chair. “Oh, please. I’m not the fainter in the family. That would be Sofia,” I said as my legs folded.

Everything went black and I crumpled to the floor.

Chapter Ten

When I opened my eyes, two faces floated directly over me. Two faces remarkably similar, both with olive skin and lush wavy black hair. Two sets of brown eyes framed by long dark lashes gazed down at her. Vertical worry lines creased both foreheads.

Sofia leaned close and whispered, “Mom, are you okay?”

I rose to a sitting position, smacking heads with her.

“Please allow me to assist you, my darling.”

Before I could protest, Antonio clamped his hands around my waist and hoisted me to my feet.

I jerked free. “I am not your darling.”

Now fully conscious, I glanced around the pro shop and discovered I was the star of my own private soap opera. A crowd had gathered to watch the drama unfold. In addition to the Mavens and Rita, Tristan and three of his buddies, beers in hand, were peering in from the cocktail lounge. Two other guys, munching hot dogs, settled into a booth, waiting for the next episode. A man and woman were at the counter, their curious gazes fixed on me. Hot with embarrassment and anger, I longed for invisibility.

“We need to sort this out. Somewhere private,” Sofia whispered.

My mind was a whirlwind of emotions. Anger.

Shock. Sadness. Humiliation. I had difficulty stringing a simple sentence together. “Um, yeah, we do, but…” Sofia glared at Antonio. “Look what you’ve done to my mother. She can’t talk straight. Maybe she’s even having a stroke. If she is, it’s your fault. After all, she’s nearly forty.”

Sofia’s ludicrous statement tickled my funny bone. Caught up in a fit of uncontrollable laughter, I managed to gasp, “Not having a stroke.”

When my laughter subsided to sporadic giggles, I gazed around the room at the people crowding around me. Their startled expressions set me off again.

Antonio slipped an arm around my shoulders. “Libby, *cara*, I think you are in the throes of hysteria. Perhaps we should continue our conversation out on the patio.”

Sofia wedged herself between Antonio and me. “Great idea, Dad. Or should I say Undad, Nondad, or Missing-in-Action Dad? Your choice.”

Antonio lifted his hands in a helpless gesture. “You have every right to be angry, my beautiful princess of a daughter. Please allow me to explain.”

He trotted to the sliding door leading to the patio, opened it and, with a slight bow, said, “After you, lovely ones.”

Sofia grabbed my arm and began towing me toward the door. I glanced through the window and dug in my heels.

“We can’t go out there.”

“Better than in here, Mom.”

“Look who just finished the last hole.”

Sofia peered through the window. Dad leapt out of his golf cart before it came to a full stop. He advanced toward the pro shop, fists balled at his side.

"News travels fast," I murmured.

Antonio's face lost color. "Perhaps we should do this another time."

I agreed.

Antonio whirled and walked briskly toward the exit to the parking lot.

Ed stomped through the sliding door, just in time to see the receding backside of Antonio Carone. His bellicose roar bounced off the walls.

"Stop right there, you slimy bastard!"

But Antonio did not stop, even after Dad chased after the sleek black sports car speeding from the parking lot.

"First, you get my daughter pregnant, then you disappear for twenty years. We need to talk, you son of a bitch," he yelled, shaking his fist.

I grabbed his arm. "Let it go, Dad. We're better off without him."

Carrying my purse, Sofia joined us in the parking lot. "Let's go home. I told Tristan to get his butt behind the counter. We needed time to process."

"Process, my ass," Dad muttered.

I linked arms with my father and my daughter. "At least we gave folks something new to talk about."

Sofia grinned. "Did we ever."

****

"You called him?" I screeched.

Sofia shrugged. "Why not? He stuck his card in my pocket and whispered, "Call me. So I did. I have questions, Mom, so don't get all huffy."

It was hours later and my father, after a fit of stomping and swearing, left the premises. He decided the best course of action was to jump in his truck, drive around town, and try to find Antonio. Though I believed it to be a fool's errand, I did nothing to stop him. I needed a break from the drama. Little did I know it was only the first act.

I gazed at my daughter. Her face was flushed, eyes flashing with indignation. I thought about my relationship with Dad. He was an open book, always there for me, always my champion. What if, like Sofia, I had no idea about the man who'd fathered me? Wouldn't I be curious as well?

I held out my arms. After a moment's hesitation, she stepped into my embrace. I hugged her fiercely. Cheek to cheek, our tears mingled together. We whispered, "I love you," then stepped away and wiped our eyes.

"Do what you have to do, sweetie. Just pray your grandfather doesn't find him first."

She gave me a tremulous smile. "Thanks, Mom. Is there anything you want me to ask him?"

Oh, so many questions. Where have you been for twenty years, Antonio? Exploring caves? Impregnating unsuspecting females? You're driving an expensive sports car, are you rich? Did you ever want to see your daughter?

I tried to act indifferent. Shrugged my shoulders. "Just one. Why is he here? This is your time to get the answers you need. We'll talk when you get home."

"Thanks, Mom."

She blew me a kiss and dashed out the back door. I went to the window and watched her back down the driveway. Though she was a straight A student, she never fully grasped the concept of backing up and often turned the steering wheel in the wrong direction. More than once, her car ended up stuck in the hedge bordering the driveway. Not this time. She zigzagged a little but managed to make it to the street without incident.

Restless and at loose ends, I wandered around the house, unaccustomed to being home in the middle of the afternoon. When my cell phone buzzed, I pounced on it. Jules.

"Oh my God, girl, what happened? I heard about Mickey Warren and stopped by the golf course to talk to you. Then, all the old biddies told me about THE INCIDENT. In case you can't tell, THE INCIDENT is in capital letters. Do you want me to come over?"

As usual, Jules made me feel better. "Sure, come on over. We'll visit Ronny and Donny, drink some Light in the Loafers and figure everything out."

"On my way, girlfriend."

My finger was poised over the off button when she said, "I'll drive us tonight."

"Drive us? Where are we going?"

Jules's annoyed sigh zinged through the cell towers and into my ear. She added a cluck of disapproval. "The meeting with Abigail Cavendish, dummy."

Oh, yeah, that.

Chapter Eleven

We had a happy little glow on when we drove through the iron gates leading to the Cavendish mansion. The word mansion was not an exaggeration.

"Wow, just wow," I gushed as we traversed the cobblestone driveway leading to the massive all brick structure.

The circular drive included its own landscape with three evergreens and manicured lawn. A multitude of gabled roofs topped the L-shaped house.

"Over 13,000 square feet," Jules said. "A five car garage, eight full baths plus two half baths, seven bedrooms, two-story man cave, and elevator."

I shook my head in disbelief. "All this for two people."

Jules glanced over at me. "You grew up on Fairway to Heaven. You've never seen this place?"

"Only the backyard and from a distance. Remember, I'm just a flunky."

Jules laughed. "Yeah, a flunky who keeps the place from falling to pieces."

We parked in front of a portico leading to a massive double front door. So far, we'd seen no signs of life. Surely they needed a large staff to take care of a place this size. It felt a little creepy.

"Maybe we shouldn't park here," I whispered. "Where is everybody?"

"Why are you whispering? Stop being intimidated. We'll be fine. Follow me."

She bolted out of the car, slammed the door and marched through the portico. I gulped back my anxiety and followed her.

Jules glanced over her shoulder. "Get ready."

Her bossiness was making me cranky. "What do you mean, get ready?"

"You'll see."

She pressed the brass button encased within an elaborate wrought iron frame. A few beats later, thunderous strains from the 1812 overture blasted from speakers concealed behind the shrubs. Startled, I jumped back, teetered on one foot and fell on my butt. Somehow I managed to hang on to my notebook and pen.

"I warned you." Jules pulled me to my feet. "They change it daily."

I brushed off the seat of my white pants. "What kind of a nuthouse is this?"

She slung an arm around my shoulders. "You ain't seen nothin' yet, kiddo."

"What's next?"

"You're about to meet Felicity Horncastle."

Before I could reply, the musical salvo ceased. The door creaked open, revealing a stern-faced woman with iron gray hair, clad in a severe black pants suit. A sprinkling of coarse white whiskers protruded from her pointed chin.

Jules proceeded to chat her up. "Oh, hi there, Miz Horncastle. This is my friend, Libby. Abigail is expecting us."

After a thorough once-over by Horncastle's icy

blue gaze, we were deemed suitable and allowed to enter the elaborate marble-floored foyer. She glanced at the tiny watch on her bony wrist despite the enormous grandfather clock adorning one wall.

"Mersus Bingham will see you in the library." After this pronouncement, she turned and marched down the hall without a backward glance.

Mersus? I shot Jules a quizzical glance. She shrugged and gave me a little shove, indicating we should scurry after the formidable Miz Horncastle. I pinched my lips together and loped down the hall.

The hallway had gloomy recessed lighting. A variety of oil paintings lined the walls. Gentlemen on horseback decked out in foxhunt duds. Voluptuous nudes reclining on velvet settees. Portraits of stern-faced aristocrats I assumed to be Cavendish antecedents. When I stopped to gape at a spectacularly endowed gentleman gripping a dueling sword, I received another push from Jules.

"Keep on steppin', girlfriend. Trust me, you don't want to get lost in this place. You could wander around for days looking for an exit."

Indeed, it seemed Horncastle had rounded a bend and was no longer visible. I scurried after her just in time. She pushed open a massive wooden door on the right, held the door open, gestured for us to enter, then disappeared down the hall.

When Jules and I entered the room, I gasped and stopped dead in my tracks. This wasn't just a library, it was a library on steroids. Two stories high, shelves lined with leather-bound books extended halfway to the top of the vaulted ceiling. A glossy wooden ladder was propped in one corner. Just looking at it made me dizzy.

What if the book I wanted was at the top? And who did the dusting?

"Wow," I whispered.

Jules grabbed my arm. "Come and meet Abigail."

She dragged me across the cavernous room toward a brightly burning fireplace. The furniture, a brown leather couch, two crimson wingback chairs, and a gleaming cherrywood coffee table were arranged in a conversational grouping.

Abigail Cavendish rose from the wingback chair enveloping her. "Oh, hello, my dears. So glad you could make it."

Everything about Abigail was round, from her chubby cheeks and twinkling blue eyes down to the prominent little tummy pressing against her pink silk blouse. Her head was crowned with a halo of fluffy white curls reminiscent of dandelion fuzz.

Jules made the introductions. At least a head taller than Abigail, I resisted the urge to curtsy and lower my chin in deference. Momentarily struck dumb, it wasn't until Jules pinched me I managed to stammer, "Pl…pl…pleased to meet you, Mrs. Cavendish."

After a trill of tinkling laughter, she said, "Oh, please. Call me Abigail. Mrs. Cavendish was my mother-in-law." She lowered her voice. "We didn't get on. Not a-tall."

Apparently I'd already screwed up. "Sorry, um, Abigail."

"Not a problem. Now you know." She patted the chair next to her own. "Come, sit down. Let's get started."

She plopped her round little butt onto the chair and then popped back up again. "Oh, Jules, I'm so sorry.

Make yourself comfy on the couch. We must have a toast to our new venture. Brandy okey dokey with everyone?"

We assured her brandy was dandy.

My mind blossomed into full-out fantasy mode. I took an imaginary photo titled Libby and Jules starring in the Vista Valley version of a British period piece and pretend texted it to Sofia.

I was jolted back to reality when Abigail shrieked, "Willard! Brandy. Now, if you please."

Willard?

Her request was greeted with a series of grunts, snorts and, quite possibly, a few toots of flatulence. Startled, I squinted into a shadowed recess of the expansive library and saw a tall, cadaverous man lurching toward us.

"No reason to yell, my darling. Brandy is forthcoming."

Abigail raised a hand to shield her mouth. "He's quite deaf. If you care to address him, you'll have to speak loudly."

Willard, gripping a brandy snifter, shuffled into our circle of light. "I heard that, Bunny."

He looked me over and winked. "My, my, you're a pretty one. Is this your new writing friend, Bunny?"

With a girlish giggle, Abigail said," Yes, it is, you horny old goat. Now, pour the brandy and resume your nap so we can get to work."

We clinked glasses, Willard staggered back to wherever he'd come from, and Jules settled herself on the couch.

Abigail sipped her brandy and beamed at me. "Here's to a long and fruitful collaboration. Maybe even a bestseller."

Startled by her comment, I gulped down a tad more of the fiery liquid than intended. Its warmth spread through my body like liquid gold and smoothed out the jagged edges of my nerves.

Suddenly brimming with confidence, I grinned back at her. "Yes, let's get this puppy going."

I heard Jules stifle a snicker, disguised as a sneezing fit. I ignored her and pulled a steno pad from my purse. "Now, give me some ideas about the type of book you want, characters, setting, that type of thing."

Abigail extracted a paperback novel jammed between the chair frame and cushion and handed it to me. "This is my favorite."

The book was obviously well-loved. The cover was worn, the pages dog-eared. A number of sticky notes marked Abigail's favorite passages. The book was titled *Passion Unbridled.* It featured a voluptuous red-haired woman draped over the brawny arm of a muscular man who wielded a wicked-looking sword. Clad in skin-tight breeches and a dashing black cloak, his shirt was unbuttoned, revealing six-pack abs. A carriage with four black horses loomed behind the couple. Although the horses were clearly bridled, apparently our hero was not.

"Okay," I murmured, somewhat taken aback by the cover and title and turned the book over to read the back cover.

Lady Sabrina Covington must marry a wealthy man to save her family's fortune. But when taken captive by the handsome, though dangerous rogue, Montague Forsythe, Sabrina's desires awaken and ignite. Little did she expect the hot flames of lust and love to change the course of her life.

"All righty, then, let's get started."

Chapter Twelve

"Hot-hot-hot-stuff," Jules sang as she drove me home.

"Oh, stuff your hot stuff," I muttered, scanning the notes I'd jotted down in my session with Abigail.

She'd also handed over *Passion Unbridled*, insisting I read it for inspiration.

Jules grinned. "She made it very clear. She wants it *hot*. Are you up for that? I know it's been a while since you've experienced an assault with a friendly weapon, a little lust and thrust, a pants-off dance off."

I fought the laughter bubbling up in my chest. I couldn't stay mad at Jules. "For the record, I told Abigail I don't write erotica. She agreed and said it should be a tender love story, but with lots of—in her words—'you know what'."

"Any ideas?"

"Actually, yes. I'm leaning toward a historical setting with a studly pirate named Striker."

"I like it. And the heroine?"

"Rowena, a prissy old maid from Boston, captured by Striker on the high seas. Think plain clothing, a corset, hair pulled back in a severe bun."

"I see where you're going. Beneath the prim exterior, dwells a fiery hellcat. She'll be awakened by our manly pirate who, before long, will be paddling up Coochie Creek."

"But there will be a tender love story."

Since Jules had been having such fun at my expense, it was time to turn the tables.

"Wow, Jules, you sure know a lot of euphemisms for sex. Apparently you and Pete must be getting busy, doing the horizontal greased weasel tango, bumpin' bellies, the old bow-chick-a-wow-wow."

She slowed the car, reached over and grabbed my hand. "Don't tell the kids. Pinky promise?"

Jules was super protective of fourteen-year-old Micah and his sixteen-year-old sister, Isabella.

The laughter I'd been suppressing burst out. "Aw, come on, Jules. They're teenagers. I'm sure they've figured it out what's going on when mommy comes home with a big smile on her face."

"We're real careful. Never do it at my house."

Now I felt bad and squeezed her hand. "You're a single woman. You don't have to apologize for having a relationship. Besides, Pete's a really good guy." I linked my pinky with hers. "No worries. My lips are sealed."

Satisfied, she nodded and rounded the corner leading to my house. The driveway was jammed with cars, totally out of order for morning departures. My ride was blocked by Sofia's car. Dad's pickup truck was parked crookedly behind it. I recognized the third vehicle parked next to the hedge and hiccupped in surprise.

Jules, who'd regained her unflappable nature, hit the brakes and parked at the curb. "If I'm not mistaken, that car belongs to Sheriff Riley O'Connor. I hear he's got the hots for you, sweetie."

"Where did you hear that?"

"Sofia. She's been egging him on. Has he asked you out?"

"He's wearing a wedding ring. I'm not going to poach a guy who's roped and branded."

"Totally bogus," Jules said. "I heard the ring's a phony."

"So he claims."

She nudged me with an elbow. "Go for it, girl. You're writing a steamy romance. You need inspiration, and I believe he's up to the job."

Before I could come up with a rebuttal, she said, "Why is he here now?"

"He asked me to keep my ear to the ground, so to speak, see if I heard anything about Mickey Warren's death. "

"And you didn't tell me? Your best friend in the world?"

"Nothing to tell, Jules. I'm no good as an undercover agent."

"Hmm. Nevertheless, here he is."

Before I could respond, she was out of the car and trotting across the front lawn to the house. I hurried after her. Knowing Jules, she'd have me hooked up with O'Connor before I made it through the front door.

Our living room was the picture of tranquility. Dad, looking bleary-eyed, was in his recliner, the TV tuned to a news channel. He raised a hand in greeting. Sheriff O'Connor, guzzling a beer, was on the couch chatting up Sofia.

"Hey, Mama, Aunt Jules, look who's here." Sofia scampered across the room, gave me a big hug and whispered, "Riley brought Pops home. He was raising hell all over town looking for you-know-who."

"Did he find him?"

"Nope, daddy dearest was with me. Come, sit. I'll tell you all about it."

She grabbed my hand, pulled me to the couch and gave me a little shove. Off balance, I plopped down, snugged up against Riley's warm body. He gave me a big, cheesy grin. Sofia sat next to me, conveniently trapping me between the two. Jeez, could she be any more obvious?

Jules perched on the arm of the couch, her eyes bright with curiosity.

"Sofia," I said. "Are you sure you want to talk about this now?" I waved a hand around the room. "In front of everybody?"

Sofia rolled her eyes. "Oh, please. It's not exactly a family secret. Half the town knows my bio dad showed up at the golf course. Then, when Pops drank a couple of beers and went off the deep end…" She paused. "Sorry, Pops."

Dad lifted a hand, "No problem, Baby Bird." He pushed the recliner back another notch and closed his eyes.

"She's right. I was at the grocery store and the check-out clerk told me some hot Italian guy was in town looking for Libby," Jules said.

Riley nodded and placed his empty beer can on the coffee table. "Yep, pretty much everybody knows."

I sighed. "Okay, so what does he want?"

"A divorce," Sofia said. "He hooked up with a rich babe who wants to marry him. She bought him the snazzy car. And since you two never divorced…"

Beside me, Riley stiffened. "Divorced? You're still married to the guy?"

Unable to meet his gaze, I nodded.

He shook his head. “Unbelievable. And you were giving me shit about wearing a wedding ring?”

“Yeah, I know it’s weird. I thought you were married and you’re not. You thought I was single, and I’m still married. But it’s not like Antonio and I had a real marriage. He took off before Sofia was born and I haven’t seen him again until today,” I mumbled, embarrassed.

With a rumble of laughter, Riley stood, folded his arms across his chest and stared down at me. “Fortunately, I have no problem going out with a married woman. Sofia said you have Monday off. I’ll pick you up at six.”

“She’ll be ready. I’ll make sure,” Sofia said.

The situation was spinning out of control. I jumped up. “Hold on a sec. Maybe I have plans.”

“As if,” Sofia said.

Jules said, “She’s writing a book, but she should have time to squeeze you in, so to speak.”

Riley looked me over and winked. “Great. See you Monday. We’ll have a nice dinner, catch up on the Mickey Warren thing and you can tell me all about your book.”

The book. Warmth flooded my cheeks.

Jules sprang up. “Oh, yeah, it’s a sexy pirate romance with—”

I held up a hand. “Enough. I’m sure the sheriff has things to do, places to go.”

“I’m off duty. Just wanted to make sure Ed got home okay.”

Dad grunted his thanks. Not wanting to appear ungrateful, I added mine.

"Okay, what's next?"

"Lawyer's office. Tomorrow. Nine a.m. I'm coming with you."

"Count me in, Chickadee," Dad mumbled.

Chapter 13

Sofia and I were breathless by the time we climbed to the third floor of the Lincoln building and staggered into the offices of Hochstetter, Schmidt, and Barker, Attorneys-At-Law. Elevator access was available, but due to my fear of tight, enclosed spaces, not an option.

Fortunately, Sofia convinced Dad to skip the meeting. He grumbled a bit, fired off a few of his favorite curses and stomped out to the backyard to tend to his new bee colony. Clawdius picked up on his mood. Tail swishing ominously, he followed Ed to the hives.

We paused inside the door to the attorneys' office and gazed around the reception area.

"Wow, nice," Sofia whispered. "Maybe I'll change my major to pre-law."

The room had all the trappings of success. Thick carpet. Walls adorned with modern art. Sleek leather chairs for those waiting to be summoned. The window wall featured a view of the city and a variety of sports memorabilia. A large framed photo of Hochstetter and Mickey Warren was prominently displayed. Clad in golf clothes, the two grinned into the camera while hoisting a trophy.

A receptionist sat behind a large barren desk adjacent to a single door, presumably the one leading to the inner sanctum. Phone pressed against her ear, she glanced at us through abnormally large, red-framed glasses and waved us into chairs.

"I wonder if he's here yet," Sofia whispered.

"I doubt it. As I remember, Antonio was late for everything. Some things never change."

She gave me a curious look. "You must have loved him once."

Not willing to go there, I shrugged. "Maybe. But then I had you to love."

"Good non-answer, Mom." Sofia was no fool.

Truthfully, Antonio shattered my tender teenage heart. Somehow, I managed to pick up the pieces and glue them back together. In doing so, I sealed off the hurt and pain of his abandonment and hid it away in the dark recesses of my mind. Probably not a healthy way to deal with trauma, but I was nineteen and had a baby to care for.

The receptionist finished her call, straightened her glasses, stood, and tottered around the desk on four-inch stilettos.

"Hi, there. I'm Gloria. Are you here for the Carone divorce proceedings? With Mr. Hochstetter?" she squeaked.

Her high-pitched little girl voice was in stark contrast to the ample bosom spilling from the neckline of a midnight blue silk blouse.

Sofia opened her mouth, but no words ensued. Apparently she was rendered speechless by the incongruity between the girlish voice and voluptuous womanly curves. I had no such problem.

"We're here about the Carone-McKenna divorce."

Gloria frowned at me. "Well, technically, yes. But since Mr. Carone's friend is paying the bill, it's been filed under his name. I'm sure you understand."

"Mr. Carone's friend?" Sofia said.

"Anne Marie Kirkpatrick. Senator Bradley Kirkpatrick's widow? Perhaps you've heard of him."

A stunned silence ensued while Sofia and I digested this new bit of information.

"Oh, here they are now," said Gloria.

The door opened and Antonio walked in. A woman old enough to be his mother clung to his arm.

"Holy Mother of God," Sofia whispered. "Is that the girlfriend?"

"Looks like it," I whispered back.

I was thirty-nine. Antonio was 4 years older, which made him forty-three. His new girlfriend was surely in her sixties. Stick-thin with tastefully frosted hair, she floated in on a cloud of expensive perfume, clinging to Antonio's arm with a bony hand tipped with scarlet, dagger-like fingernails. The skin on her face was tight and shiny, giving her a blank, doll-like expression. I assumed it had been cinched up a time or two. She wore a white pants suit over a silky black blouse. Black pumps completed the outfit. Simple, but classy.

Antonio acknowledged us with a quick smile and a nod, but made no attempt to introduce us to his new squeeze. His new, very wealthy squeeze. She looked me over briefly and then gazed at Sofia. Something dangerous flared in her eyes. I immediately morphed into mama bear.

I took Sofia's hand and stood. "Hello, I'm Antonio's wife, Libby McKenna Carone and this is our daughter, Sofia. And you are…"

I knew, of course, who she was, but couldn't resist a jab at the woman who'd shot an evil glance at my

Sofia. My words had the desired effect. Especially the word *wife*.

She blinked rapidly and drew herself up. "I am Anne Marie Kirkpatrick, formerly married to the honorable Bradley Kirkpatrick, United States senator from the great state of Arizona," she said in a deep smoker's voice. I gave Antonio a sweet smile. "So that's where you've been all this time, Antonio. Are there a lot of caves in Arizona? Or maybe just one special cave?"

Antonio flushed and opened his mouth. Before he could utter a word, Anne Marie snapped, "I'll handle this. Yes, there are caves in Arizona. My husband and I were happy to sponsor Antonio in his efforts. He's a very accomplished spelunker."

"Oh, yes, I know all about Antonio's spelunking ability and his affinity for caves. Actually, Sofia here—"

"Mom! Let's not go there."

Gloria clapped her hands to get our attention. "Well, goody, we're all here. I think Russell is ready for you. Please follow me."

Anne Marie mouthed the words, You won't be his wife much longer. Still clinging to Antonio's arm, she trailed behind Gloria.

"Best news I've heard all day," I called.

Sofia pulled me along. "Mom, what's the matter with you? Please, just shut the hell up. You're making it worse."

"But I feel sooo much better."

And, strangely, I did. The big ball of grief I'd hidden away came to life, caught fire and erupted into a red-hot blaze of anger. Like a rocket on Independence Day, my snarky comments could not be controlled.

Maybe I should declare it Libby Independence Day. Was it unfair of me to direct it at Anne Marie instead of the person who had caused me anguish? Probably. I figured she could handle it. Whereas Antonio would simply hang his head and mutter an insincere sorry.

As our merry little party of four headed for the conference room, the door to the office burst open once again. Two women entered, both of them red-faced and spitting mad. The resemblance between the two was obvious. Had to be mother and daughter.

"Uh, oh." Sofia gripped my arm and leaned close. "I know the younger one. She's Sierra Warren. I think the older one is her mother Patty, Mickey Warren's starter wife."

Astonished, I gaped at my daughter. "How do you know these things?"

She grinned. "Ear to the ground, Mama. You learn a lot that way. Besides, I was in school with Sierra. She was in the class ahead of me."

Gloria peeked around us. "May I help you?"

"You sure as hell can. I'm Patty Warren Taylor and this is my daughter, Sierra. We've been hearing some ugly rumors about rat bastard Mickey Warren's will. We need to see Russell Hochstetter. *Now*."

"Do you have an appointment?" Gloria made sure she was tucked behind the rest of us.

Patty Warren gripped her daughter's arm and plowed her way to the front of the line.

"Well, of all the nerve," Anne Marie huffed.

Patty Warren got up in Gloria's face. "No. I. Do. Not. Have. An. Appointment. Get Russell out here right now or, by God, I'll go find him myself."

Gloria's face lost color. Clearly, this was not in her

job description. "Please, everyone, have a seat. I'll go find Mr. Hochstetter and we'll get this straightened out."

She darted through the door and shut it behind her. The lock clicked and her heels clattered down the hall.

Patty and Sierra stood by the door, breathing angrily. The rest of us found seats. As I walked by Anne Marie, I smiled and said, "Looks like I'll be married to Antonio a little longer."

Two red spots burned high on her artificially smooth, porcelain cheeks. She pinched her lips together in anger.

Sofia, shaking with silent laughter, tugged me into a chair. "I don't know what happened to my mother, but I like her replacement."

Two hours passed before I became a free woman, unencumbered by the memory of an absentee husband. Papers were signed. Dirty looks were exchanged. Fortunately, no blood was shed. However, we did have one sticky moment.

Anne Marie tilted her head back so she could look down her nose at Sofia. "We are prepared to offer a generous lump sum payment to make up for Antonio's lack of monetary support over the years."

Sofia flushed and inhaled sharply. I gripped her hand and squeezed it, willing her to hold back the rush of angry words ready to burst from her lips.

I ignored Anne Marie and fixed my gaze on Antonio. "Does the word *we* include you as well? Or is this Kirkpatrick cash?"

"What does it matter? Money is money," Anne Marie snapped.

"Russ, in your final statement, please include the

following… ” I leaned over the table. “No, thank you, Anne Marie. I would rather set my face on fire and put it out with a fork than take your money.”

With that, we took our leave.

Chapter Fourteen

Three hours late for work, we sped toward the golf course. I began to have second thoughts about my bitchy attitude regarding Antonio's newfound love, the formidable widow Kirkpatrick.

"Sofia, I should have checked with you before I turned down the money. You've got three years of college left. It would have helped a lot."

Her head swiveled toward me. "Are you nuts? I don't want a penny of her money." She burst into fit of giggles.

"What's funny?"

"Your last remark was classic, Momser. The one about setting your face on fire."

"Something about that woman gets under my skin."

The entrance to Fairway to Heaven's parking lot was clogged with a group of protesters carrying picket signs including, 'Golfers, you will burn in hell.' 'Repent before it is too late.' 'CHANGE THE NAME, NOW!'

"Geez, I thought Christians were supposed to love their neighbors."

Sofia hopped from the car before it came to a full stop. She headed for the parking lot, dodging the picketers like a running back sprinting toward for the goal line.

As I headed for the clubhouse, Reverend Farley Faraday stepped in front of me. “I warned you. Do you remember what I said?”

Still fuming from my altercation with Anne Marie Kirkpatrick, I snapped, “You’re on private property. Get out of my way. I’m late for work.”

I darted around his bulk. He trailed after me.

“I told you to ignore us at your own risk. I told you God punishes sinners. And now, a man was murdered on your golf course. Maybe you should have listened to me,” he shouted.

I whirled and met his angry glare with one of my own. “Now, you listen to me. It is not my golf course. I work here.” I paused and stepped closer to him, even though every fiber in my being wanted to back away. “Here’s a thought. Since you’re the one all worked up about Fairway to Heaven’s name, maybe you and your followers decided to leave a calling card on one of our fairways to help your cause. So tell me, Reverend Farley, where were you when Mickey Warren met his Maker?”

His eyes widened in surprise. “How dare you speak to a man of God in this manner?”

I forced a phony smile. “A true man of God wouldn’t be marching around threatening people and carrying signs with hateful messages.”

Shaking with anger, I marched toward the clubhouse. Maybe I wasn’t cut out for more than one confrontation a day. When I stepped into the pro shop, another surprise awaited me. A complete stranger was behind the counter where Tristan was supposed to be. His gaze was fixed on the computer screen.

I looked for Rita and found her in the kitchen

dishing up three plates of burgers and fries.

"Do we have a new employee? Did I get fired?"

She rolled her eyes and shook her head in disgust. "When our favorite golf pro showed up to cover for you—late as usual—this guy was with him. Apparently he's Tristan's new best friend. About twenty minutes ago, Tris had pressing business to take care of—probably a new hot blonde—and asked me to take over the counter. I said I had hungry golfers to feed. Not a lie, by the way. So he stomps off in a huff and the next thing I know, his buddy is behind the counter."

I mumbled a few of Dad's favorite curses under my breath and patted Rita on the shoulder. "Not your fault. I'll take care of it."

As I walked away, she said, "Um, maybe you should cool down a bit. Bad morning?"

I grinned at her. "Actually, it was a pretty good morning. I'm no longer a married woman."

She snort-laughed. "Pretty funny since none of us knew you were married until a few days ago."

I approached the counter. The guy didn't bother to look up. I wanted to say, 'Great customer service,' but thought better of it. I was more interested in what he found so fascinating on the computer screen. I slipped behind the counter and sidled up next to him. He studied the member list, which included personal information. Totally none of his business.

I bit back my outrage and attempted a civil tone. "Hi, I'm Libby McKenna, and you are…?"

Not in the least perturbed, he closed down the member list and looked down at me through pale blue eyes. I'm fairly tall, about five-eight, but this guy was well over six feet with a muscular build. His wavy brown hair was swept back and jelled. Clad in pricey golf duds, he would have no trouble fitting in with Fairway to Heaven's wealthiest clientele.

He stuck out a hand. "So you're Libby. I've heard a lot about you from Tris. I'm Jonathan Dumas. Call me Jon."

I gripped his hand, a little harder than necessary. Yeah, I bet you got an earful about me from Tristan. "Speaking of Tris, He's supposed to be covering for me."

Jon freed his hand and flashed a teensy, condescending smile revealing perfect white teeth. "Here's the thing. He forgot he'd scheduled a lesson. So I'm covering for him. Is that a problem?"

"Actually, it is. The information on the computer is private. Our members expect it to be safeguarded. May I ask your interest in the member list?"

"I've been away for a few years. Thought I'd check to see if any of my buddies play golf here." One perfect eyebrow shot up in disbelief. "Surely you don't think I was doing something shady."

Actually, the thought had crossed my mind. I struggled to speak in a non-judgmental tone. "Any luck?"

"Luck?"

"Yeah, did you find any of your old buddies?"

He shrugged and pushed by me. "I'll leave you to it."

Later, when Rita's lunch crowd thinned out, I asked her to take over for me. "I need to talk to Tristan."

She tapped the side of her head. "Tristan the Turd. No toys in the attic. Nothin' at all."

I found him on the putting green with two teenage girls who were half-heartedly tapping a ball back and forth between them. Tristan didn't see me coming. He was leaning on his putter, checking the girls out.

"Hey, Tris, we need to talk."

Startled, he spun around. "Oh, hey, Libby. What's up?"

"Over here." I pointed out a shady spot next to the cart shed. "And FYI, girls," I called. "The point of putting is to put the ball in the hole."

"Golf is boring. Dad is making us take lessons," one of the girls said.

"Easy money, huh Tris?"

"I'm guessing you're pissed off."

"I'm guessing you're right. Why the hell would you let this Dumas guy cover for you? People hand over their credit cards, Tristan. There's information on the computer we need to keep private. I don't care if he's a friend of yours. He was scrolling through the membership on the computer. That's unacceptable."

Tristan flushed. "He's totally responsible. You know Janice Pomeroy. Right?"

"Yes. She's on the board. Recording secretary."

He placed his hands on his hips and glared. "For your information, Jon is practically a member of her family. He's Serena's boyfriend."

"Who's Serena?"

"Janice's daughter."

"But Janice doesn't have children. Everybody knows that."

Tristan stroked his chin and smirked. "Well, guess what? She does. Years ago, before she was married to Pomeroy, she gave a baby up for adoption. Serena reached out to her and they re-connected. One big happy family. Right?"

I took a moment to process and then chose my words carefully. "Tristan. Jon may be an upstanding citizen, but taking care of customers is your responsibility. Are we clear?"

"Crystal. Bitch," he muttered as I walked away.

Chapter Fifteen

The rest of the day passed without incident. Thank you, God. Tristan showed up promptly at five p.m. His new bestie, Jon, was not around. Tris was still pouting and wouldn't make eye contact. I was tempted to channel my teenage daughter and say, 'Whatever.' I resisted the urge and praised him for being punctual. Roses, not sour grapes. That's my philosophy until something else goes sideways.

Frazzled by the events of the day, I pulled into the driveway and slammed on the brakes. Strung across the driveway was an enormous banner saying 'HAPPY DIVORCE DAY!' I climbed out of the car to read the small script printed below. "Get your butt next door. There's a party going on at R and D's!"

I stepped through the gate leading to Ronny and Donny's yard. The back door was open. The sounds of hilarity stemming from copious amounts of alcohol spilled out.

Jules appeared in the doorway. She spread her arms wide. "Hey there, girlfriend! We started without you."

"You're here? Where's your car?"

"Ed picked me up. We wanted it to be a surprise. Are you surprised?"

I bounded up the stairs and gave her a big hug. "Yes, in a good way."

She took my hand and led me through the kitchen.

The house was every bit as old as ours, but the boys had modernized it. The gleaming granite countertops with a colorful backsplash made me realize how pathetic our house looked. I made a mental note to talk to Dad about updating the kitchen. I would probably be greeted with a dismissive flap of the hand and 'it's fine.' Worth a try.

A chorus of cheers welcomed me, along with a glass of Light in the Loafers.

Donny made the toast. "Here's to our dear Libby. She's a free woman, ready to dip her toes, and perhaps other body parts, into the dating pool."

Hoots of laughter and a resounding, "Amen," from my dad greeted his words.

What?

After we clinked glasses, I said, "Really, Dad, you think I should be dating?"

"Well, duh."

Sofia chimed in, "Why do you think I've been trying to hook you up with Riley?"

Ronny said, "By the way, we invited him. At first he thought we were just, um, well, you know how we feel about Sheriff Stud Muffin. He claimed he had a heavy caseload and couldn't make it. Then,we told him the party was for you and, suddenly, his load got lighter."

I ran a hand through my hair, aware of how frazzled I looked.

"No worries, Mom," Sofia said. "He likes the way you look. He told me painted up ladies aren't his type. His words, not mine."

"It wouldn't hurt to freshen up your lipstick," said Jules.

I shook my head. “If my looks scare him away, so be it.”

Donny filled everyone’s glass again and offered a second toast. “Here’s to Libby, a natural beauty inside and out.”

As everyone lifted their glasses, I realized how special my family and friends were, especially after a rough day. “Thanks, guys, I needed that.”

Dad hoisted himself off the couch, crossed the room and wrapped me up in a big hug. He whispered, “I’m proud of you, Chickadee. Look at Baby Bird. She’s our pride and joy, and it’s because of you.”

His words were so sweet, so unexpected, my eyes filled with tears. “Damn it, Dad, you’re gonna make me cry.”

Our sentimental moment was interrupted by the arrival of Dad’s girlfriend, Suzy Reynolds. Clad in skin-tight blue jeans and a fluorescent lime v-necked tee that displayed her ample bosom, she held a wooden tray aloft.

“Behold,” she said. “Our new venture. Suzy’s Bodacious Booty Bunz and Ed’s Special Dark Honey, hand delivered with an original greeting card from Lib&Jules. Ta-da!”

Suzy and Dad had been “keepin’ company”—his words—for the last five years. Suzy was a self-described entrepreneur. She ran two businesses, Suzy Rentz and Suzy’s Booty Buns Bakery. The former featured houses she’d flipped. She bought them on the cheap, hired a bunch of day workers to do renovations and sold them outright or used them as rentals. Her bakery specialized in buns formed in the anatomically correct shape of human buttocks and came in a variety of flavors. When Suzy's buns came out of the oven, crowds of people waited to hand over their hard-earned money.

Dad joined her, beaming with pride. "This here is genius. People want my special honey and they love Suzy's buns." He patted her butt. "I love them, too."

This earned Dad a standing ovation and cheers of, "Right on, Ed."

"Anyhoo," he continued, "my smart little sweetie here came up with a killer plan."

I glanced over at Jules. Did she know about this? She grinned and gave me a thumbs-up.

"Here's the deal," Suzy said. "We have the whole package. Honey and buns along with a special card from our creative girls, Libby and Jules. We're starting a delivery service. And who knows! Maybe Ronny and Donny might want to join in with a bottle of wine."

As Donny opened his mouth to reply, Ronny exclaimed, "I do believe Sheriff Sweet Cheeks just pulled in."

"Might be best if we don't mention the special honey, him being the law and all," I said before the two could rush to the door.

"Oh, please, he's probably a customer. Right, Ed?" Jules said.

Dad made a zipping motion across his lips. His action resulted in applause and laughter. Was I the only innocent in the crowd?

Ronny and Donny tripped over each other in their eagerness to open the front door.

"Welcome to our humble abode, Sheriff O'Connor."

Riley entered the living room, spotted me and

smiled. "It's not like I haven't been here before."

"Yes, in your official capacity. You're off duty now. Donny, get the sheriff a glass of wine. Not Light in the Loafers, maybe a hearty red," said Ronny.

"No offense, boys, but I'm more of a beer guy."

Dad approved. He plunged a hand into the cooler by his chair, pulled out a local beer, uncapped it, and handed it to Riley. He took a big slurp and walked over to me.

"I need to talk to you." He looked around the room. "In private."

Ronny and Donny looked disappointed, but led the two of us to their office. They left the door open a crack.

Riley closed it tightly. "I think I hear breathing. Are they out there, listening?"

"Probably." I opened the door. "Get lost," then whispered, "I'll fill you in later."

I closed the door firmly and leaned against it. "So is this about Mickey Warren?"

Riley leaned against the desk and looked me over. "The boys said this is a divorce party. How did it go?"

"Fine. Is that why you wanted to talk to me?"

"One of the reasons. But it's also about Warren. What do you know about Earl Tomlinson?'

"Earl was Mickey's best buddy. They were in the same golf foursome and worked together at Mickey's car business. Why?"

"Tomlinson was Warren's finance guy and apparently has a gambling problem. I talked to people at the car dealership. Warren and Tomlinson had a huge blow-up last week. It was behind closed doors, but folks heard them yelling. Apparently there were large sums of money missing and unaccounted for."

"So if he was embezzling money from the dealership and Mickey found out…."

"It's a good motive for murder."

I gnawed on my lip, thinking it over. "A lot of people hated Mickey." I filled him in on Patty Warren and her daughter. "Have you talked to Reverend Farley Faraday? He showed up at our board meeting the night before Mickey was killed and made threats about changing the name of our golf course. He and I had a confrontation today at the golf course. He basically told me Mickey's death was proof that God punishes sinners. You might want to find out where he was when Mickey was killed."

Riley nodded. "I'll check it out. Anything else?"

I shook my head.

He walked over to me, placed his hands on my shoulders and gazed into my eyes. The heat from his hands spiraled through my body, heading south.

He gave me a knowing grin.

"Then let's join the party."

Chapter Sixteen

On Sunday evening, I stood outside the Cavendish estate, one finger poised over the doorbell. I steadied my nerves, ready for thunderous sound to pour from the hidden speakers, not to mention the formidable Felicity Horncastle.

I arrived armed with a detailed synopsis and two chapters of *Pirate's Plunder.* Bowing to Abigail's request for 'hot stuff' I'd dashed off a couple pages describing Striker's first paddle up Coochie Creek. I'd written the purple passion on my laptop in the breakfast nook. Since Dad and Sofia kept trying to peek over my shoulder, I waited until they'd gone to bed. Even then, I blushed as the words appeared on the screen.

To my surprise, the door opened before I could press the button. Instead of Felicity Horncastle, a smiling Abigail greeted me.

"Libby, my dear, please come in. I can't wait to see what you've written."

I followed her circuitous route through the massive house. She led me through glass doors and onto a patio overlooking the golf course. The sun, dipping down in the west, cast a golden dappled light across the fairway, highlighting a house equally as impressive as Abigail's. This perspective was vastly different from what I'd experienced zipping around on a golf cart sorting out problems. Instead of outside looking in, I was inside looking out. Not my world, but why not enjoy the view?

Abigail pointed at wicker chairs with deep blue cushions grouped around a glass table topped with a matching sun umbrella. "Have a seat, dear."

Binoculars and a highly polished silver bell were placed next to the umbrella.

I quickly joined her when I realized I'd been gaping, open-mouthed at my surroundings. All business now, I gave her the synopsis.

"Let me know if this is what you have in mind. I can make changes if you want."

Heart fluttering with nervous anticipation, I waited for her reaction. Abigail would not be a good poker player. Her emotions were easy to read as she scanned the pages. At first, her brows pulled together in consternation. Had I chosen the wrong words? Shortly after, the corners of her mouth lifted in a smile of delight, accompanied by a humming sound. I wasn't sure what to make of the humming, but she seemed to be enjoying herself.

She placed the synopsis on the table and gazed into my eyes. "Oh my, I do believe I like Striker very much. Yes, I know I do. And this Rowena woman. Will she shed her corset at some point?"

I assured her Rowena would turn into a veritable sex kitten. I handed over the first two chapters and the standalone *hot* scene. "Two chapters and a little something else. I anticipate it will happen around Chapter Eight."

When Abigail finished reading, her cheeks were pink and she fanned herself with the papers. I hoped this was a favorable response, not a heart attack about to happen.

Abigail's eyes twinkled but she said not a word. She picked up the silver bell and rang it. Felicity Horncastle, apparently lurking close by, popped through the door.

"Yes, Mersus Cavendish?"

"Felicity, please fetch my checkbook and a pen."

I held my breath. Should I keep quiet? Ask if she liked it? Not wanting to appear too eager, I opted for silence.

It was worth the wait.

With a flourish, Abigail presented me with a check for $10,000. "Here's to a wonderful beginning. The remainder will be paid upon completion. I so look forward to the rest of the book."

I thanked her profusely and rose from my chair.

"You sit right back down, my girl. We must have a small libation and social chitchat before you leave." She clapped her hands. "Felicity? Champagne, post haste. The good stuff. There's a bottle in the fridge."

Though I had bajillion things to do at home, I didn't want to appear ungrateful, and honestly, how could I refuse?

As we sipped the expensive bubbly, Abigail chattered non-stop.

At one point she stood and squinted into the fading sunlight. "Hmm, I wonder what's going on over there. I'd best check it out." With a naughty wink, she said, "Just call me the neighborhood watch."

She lifted the binoculars, sweeping them back and forth as she focused on her neighbors across the golf course. It was almost dark, but a few hardcore golfers were hacking their way to the finish line.

Abigail pointed at the house directly across from us. "Herb Talcott, checking out the stragglers. What a busybody. Let's see who else is out and about." She moved the binoculars to the right. "There's Stella Roy taking her yappy little dog out for a pee."

She peeked over the binoculars at me. "She married up, you know. When Miles Roy lost his first wife, she started coming around. Bringing him covered dishes. Practically threw herself at him. Guess he likes big boobs, because it wasn't long before she moved in."

I wanted to clap my hands over my ears and mutter about too much information. But since Abigail was my own personal goose with the golden eggs, I nodded and kept quiet.

She swept the binoculars to the lcft. "And there's Janice Pomeroy snippin' her roses. Have you heard the latest?"

Not sure where she was headed, I shook my head.

Abigail's eyes flashed. "Well," she huffed, "Apparently some long lost daughter of hers turned up and moved in with her boyfriend. What do you think of that?"

I tried to couch my words as diplomatically as possible. "Not knowing the situation, I really don't have an opinion. Is Janice okay with it?"

Abigail clucked her tongue. "Who knows? She's such a mousy little thing. If you ask me, it's all about her money. When Elmer Pomeroy kicked off, he made Janet a very rich widow. Then the daughter shows up? Bit too coincidental, if you ask me."

Since Abigail had an abundance of information regarding her rich neighbors, I asked, "Did you know Mickey Warren?"

She blew out air. “Dreadful man. I heard it wasn’t a heart attack after all, that somebody offed him.”

“Any idea who?”

“Where do I start?”

I wanted to reach for paper and pen, but thought better of it. She used her fingers to keep track of her favorite suspects, beginning with Warren’s current wife and girlfriend.

“Did you know his first wife?”

Two more fingers shot up. “Yes, I know Patty Warren and Sierra. I hear they were cut out of the will.”

“Anybody else?”

“Maybe the golf pro, Tristan something or other.”

I shook my head. “Don’t think so. Mickey and Tris were buddies.”

Abigail frowned at me. “I respectfully disagree. Rumor has it Tristan’s parents were disgusted with his profligate ways and cut off the family funds. Apparently, he was borrowing money from Warren to maintain his status and lifestyle.”

“If that’s the case, why would Tristan kill his cash cow?”

Abigail’s shoulders lifted in a shrug. “Who knows? Maybe Warren threatened to stop supporting him.”

“Maybe. Anybody else?”

“Probably everyone in his foursome. He was a cheater, you know. Word gets around.”

“Do you really think someone would commit murder because the person cheated at golf?”

“Murder has been committed for less.”

Her words rang in my ears on the drive home.

Should I add Tris’s name to my list of suspects?

Chapter Seventeen

"Stop!"

Sofia was coming at me with a make-up case and curling iron. Jules trailed after her, a pink sundress in one hand, a pair of wedgie sandals in the other. My command did nothing to deter them.

"Sorry, Momser," Sofia said. "Tonight's the big date. I heard he's taking you to someplace nice."

"Define *nice*."

"Nice, as in white linen tablecloths and china."

"I heard that, too," Jules said. "I bet Riley O'Connor is a carnivore. Therefore, he's probably taking her to the new steak place. It's pricey but super nice. They even have an enclosed patio for outdoor dining."

I shook my head in disbelief. "How do you guys know the details of my upcoming date before I do?"

Jules grinned at Sofia. "We'll never tell."

Both busted out laughing. Why did I sense a conspiracy was afoot?

Fighting a losing battle, I gave in to their beautification attempts.

"Remember what you said. Riley doesn't like painted-up ladies."

Sofia studied my face like an artist perusing a blank canvas. "No worries. I'll make you look like a natural beauty."

"Which you are," Jules added quickly. "Now, what about some jewelry?"

I couldn't resist. "I thought I was a natural beauty. Now you want to gild the lily?"

"A little bling never hurts," Jules said, fastening a silver pendant around my neck.

"Wear your charm bracelet," Sofia ordered. "It's all about you. It even has a Libby charm."

I pawed through my mostly junk jewelry, searching for the bracelet Dad and Sofia gave me for my thirty-fifth birthday. "It's gone. Sofia, did you borrow it?"

She rolled her eyes. "Oh please, would I borrow a bracelet with the name Libby on it? When did you last wear it?"

"Not sure. I may have worn it to work."

"Maybe the clasp broke. Want me to look in your car?" said Jules.

I glanced at the time. "No, I'll look for it later."

In the midst of my makeover, Dad stormed in. "That son of a bitch! If he doesn't quit driving by our house, I'm getting my shotgun."

I darted around Sofia who was wielding a mascara wand. "What son of a bitch, Dad?"

"That fake minister, the one who came to our board meeting."

"Farley Faraday?"

"Yep, Farley on a Harley and his teeny weeny wife who's stuck to his back like a baby monkey. They keep cruising by our house."

Sofia nodded. "Last night, I kept hearing a Harley drive by. I looked outside and it was the Faradays. He'd drive real slow by the house and then gun the motor."

"How many times?" I asked.

"At least five times."

A shiver of fear snaked through my body, followed by anger. "Sofia, why didn't you tell me? You were here alone. Those two are wing nuts. Who knows what they might do?"

Sofia shrugged. "It wasn't a big deal, Mom. Yeah, they're definitely weird, but I doubt if they're dangerous. Besides, I know how to use the shotgun. You taught me. Remember?"

Sofia was trying to distract me by dredging up a fond family memory, namely the two of us in a vacant lot, plinking at tin cans.

I placed my hands on her shoulders and gazed into her guileless brown eyes. "I know you think you're invincible, my darling, but you're not. So, please, if it happens again and you're here by yourself, call Pops or me. Promise?"

She didn't like it, but nodded. "Yeah, okay. Whatever. I promise."

"Right on," Dad said. "In the meantime, I'll hang around tonight so you don't have to worry about anything while you're on your hot date."

"Absolutely," Jules added. "No worries. We've got it covered."

I flapped my hands at them. "I think all of you are more invested in my so-called hot date than I am."

Sofia snickered. "Just remember, Mom, you don't have a curfew. Now get your buns back to the beauty parlor."

****

Fifteen minutes before Riley's arrival, I was trotted out to the living room for Dad's approval.

"Presenting the lovely lady of the evening,

Elizabeth McKenna."

"Jules, lady of the evening makes her sound like a ho. Please don't say that when Riley arrives." Sofia scowled.

Dad clapped and whistled. "Chickadee, you look beautiful. It's about time you went out and had some fun."

Actually, I was feeling pretty good in the pink cotton sundress with wide straps and square cut neckline. It showed a bit of my barely adequate cleavage. Jules had strapped me into a push-up bra, claiming the girls needed a little help. Also the three-inch sandals, insisting I had beautiful long legs and to show them off. When Jules was on a roll, there was no stopping her.

Riley arrived promptly at 6:15. Like me, he looked nothing like his former self. I wondered who had done his makeover. No uniform tonight. The little paunch he always sported—probably due to his preference for hoppy beers—was totally sucked in and tucked inside a pair of crisply pressed jeans. He wore a collarless silk black tee topped with a sport coat. Cowboy boots completed the image.

He looked me over, his eyes widening in appreciation. "Damn, how did you get away from Hollywood? You look gorgeous, girl."

I linked my arm through his. "You look pretty good yourself."

"Mom," Sofia called as we headed for the door.

I turned around. She had her cell phone in hand and snapped a picture.

I groaned. Riley laughed.

"Sofia," I scolded. "We're not going to the prom.

Okay?"

Sofia flashed a thumbs-up.

"Have fun, kids. Stay out as late as you want," Jules said.

As we walked to Riley's classic muscle car, I said, "Sorry about the dithery-do. Guess I haven't been out for a while."

"Then it's about time. I'll try to make it worth your while."

He opened the passenger door and helped me inside then backed out of the driveway and headed toward town. "Thought we'd try the new steak place. Okay with you?"

We were just minutes away from the restaurant when I heard the unmistakable sound of a Harley Davidson. It tucked in behind us, riding our bumper.

Riley glanced in the rearview mirror and tensed. "It's that asshole Faraday. I talked to him yesterday. He mentioned your name. Said you made some sort of accusation. I told him you had nothing to do with my investigation. He must be watching your house."

"He is." I filled him in on last night's events.

A flush of anger rose in his cheeks. "Well, damn. Maybe I need another word with Farley on a Harley."

He pulled over to the curb and hit the brakes. Faraday zipped around us and took off.

Riley glanced over at me. "Mind if we're a little late for dinner?"

"Not at all. Go for it."

"Hang on."

He punched the accelerator. My head snapped back as the powerful V-8 engine sprung to life. I wanted to holler, "Yowser, let's get the son of a bitch." Instead I braced my body against the door and enjoyed the chase.

When Faraday realized we were now riding his bumper, he gunned the motor and tried a couple of half-hearted evasive moves. Left turn into a residential neighborhood. Quick right turn. Oopsy daisy, cul-de-sac.

Riley grinned at me. "Got him."

Faraday dismounted. Faith remained on her perch.

"Stay in the car," Riley said before climbing out.

Stay in the car? No way. First of all, I don't like men barking orders at me. Secondly, I was the one being harassed. And finally, I wanted Faraday to know he couldn't intimidate me.

Riley strode up to Faraday. "You and me need to talk, podner."

Though Riley was a solid six-footer, Faraday loomed over him. "We got nothin' to talk about."

I peered around Riley. "Why are you driving by my house?"

Riley jerked in surprise. He tilted his head toward the car. I shook mine.

"Nice neighborhood. Might want to buy a house on your block. Probably not, though. I try to steer clear of sinners," Faraday said with a mirthless chuckle.

Riley stiffened. "Word of warning. Stay away from the lady and her family. Got it?"

Faraday shrugged like he didn't have a care in the world. "It's a free country and I have civil rights. It would be a shame if your personal relationship with this so-called lady endangered my freedom of speech. Right, *podner*?"

He mounted his bike and tooled away.

Stiff with anger, Riley clenched and unclenched his

fists. I linked my arm through his. “Let’s go eat steak.”

As we walked to the car, his body relaxed. He gave me a sideways glance. “Didn’t like me giving you orders, huh?”

I smiled up at him and squeezed his arm. “Best you should find out now.”

Chapter Eighteen

Despite the rocky start, the drinks we had before dinner smoothed out the rough edges. Wine for me, beer for him, even though the prices made me cringe. When I offered to go Dutch, he waggled a finger in warning.

"I asked you out. My treat."

"Next time, it's my turn."

The second I uttered the words, I wanted to take them back. Next time? This is hound dog Riley O'Connor you're with, dummy. The contact list on his phone is probably chock full of willing women. He picked up on my embarrassment, reached across the table and covered my hand with his.

"Trust me, there will be a next time."

The comment earned him a bunch of brownie points.

Throughout the evening I learned a great deal about Riley. After graduating from law school at UCLA, he passed the bar, but hated being a lawyer. A brief, unhappy marriage followed. No kids. Feeling at loose ends, he joined the Army as an MP. It was there he discovered his affinity for law enforcement.

"How did you end up in Eastern Washington?"

"I needed wide open spaces. No such thing in So Cal."

"So I've heard."

I looked around at the suddenly overflowing restaurant. The Sagebrush Bar and Grill was definitely upscale for Vista Valley. But Monday night? Really? When did Monday become a date night?

"Oh, no." I spotted a familiar couple following the hostess to the table next to ours and groaned.

Riley's head swiveled left and right. "What?"

"Remember my divorce party?" I whispered.

"Yes."

"You're about to meet my ex and his very rich girlfriend."

Riley's gaze swept over the two. One eyebrow shot up. "That's his girlfriend?"

"Yes. Don't be alarmed at what happens next. It's something I have to do."

"Go for it, girl."

The hostess pulled out their chairs, but Anne Marie didn't sit. She snagged Antonio's hand and dragged him to our table. He was muttering in Italian and obviously embarrassed.

Anne Marie extended her left hand to display the enormous diamond on her claw-like ring finger. "Antonio and I were wed today. I am now Mrs. Carone."

Don't go there.

But I did. Something about this woman brought out my inner beast. It always lurked beneath the surface, but I usually kept it under tight rein. Not tonight.

I jumped from my chair and threw my arms around a stunned Antonio. "*Congratulazioni*, Antonio! *Molto bene. Sarai ricco.*"

He quickly pushed me away but managed to say, "*Grazie*."

Anne Marie whirled toward Antonio. "What did she say?"

"Just congratulations," he said.

I forced a phony smile. "Allow me to translate. My exact words were, congratulations, Antonio. Well done. You will now be rich."

"Sore loser," she hissed.

"Happy loser."

She turned her back and snapped her fingers at a waiter. "We would like another table. This woman is bothering us."

Riley and I burst into laughter. He raised his glass and tipped it toward me. "Good job."

On our way out of the restaurant, I spotted Tristan and his buddy Jon. They sat at a table with Janice Pomeroy and a woman I presumed was the long-lost daughter. With her curly light brown hair and strong features, she bore no resemblance to Janice. Still, there was something familiar about her. Tris raised a hand in greeting and whispered something to Jon. I felt the heat of their gazes as we made our way through the tables, Riley's hand on my back.

Once outside, I said, "Sorry I made a scene. Anne Marie pushes all my buttons."

He slung an arm around my shoulders and squeezed me. "No apologies. It was epic. Wouldn't have missed it for the world."

Back in the car, Riley said, "Too early to go home. Let's find someplace to dance."

"You dance?"

"Hell, yeah, like a dancing bear in the circus. Why are you so surprised?"

"Well, um, guess I didn't think you were the

dancing type."

He gave me a heated look. "Maybe I have an ulterior motive. If we find someplace to dance, I can wrap my arms around you, hold you close and it's all legit."

I laughed. "At least you're honest."

My cell phone buzzed. I dug it out of my purse. Sofia. Alarm bells clanged. Sofia wouldn't call unless it was important.

"Sorry," I told Riley. "It's my daughter."

"No problem."

Sofia's voice was tinged with panic. "Mom, I'm so sorry to bother you. I'm with Gabe Espinoza. We were having dinner when Sammy called. Someone vandalized their place. We're here now. Oh, Mom, it's awful. Somebody splashed blood all over their fence. And left a sign that says, 'Blood of the lamb has been shed for sinners like you.'"

I quickly relayed the message to Riley.

He took the phone from me. "Hey, little girl. No worries, we're on our way."

I grabbed the phone back. "Are you okay, Sofia?"

Her voice was quivering. "It's just seeing that blood. You know…"

I did know. Sofia will never work in the medical field. The sight of blood makes her weak, dizzy and prone to fainting.

Before we clicked off, Riley jotted down the address. "I'll contact my deputy and we'll meet up there. Okay, honey?"

Five minutes later we parked in front of the blood-spattered white picket fence. Sofia's face was ashen and she was shaking.

Sammy was beyond furious. His family home was his pride and joy. He took care of it as lovingly as he did the golf course.

Upon questioning, he shook his head. “I hear nothing. Watching video with lots of loud bangs. You understand. *Si*?”

I hugged him. “I’ll come over tomorrow and help you clean up.”

He shook his head. “No, no, Libby. You have enough to do. I have many sons. We will take care of it. Is baby girl okay?”

Sofia stood with Gabe. He had his arms wrapped around her, holding her upright.

“I think so. It’s the blood. She can’t handle it.”

“My Gabe will help her.”

“I know he will.” Fighting tears, I gripped his calloused hand in both of mine. “Don’t worry about coming to work tomorrow. You’ll want to get this cleaned up.”

He shook his head. “No, no, Sammy will not miss work.”

Of course not. Silly me.

“Okay, see ya tomorrow.”

Gabe loaded Sofia into the car and we headed home. Sofia dashed out, leaving Riley and me alone.

“Had to be Faraday,” I said.

“Sneaky bastard,” Riley said. “He’ll slip up soon and we’ll be ready.”

He walked me to the front porch. I turned and slipped into his arms, feeling the comfort of his warm, solid body.

He dropped a kiss on top of my head. “Go take care of your daughter. No worries. We’ll try this again soon. I haven't given up on my quest to get to know you a whole lot better, if you get my drift."

I looked up at him. "Oh, yeah, I get your drift. Is that a flashlight in your pocket, Sheriff?"

He stepped away from me with a bark of laughter. "You're something else, Libby. Bet you'll never forget this date, huh?"

I put my hand on the doorknob and then turned to face him. "You're right about that. See ya."

"Yep," he said with a two-finger salute. "You sure will."

Chapter Nineteen

For the next few days, peace reigned, a welcome relief after the emotional upheaval we'd been through. The Last Bus to Salvation people seemed to be losing steam. Only a few sign-carrying folks showed up on the sidewalk and they didn't look happy about it. Maybe the Faradays opted for a low profile after their Monday night antics. Even Tristan the Turd was cooperating. After our altercation, he showed up on time to relieve me. Sulky, but on time. His buddy, Jon, was still around but taking care to stay out of my range.

Shortly after our abbreviated date, Riley dropped by the clubhouse. He patted his tummy. "Need to feed the beast. Hear it growling? It wants a bowl of Rita's chili and a big old hunk of corn bread. Care to join me?"

Before I could answer, Rita said, "Chili for two. Coming right up."

I closed down the computer and joined him. "I need to keep an eye on the counter. Might have to dine and dash. Nothing personal."

Between bites, he filled me in on the latest Mickey Warren news. "The coroner released his body. Apparently wife number two is planning a memorial service."

"Should be interesting. I wonder if wife number one is invited. They had a daughter together."

Riley shook his head. “What a mess. Two exes and a girlfriend, all madder than hell. Could be a real catfight. I plan to attend. How about you? Shall we call it our second date?”

I wiped a bit of chili from my chin and smiled. “Hard to top the first one.”

Rita, who had ears like a bunny, called from the kitchen, “No worries about the girlfriend. Tammy has moved on.”

Riley arched a brow in surprise. “What are you, Rita, the town crier?”

She appeared, one hand on her hip. “You betcha, Sheriff. You need my help figuring stuff out, just ask.”

“Good to know,” Riley said.

She pulled up a chair and lowered her voice to a raspy whisper. “I hear there’s some hanky panky going on with the will. Mickey was loaded with money. He bragged about it all the time. Now everyone wants a cut. Apparently Heather, wife number two, is challenging the pre-nup. And Patty, the first wife, thinks Heather is trying to grab it all for herself.”

She paused, leaned close and shielded her mouth with one hand even though we were the only ones present. “Now for the good stuff. A source who’s close to the family and will remain nameless, told me Heather thinks Patty shouldn’t get anything because she re-married, and Sierra, the daughter, is an adult.”

She stood and made a zipping motion across her mouth. “Don’t let on you heard it from me, Sheriff. I’d hate to be accused of gossiping.”

When she sashayed away, Riley said, “I think that ship has sailed.”

He’d barely finished his lunch when his transmitter

crackled to life. "Naked guy running down Main Street."

He dropped a wad of bills on the table. "Duty calls. Gotta go stop a nude crime wave. See you soon."

I scooped up the money and took it to Rita who counted it. "That's way too much. Tell him he gets free chili next time."

Jules breezed in clutching a large gift-wrapped basket. "Guess who I just ran into? Guess who's no longer wearing his wedding ring?"

"I noticed."

"Good girl."

She set the basket down on a table and fished out a card. "Our first delivery is to Abigail Cavendish. Here's the greeting card. My illustration. Your words. If you like it, I'll print off more. Suze says she's getting a ton of orders."

I've always loved Jules's artwork and this was no exception. The top of the card featured a bee with antennas and a big, goofy smile, perched on a rosebud. The stem of the rose trailed gracefully down the left side of the card and wound around an extremely accurate drawing of a booty bun. The words I'd penned filled the center of the card, done in intricate calligraphy.

Ed's Special Honey and Buns by Suze
Will Lighten Your Load and Help You Snooze
When the Daily Grind Leaves You Tired and Testy
There's Plenty for Two, so Share with your Besty.

"Love the illustration, but the poem's kind of cheesy," I said.

"Stop that." She shook a finger in my face. "People love cheesy. By the way, I heard from Cheryl Abbot.

She was raving about our anniversary card. Said she showed it to all her friends and we'll be getting more orders. So no more talk about cheesy. Let's talk about horny. How's my favorite pirate, Striker the plunderer, coming along?"

"Chapter Eight coming up."

"Has he scored yet?"

I lifted a hand in protest. "All in good time. Remember, Jules, this is a tender love story."

"Riiiight," She drew the word out as long as possible and her eyebrows did the up and down thing.

The phone shrilled, two people came in for a bucket of balls, and I fielded a couple of complaints about slow play. When the hubbub subsided, I found Jules staring out the windows overlooking the driving range. She motioned for me to join her.

"Who's the guy with Tristan? Looks like they're having an issue."

I squinted through the sun bouncing off the window. "It's Jonathan Dumas. Tris told me he's the boyfriend of Janice Pomeroy's long-lost daughter."

Jules frowned. "No way."

"So he says."

"He's a big dude and he looks pissed off."

I went to the door, opened it and looked out. The two were deeply involved in intense conversation. They didn't notice me noticing them. Jon loomed over Tristan. His chin jutted forward and his fists clenched. Tris wasn't backing down. He was talking a mile a minute, but I was too far away. Couldn't hear a word. I hoped it wouldn't become physical, but checked the location of the nearest hose in case I had to spray them down.

Jon leaned closed to Tristan, poked him in the chest, then whirled and stomped away. Tris stood stock-still for a moment, and then, hands thrust in his pockets, walked toward the clubhouse. Spotting me, he pivoted to the left and headed for the practice green. Something about his sad, slump-shouldered demeanor plucked at my heartstrings. Was Jon the bully and Tris the victim? I didn't know for sure, but I surely owed more to Tristan than to Jon Dumas.

"Hey, Tris, you okay?"

He stopped and turned. He was breathing hard and fighting back tears. "I'm fine, Libby, Just a little personal problem. It won't affect my work. Thanks for asking." His voice was soft, almost apologetic.

"If you need to talk, let me know."

My offer brought back the Tristan of old. "Yeah, right. Like I don't have anyone else to talk to."

So much for caring comments. Somehow, the sneer and sarcastic remark made me feel better.

What can I say? I don't like change.

Chapter Twenty

The entire McKenna family was en route to Mickey Warren's memorial service. The only missing member was Clawdius who preferred to remain at home. He wasn't the only one. We were crammed in Dad's battered pick-up truck and forced to listen to his bitching and moaning all the way to the funeral home.

"Don't see why I have to go. I didn't even like the guy."

I took a deep breath and prayed for patience. "We've been over this a hundred times, Dad. He was president of the board. You're the treasurer. Sofia and I work there. They've closed the golf course so everyone can attend. You think nobody would notice if we missed it?"

He shrugged. "Probably not, but just the service. We're not staying for the social doohickey afterward. Okay?"

"Pops, if Mom and I want to stay for the social doohickey, we'll get a ride home with somebody." She gave me a significant look. "Possibly Riley."

Dad sped through a yellow light. "By the way, Chickadee, when are you inviting him over for dinner?"

I shrugged. "As soon as one of us learns how to cook."

Sofia giggled. "Yeah, we're all shitty cooks, Pops. You know that."

"Is take-out food out of the question?"

"As a rule," I said. "When you invite someone for dinner, he or she expects a home-cooked meal."

"I'll talk to Suze. She knows catering people. I'll take care of it. In fact, I'll talk to Riley at the service. Set the date."

Sofia elbowed me in the ribs. "Don't even try to stop him. Not worth the effort," she whispered.

"What did you say?"

"I told Mom to save her breath. You know what, Pops? You're sounding more and more like a crabby old coot."

"Really?" Dad chuckled. "Did you know a coot is a duck?"

"Then you'll fit right in with the rest of us birds," Sofia said.

"Actually, you look pretty good for an old coot," I said. "The suit still fits."

He puffed up at my compliment. "Little tight around the waist. Had to leave the button on my pants undone. Hope the zipper holds."

"So do we."

"Will the viewing be over when we get there?" Dad asked. "The last thing I want is to check out Mickey Warren in his big, fancy coffin. Hell, he's dead. Let's get him in the ground and carry on."

I patted his arm. "No worries. The viewing is in a separate room. We're only attending the service."

He grumbled a bit more. I tuned him out in order to preserve my sanity.

When we pulled into the spacious lot of the Vista Valley First Baptist Church, I spotted Riley on the sidewalk standing toe-to-toe with Farley Faraday. A couple of Sammy Espinoza's sons, including Gabe, flanked Riley. Faraday had called in the troops. Several dozen parishioners strolled up and down the sidewalk carrying signs, the predominant message being God punishes sinners.

"Look at that!" Dad exclaimed. "Mickey wasn't my favorite person, but for God's sake, this is too much. I'll go see if Riley needs backup."

He vaulted from the car and headed for the sidewalk.

"Pops," Sofia called. "Be careful. Remember the only thing holding up your pants is a twenty-five-year-old zipper."

In spite of the situation, I laughed.

Sofia linked her arm in mine and tugged me toward the church. "Men are so stupid," she muttered. "Nothing like having a pissing contest in front of the church."

We made our way through the crowd gathered in the narthex as people filed in and out of the viewing room.

"Want to take a little peek?" I whispered.

Sofia's face lost color. "Are you crazy? No way. I'll save you a seat."

She peeled off. I entered the viewing room. The pallbearers, all dressed in black suits, stood behind the casket. They consisted of Mickey's golf foursome along with Tristan and handicap chairman Herb Talcott.

I joined the line filing by the casket for one last look at our chairman of the board.

The man ahead of me murmured, "Godspeed, you old hacker," and tucked a bottle of single malt Scotch beneath the satin pillow, apparently intended for

Mickey's journey into the Great Beyond.

A sleeve of golf balls and his driver were also enshrined in the casket, along with a bag of tees and a visor. For a fleeting moment, I felt guilty about being empty-handed. Was this a new thing, bringing gifts to the deceased?

The mortician had done his best to give Warren the rosy glow of health. He failed. Mickey's face was artificially tan with two pink spots high on his cheekbones. The corners of his mouth had been tugged upward into the facsimile of a faint smile and topped off with pale pink lip gloss. The result was slightly clownish, if not a bit creepy.

I joined Sofia in the fourth row of the sanctuary and filled her in on the bizarre viewing. A few minutes later, Riley slid in next to me, trailed by Dad. The two of them were still riled up and grumbling about 'that damn Faraday fool.' They were silenced by the appearance of the Baptist minister and a thunderous chord from the pipe organ. The ornate casket, ensconced on a wheeled device and flanked by the pallbearers, made its way down the center aisle.

A traditional funeral service followed. It featured lengthy prayers for Mickey's soul along with a number of hymns sung by a mezzo-soprano whose high notes were painfully shrill.

Though probably not proper funeral etiquette, I entertained myself by surreptitiously scanning the gathered crowd. The Fairway to Heaven folk had turned out in large numbers. Despite declaring Mickey to be a 'dreadful man', Abigail Cavendish was in the second pew along with Winston. I spotted all the Mahjong Mavens, including Janice Pomeroy, her daughter,

Serena, and Jonathan Dumas. Perhaps the younger woman felt the heat of my gaze, because she shot a brief glance over her shoulder in my direction and then flipped her artificially sun-streaked light brown hair and whispered something to Janice. Once again, I had the feeling we'd met before. If she was new in town, how could that be?

The front pews on each side of the church were filled by Warren's family. Current wife Heather and her entourage were on the left. Patty Warren and her daughter, along with various and sundry friends, were on the right. Thankfully, both the widow and ex-wife, aside from a few vicious glances, behaved with decorum.

As the minister droned on about the wonderfulness of Mickey Warren, I leaned into Riley's warmth, enjoying the slight tingle it evoked. He smiled and folded my hand into his. Probably another funeral no-no.

Ninety long minutes later, the service was over. We were invited to attend the social doohickey so dreaded by my father. After extracting a promise from Riley to deliver Sofia and me to our doorstep, Dad vanished like mist in the wind. We headed for the refreshment table.

"Well, as I live and breathe. I thought I spotted you earlier, Elizabeth McKenna Carone," said a venomous voice directly behind me.

I didn't have to look because I knew who had spoken. I have a theory. I believe each of us has an archenemy, someone who hates us for some trivial reason or, perhaps, no reason at all. Annabelle Snodgrass had despised me since we were both sixteen and mad about the same boy, Seth Hoofnagle. Long story short, he picked me. Until later, when he married and then divorced Annabelle.

In my previous life, I would have feigned deafness and walked away. Not now. Evoking the spunky spirit of Libby Independence Day, I whirled to face her.

"And, hello to you, Annabelle Snodgrass Hoofnagle. I see you have a new, young boyfriend. Hi, Tris," I purred.

She was, in fact, clinging to the arm of Fairway to Heaven's golf pro, our very own Tristan Kensington the Third, who was at least ten years her junior.

Her eyes narrowed ominously. "Don't you dare judge me, Elizabeth McKenna Carone. At least my husband didn't ditch me when I got pregnant."

Based on previous encounters, she expected me to scurry away to avoid more unpleasantness. I did the opposite and stepped closer, invading her space. She recoiled and tightened her grip on Tristan's arm.

I smiled. "FYI, Annabelle Snodgrass Hoofnagle, your husband hit on me a bunch of times before you were divorced. I turned him down. Not my type."

Her mouth opened and closed in rapid succession, not unlike a goldfish. I'd rendered her speechless. My work here was done. I pivoted and bumped into Riley. He wrapped an arm around my shoulders and led me away, his body vibrating with barely concealed laughter.

He leaned down and whispered, "What was that about?"

"Nothing important."

How wrong that statement would prove to be.

Chapter Twenty-One

When Ed Montgomery focuses on a goal, it consumes every waking moment. Sometimes it's a good thing. Sometimes not. After Mickey Warren's funeral, he became obsessed with the idea of hosting a home-cooked meal for Riley O'Connor. It's possible he was trying to be helpful. Or maybe he considered Riley O'Connor the answer to my prayers and wanted to seal the deal. Riley was a good guy. I enjoyed his company. That said, I was content to let things unfold naturally. If our relationship deepened, fine. If not, it wasn't meant to be. Dad did not agree.

Since the three of us had questionable, if not downright dangerous culinary skills, the words home-cooked took on an entirely new meaning. Suzy was consulted.

Giddy with enthusiasm, she exclaimed, "I'm happy to help. I know the perfect caterers for this event."

So when did it become an event?

"Who?"

"B&B Caterers. Bill and Brenda Bradshaw. I'm thinking lasagna, a crusty French bread, green salad and one of their signature desserts. What do you think?"

I lifted my hands in a helpless gesture. "Sounds okay to me."

She leaned close."Here's the thing, Libby. You can't screw up with lasagna. It's easy and everyone knows how to make it." She paused and patted my hand. "Well, maybe not everyone. We'll have it delivered before he arrives and get rid of the telltale packaging. He'll think it's homemade; I guarantee it."

This was wrong on so many levels. "I'm not trying to fool the man, Suze," I said. "I just want to give him a good dinner. Forget the signature dessert. We'll have Dad's favorite, a bowl of vanilla ice cream."

She heaved an exasperated sigh. "I'm trying to help."

"You are helping, but I want to be upfront about the food. So, no hiding the packaging. Okay?"

She cast her gaze heavenward as if praying for divine guidance. "You've probably heard this before, Libby, but the way to a man's heart is through his stomach."

"Among other parts."

Her eyes widened in surprise. "Oh, really? You and he have…?"

"No, we haven't. But I assume it's true. Take you and Dad, for instance. Please don't misunderstand, but you guys eat out a lot. I don't recall a lot of home-cooked meals, so I'm guessing his attraction to you isn't food-based."

She started to sputter a protest, but it morphed into hearty gusts of laughter. She held up a hand for me to slap. "High five. Keepin' it real, girl. No lies. Got it."

That settled, it took a bit more wrangling to find an evening when I was free, Riley was off duty and the caterers could work us in. My original plan was a nice dinner shared by the two of us. I didn't factor in the fervent desire of my extended family to attend The Event. Dad. Sofia. Suze. Dad managed to deflect

Donny and Ronny although we invited them for pre-dinner drinks.

Finally, schedules were juggled and we were about to assemble for the McKenna version of a home-cooked meal. The caterers delivered the goods. Dad manned the kitchen. I set the dining room table—unused since Mom's death—with a lace tablecloth and her good china dishes.

"Chickadee, I need some raspberry jam from the fruit room. Suze is bringing scones and says nothing will do but raspberry jam," Dad hollered from the kitchen.

An involuntary shiver crept through my body as a visual of the dark, creepy fruit room appeared in my mind's eye.

"Have Sofia get it," I called.

"She's next door with the boys. Buck up, Buttercup, you can do it."

Well, crap. Dad knew how to push my buttons since he installed them. I didn't want him to think I was a craven, faint-hearted scaredy-cat, so I took a deep breath and made my way to the entry leading to the basement. I flicked on the light and started down the slippery stairs, bracing one hand against the wall. I'd been nagging Dad for years about installing a handrail for safety's sake. His response was we don't need one. Nobody goes down there but me, and I know those steps like the back of my hand.

So apparently a handrail would not be installed until Ed McKenna was a doddering old fogey, and by then he wouldn't be capable of building it.

When I hit the bottom stair, the hair on my arms prickled and stood to attention. I turned right, steeled myself, and marched to the wooden door leading to the fruit room. The door creaked when I pushed it open, evoking memories of horror movies. It was pitch-black inside.

"Why didn't you bring a flashlight, dummy?" I mumbled.

I waved a hand in the air, reaching for the string attached to the single bulb installed in the ceiling. My pulse sped up as I imagined grabbing a handful of sticky spider web instead of the string. My fingers finally located the clammy string. I yanked and the low wattage bulb flickered to life.

I was surprised to see a number of dusty jars filled with canned peaches, pears, tomatoes, and raspberries lining the wooden shelves. Because of my fear of dark, enclosed spaces, I was not a frequent visitor to the basement room. All these years, I'd assumed my father had been gleaning the fruits of my mother's labor.

A wave of sadness briefly quenched my anxiety. Maybe Dad didn't like this room anymore than I did, but for different reasons. Perhaps, like me, he remembered her standing over the stove, stirring a fragrant mix of fruit and sugar and flashing her dimpled smile at the man she adored. Maybe it was too painful to remember.

Suddenly ashamed for being so self-centered, I did a quick scan of the dreary, cave-like room. Other than a few dusty webs, I didn't spot a single eight-legged critter preparing to rappel down from the rafters and nest in my hair. I grabbed a jar of what looked like raspberry jam and exited the room of my nightmares.

Actually, in my lengthy index of nightmares, it's number two. Number one is the cave dream. Yes, I know. I'm likely a prime candidate for some heavy-duty psychological therapy. It might happen someday, when I have the time and money.

I ascended the stairs and found Suze had joined Dad in the kitchen.

"Here's your damn jam." I thrust the jar into her hand.

Her eyes widened. "You look a little pale, dear. Everything okay?"

Dad stepped close to me. He held back a grin as his gaze flicked over my head. "No worries, Chickadee, it's just a little one."

Alarm shot through my body. "What? What?" I screeched, jigging in place and flicking my fingers through my hair.

"Just kidding," he said. He turned toward Suze and extended his hand. "Told ya she'd do her spider dance. Pay up."

Suze started to snicker, but sobered quickly when she checked out my expression. "Um, Ed, I don't think Libby appreciates your sense of humor."

I narrowed my eyes and placed my hands on my hips. "She's so right. That wasn't funny. It was downright mean-spirited. Let me make this perfectly clear. From now on, if you want something from the fruit room, you can damn well get it yourself."

I whirled and pushed through the swinging door leading to the dining room.

"Aw, come on, Libby, it was just a little joke. You need to conquer your fears."

"Shut the hell up, Dad!" I called, just in time to see Riley peering through the front screen door.

Still seething, I pasted a phony smile on my face

and opened the door. "Hi, come in. Welcome to the McKenna family zoo."

He clapped his hands on my shoulders and studied my face. "You okay? I'm guessing you're one of the following: mad, sad, definitely not glad, frustrated, disgusted, probably not scared, terrified, horrified, let's try peeved, slightly annoyed… stop me when I come to the right adjective."

My anger evaporated, replaced by a smile. "Check off all of the above. Damn, Riley, somewhere, somehow, you learned how to read a woman's face. Rest assured, the incident precipitating those emotions is the result of a father-daughter issue soon to be resolved."

He grinned down at me. "Hey, as long as you're not pissed at me, I'm all right."

I assured him he was solidly on the side of the good and righteous.

Dad and Suze joined us for pre-dinner drinks. Riley and Dad opted for beer. Sofia arrived with Donny and Ronny who, with a flourish, presented their best wine.

Sofia gave Riley a quick hug, "Hey, lawman, glad you're here. Be prepared for a dinner to blow your socks off. By the way, my mom didn't cook it."

Suze inhaled sharply. Donny and Ronny gasped in tandem. Dad's mouth dropped open. Not an attractive look. Actually, Sofia and I hatched this plan earlier. I had no intention of passing myself off as a gourmet chef. Too many expectations. I felt it was best Riley should know the scoop right from the start of our relationship, assuming this was the start of a relationship.

No worries on that front.

Riley lifted his beer in a toast. “Here’s to dining with friends, no matter who cooks.”

Suze was right. The lasagna was yummy, the green salad fresh as the morning dew and for dessert, my favorite, lemon meringue pie instead of Dad’s generic vanilla ice cream.

Riley had just scraped his dessert plate clean when his work phone buzzed. He excused himself from the table and stepped onto the front porch to take the call. When he returned, his face was grim. His gaze zeroed in on me.

“Libby, I have bad news. Tristan Kensington is your golf pro. Right?”

Alarm bells clanged. “Yeah, he is. Why?”

Chapter Twenty-Two

"Apparently his parents were trying to reach him. They drove to his condo and found his car parked in the driveway. All the doors were locked and he was slumped over the steering wheel. They tapped on the window. When he didn't respond, they called 911. Doesn't sound good, Libby."

After a moment of stunned silence, I pushed my chair back and ran after Riley who strode toward his car.

"I'm coming with you," I called.

"No, you're not." He hopped in the car, locked the doors to emphasize his point and sped away.

"Well, guess what? I know where Tris lives so I'll see you there," I yelled at his vanishing car.

Dad fired up the truck. Sofia and I piled in. Donny and Ronny went home after we promised to dish the details later.

I glanced over at Sofia. Her olive complexion—compliments of Antonio—looked a little yellow. Her eyes were wide and fixed straight ahead.

I took her hand. "Are you up for this? Especially after finding Mickey Warren?"

Her fingers wrapped around mine and held on tight. "You know what Pops always says. You gotta conquer your fears. Blood, guts and dead bodies are mine."

"Dad and I had that very conversation a short time ago. In my humble opinion, his words of wisdom are highly overrated."

"Hey," Dad said. "I'm sitting right next to you and I'm not deaf yet."

I patted his knee with my free hand. "Good. Maybe you'll stop giving unsolicited advice to the women in your life."

"Or maybe not." He grinned and turned onto the street leading to Tris's condo. He parked next to the curb. We scrambled out, joining the crowd gathered in the street.

I spotted Riley behind the yellow crime scene tape. He huddled with a handful of uniformed officers who peered inside Tristan's car. An ambulance, horn blasting, made its way through the crowd. It reversed and backed into the driveway. A pair of burly EMTs unloaded a gurney and wheeled it next to the car.

"Just in time to see poor, dead Tristan's trip to the morgue," whispered Sofia, still gripping my hand.

I pulled her closer. "You don't have to look. Close your eyes if you're feeling woozy."

She slipped an arm around my waist, closed her eyes and pressed her forehead against my shoulder.

Dad pinched his lips together and shook his head in disapproval.

"Not now, Dad," I murmured.

He shrugged and wandered away, looking for someone more agreeable than his daughter.

Scanning the crowd, I recognized most of the people. The Mahjong Mavens were huddled in a tight group. I caught a glimpse of fluffy white curls atop a plump little body. Abigail Cavendish clung to Willard's arm. She spotted me and waved. Jonathan Dumas stood apart from the crowd. His arms were folded across his chest, his gaze fixed on Tristan's sports car. Handicap chairman Herb Talcott, chatted up B-4, big, blond, busty broad, Stella Roy, president of the women's golf division.

Dad walked up behind them and clapped a hand on Herb's shoulder. Startled, Herb nearly levitated out of his baggy golf shorts.

I tried to choke back my chuckle of amusement. It sounded like someone choking on a dry bagel.

"What?" Sofia asked.

I patted her back. "Nothing. Just your mother being inappropriate."

"Have they loaded him up yet?"

Riley and his colleagues circled up around the gurney, shielding it from view. The crowd grew quiet.

"Looks like they're in the process."

"Tell me when I can look."

"Now is fine. Can't see anything."

She opened her eyes. "Thanks, Mom. Sorry I'm such a wuss."

"No problem. You got it from me."

Our mother-daughter moment was interrupted by a battered sedan going way too fast. It screeched to a stop directly behind Dad's truck. The driver's side door flew open.

Sofia gripped my arm. "Oh my God, it's…"

Annabelle Snodgrass Hoofnagle slammed the door, scanned the crowd and spotted me. She aimed her pointer finger in my direction, her eyes glittering with rage.

"It's because of you!" she shouted. "This happened

to Tristan because you bullied him."

Totally blindsided, I was rendered speechless. Sofia was not similarly afflicted. She got up in Annabelle's face.

"Are you crazy? My mom and Tris worked together. Yeah, she was his boss, but he was lazy and irresponsible, so she had to get on his case. All she wanted was for him to do his job."

"Aha!" Annabelle played to the fascinated crowd. "Lazy and irresponsible? So your mom nagged him to death. Is that about right?"

Sofia paused for a moment, possibly realizing she'd added fuel to the fire. This wasn't her fight. I stepped forward and pushed her behind me.

I took a deep breath and attempted to sound sane and non-homicidal. "Come on, Annabelle. This has nothing to do with me. Tris and I had our differences, but basically, he was a good guy trying to find his way in the world. I know you want to blame somebody, but I'm as sorry as you are that he's dead."

Her eyes narrowed. She glanced over at the ambulance and then at me. "So, Elizabeth McKenna Carone, how do you know he's dead? Maybe he just passed out and they're taking him to the hospital to revive him. You are the one who said he's dead. In other words, how would you know that?"

I bit my lower lip to keep from screaming, 'Because, you stupid bitch, they just zipped him into a body bag.' Instead, I said, "I'm sorry about your loss, Annabelle. Really, I am. We'll miss him, too."

I turned away. The crazed look in her eyes told me I was wasting my breath. She'd lost her ability to use logic or reason.

“Don’t think I’ll forget about this, Libby. You know why? Everybody knows you’re screwing the sheriff, so he’ll let it slide,” screamed Annabelle.

The crowd went silent, their fascinated gazes sweeping over me. My face burned with embarrassment. There was nothing I could say that wouldn’t sound like a lie. Sofia bristled up.

“You’re so full of shit, Annabelle. She’s not screwing the sheriff, and even if she was, it’s none of your damn business, so butt out!”

I took her arm. “Let it go. She’s not worth it.”

I glanced over my shoulder and saw my dad, fire in his eyes, striding toward us. I shook my head and gave him a warning glance, not trusting my voice. How had things spun out of control so rapidly?

As he bore down on us, I spun on my heel and latched onto his arm. “Don’t bother, Dad. She won’t listen to reason.”

Dad narrowed his eyes and took a couple of deep, calming breaths. “We’ll see about that.”

He shook me off and closed in on Annabelle. She stumbled backward and almost fell on her butt.

“You need to be very careful with your words, Annabelle. Libby and Tristan worked together. They had their differences, but for you to stand in the middle of a crowd and accuse her of murder, well, that’s going too far.” Dad’s voice was soft and reasonable. “I know you cared about him and you’re hurting. Come on, I’ll walk you back to your car.”

Annabelle’s eyes welled up, and she hung her head. Dad placed a hand on her back and urged her forward. Docile as a lamb, she allowed him to lead her away.

"An apology would be nice," Sofia sniped.,

"Shush," I said. "Your grandfather is handling it just fine."

The ambulance bearing Tristan's body pulled out of the driveway and drove slowly down the street. No flashing lights. No sirens. Not for the dead. Riley was still deep in conversation with fellow officers. I wondered if he'd heard Annabelle's loud, ridiculous accusations. I really needed to fill him in before we left for home.

Perhaps he felt the urgency of my gaze. He left the group and ducked under the tape perimeter. "I was a little preoccupied, but did I hear something about you screwing the sheriff? Did I sleep through it?" he whispered.

Trust Riley to lighten up a grim scenario. I gave him a quick smile.

"No. If and when it happens, it will be memorable."

A full-out Riley mega-watt grin this time. "Promise?"

I sobered quickly and told him about the ugly scene with Annabelle.

His brow furrowed. "She actually accused you of killing him?"

I tried to remember her exact words. "She sort of implied it. Like maybe I'd driven him to harm himself because I was so mean to him."

"That's one crazy bitch," he muttered. "We don't even know cause of death at this point." He patted my cheek. "Don't worry about it. I'll handle it. Gotta get back. See you later."

I looked past him and spotted Tris's parents, their

arms wrapped around each other, sobbing in grief. I tried to swallow the golf ball-sized lump in my throat and swiped at my eyes as I hurried to catch up with Sofia.

"Libby, wait up. I need to talk to you."

A woman's voice. Friend or enemy? I was almost afraid to look. A quick peek over my shoulder revealed Abigail Cavendish heading my way, practically dragging Willard.

"For the love of God, woman, slow down. You want me to fall and break a hip?" shouted Willard.

To prevent another catastrophe, I walked to the couple. Abigail took my hand. Her eyes were sparkling with curiosity.

"I heard what that awful woman said to you. Not that I believe a word of it."

I nodded my thanks.

She motioned me to come closer and stood on tiptoe. "Are you really screwing the sheriff?" she asked in a stage whisper.

I prayed for patience. "Abigail, you just told me you didn't believe a word of Annabelle's accusations."

She squeezed my hand. "Well, if you are, more power to you. He's quite the hunk, and from what I hear, good in the sack. Look at it this way, my dear. You'll be doing research and gaining valuable experience for writing spicy love scenes. By the way, how's the book coming along? When can I see the next chapters?"

I promised I'd call her soon and trotted to the car. My head was swimming from information overload.

Poor dead Tristan. Annabelle, who thought I was a controlling evil bitch. Riley, who told me not to worry, he'd handle it. Abigail, who viewed the evening as a plus, urging her ghostwriter to hook up with the sexy sheriff so she could write more inspired prose. The only missing element was Farley on a Harley and his whacky band of wing nuts.

I didn't know what to think. Should I laugh or should I cry?

Only time would tell.

Chapter Twenty-Three

After a fitful sleep, I awoke early, made coffee and settled into the breakfast nook, determined to write a couple of chapters before I headed for the golf course. I knew what awaited me at Fairway to Heaven. Chaos. We'd be dealing with shock and grief, curiosity and questions I probably couldn't answer. We needed to hire a new golf pro. We also needed to hire someone to relieve me so I didn't have to work twelve-hour days. Dad, bless his heart, promised to help me out for the next few days, until the remaining board members could meet and make decisions.

Resolutely, I pushed work issues to the back of my mind and immersed myself in the story. Dastardly but sexy pirate Striker continued his lustful assault on the repressed Boston spinster, Rowena, sensing a fiery vixen lurked beneath her whalebone corset and starched petticoats. The very soul of determination, Striker, tight breeches bulging, devoted most of his time pursuing Rowena.

Sudden thought—somebody has to make sure the ship was in good hands and ready for the next big skirmish. Striker needed a responsible first mate, so I added Hamish, a sexy Scot. Who knows, maybe Hamish would be the star of a spin-off novel after Striker and Rowena lived happily ever after.

I'd already written a couple of scenes that Abigail

deemed *spicy*. Whenever the opportunity arose—which happened frequently—Striker cornered Rowena, kissing her and stoking her fire. Her resistance was, at best, half-hearted, further convincing the horny pirate he was on the right course. I sensed Abigail wanted me to get to the main event. So I put my inner prude in an imaginary lockbox and set the kitchen timer for thirty minutes. Flexing my fingers, I took a deep breath and plunged in, so to speak.

When the timer dinged, I leaned back and fanned my warm cheeks with a dishtowel. I scrolled down the screen, re-reading words that had poured out with unaccustomed ease. Not too shabby. Maybe I'm a romance author after all.

While in the midst of patting myself on the back, my cell phone rang. I trotted across the kitchen and extracted it from the depths of my handbag. Jules. Her tone was uncharacteristically hushed.

"Oh, my God, Libby, I just heard about Tristan."

"You and Last Bus Stop to Salvation people were the only ones missing."

There was a slight hesitation. "I was with Pete."

"Mmm. No judgment here."

"What happened?"

"Looks like suicide, but we won't know until the medical examiner does his thing."

I filled her in on the previous night's drama, including my run-in with Annabelle Snodgrass Hoofnagle."

"She's always been a bitch," Jules said. "Wish I'd been there to rip her a new one. Glad your dad was there."

"He was pretty amazing. The whole scene felt

surreal. Tristan dead. The scene with Annabelle. Dad being reasonable."

"Yeah, weird, huh?"

We stayed silent for a long moment, trying to make sense of the bizarre evening.

Finally I said, "So what's going on with you?

"It's why I called. We've got deliveries to make. I know you're busy so I'll try to handle it myself."

"No way. I'll work it out."

While we chatted, Sofia wandered into the kitchen, poured a cup of coffee and plopped down in the breakfast nook, her wide-eyed gaze fixed on my laptop screen. I cursed myself for not hitting the sleep button.

"Gotta go, Jules. I'll call you back."

I stepped over to the breakfast nook. "Um, Sofia, it's rough draft, not quite ready for prime time."

She waved me away. "Are you crazy? This is hot!"

"Well, you know," I stammered, "Abigail likes the hot stuff, so I needed to, you know, get on with it."

She raised a fist in the air. "Yes! Prissy Rowena is getting laid."

"Is it too much?" I asked, suddenly insecure.

She grabbed my hand. "No, Mom, it's absolutely perfect and Abigail will love it."

Dad, wearing his ratty old robe over a white undershirt and pajama bottoms, emerged from the basement and made a beeline for the coffee pot. His hair stuck up like a rooster tail. He retrieved the glasses from atop his head and scowled at the cellphone clutched in his right hand.

"What's his problem?" I asked Sofia.

"He's trying to track down Bruce Hargraves and see what he wants to do about hiring a new golf pro."

Hargraves, the globetrotting owner of Fairway to Heaven, was not an easy man to locate. A member of the rarified species known as filthy rich, his grandfather was one of the first to realize Vista Valley had the soil, weather, and perfect growing season for hops. Since you can't make beer without hops, the product was in great demand and shipped all over the world. He leaves the mundane task of everyday operations to trusted managers and continues his goal of visiting every country in the world. His interest in our golf course was minimal, as long as we remained in the black. My father made sure it was.

Dad glared at me, like it was my fault he was forced to take time from his precious bees and funny honey business.

"Damn fool's in Denmark. What the hell time is it in Denmark?"

Sofia chirped, "It's seven thirty a.m. here. Denmark is nine hours ahead of us which would make it—"

"Four-thirty p.m.," I said, happy to be of help. "What's he doing in Denmark?'

Dad snorted in disgust. "He just married a woman from Copenhagen. Fourth wife, if I'm counting right. His brother said the new wife, Elinor with an *i*, is introducing him to all her Danish relatives and then they're off for a honeymoon in Paris."

He fished a scrap of paper from his robe pocket, punched in a series of numbers on his cell phone and stomped out the back door.

After his dramatic exit, Sofia said, "Mom, I've got an idea. I'm not asking for an answer right now, but just think about it, okay?"

I nodded.

"Gabe has been working part-time. What if he worked fulltime on maintenance, freeing me up to help you in the pro shop. I know the system. I know all the people and I promise I'll work hard."

I thought about it for maybe thirty seconds. "You'd have to work longer hours. It would cut into your social life."

She waved a dismissive hand. "No worries. I have plenty of social life at school. Besides, I could use the money."

Now I felt guilty. "Maybe I shouldn't have been so arrogant about Anne Marie's offer. After all, your father has done nothing to support you."

She gave me a huge eye roll. "Mom, I already told you I don't want a penny from either one of them. Got it?"

"Got it."

Somewhat relieved, I picked up my cell phone to call Jules back. Before I could punch in her number, the landline phone in the living room rang.

"Probably for Pops," Sofia said, still avidly perusing Striker and Rowena's four-page paddle up Coochie Creek.

I lifted the receiver.

"You might want to be careful. Death is at your doorstep, Libby. Tag, you're it," said an eerie mechanical voice, entirely without inflection.

Maniacal laughter followed the message.

Chapter Twenty-Four

I froze in place, my heart thundering in my chest. The receiver slipped from my hand and clattered to the floor. Stars danced behind my eyes. I placed my hands on my knees, took a couple of deep breaths and picked up the receiver. My hand shook.

It was the anonymity of the call that freaked me out. Could have been male or female, young or old. Obviously, the person used a voice-changing device. If the person's goal was to inflict terror, he or she had succeeded spectacularly.

Now I had a decision to make. Tell Sofia and Dad or wait until I talked to Riley. The voice identified me by name. I was the target. Even so, the rest of my family might also be in danger. I pushed into the kitchen.

"Phone for Pops?"

"Crank call." I headed for the back door. I'd made my decision, knowing my dad would do everything in his power to protect us.

"You okay, Mom?" Sofia called. "You look a little pasty."

I waved her off and joined Dad in the garage where he was checking the marijuana plants hung to dry from the wooden rafters crisscrossing the ceiling. Dad's illicit operation was the reason none of us parked in the huge garage. Because I was in deep denial about Dad's lucrative hobby, I rarely ventured out there. Guess I'd have to change my attitude since I was now part of the delivery service. Did that make me an accessory to crime? I sighed. Don't worry about it now. Bigger fish to fry. Like trying to stay alive.

After his little temper tantrum, Dad looked positively serene, humming as checked his drying buds.

"Hey, Chickadee, finally tracked Bruce down. He told me it was my decision. Said, 'Ed, I'm on my damn honeymoon. Hire whoever the hell you want.' So I guess we'll start looking around, maybe poach some kid from the Vista Valley Country Club. A lot of those boys would jump at the chance."

"Or girls," I added.

He flapped a hand, "Yeah, yeah, whatever."

"Um, Dad, I just had a weird phone call. I didn't mention it to Sofia, but I want you to know."

As I related the message, his eyes narrowed and his expression hardened. A flush rose in his leathery cheeks. He walked to a tall, metal cabinet propped against the wall, unlocked it and pulled out a twelve-gauge shotgun.

"No worries, Chickie, me and my new best friend will be together at all times."

I leaned close and gave him a thankful smooch. He looped an arm around my neck and pulled me close. The last bit of fear gripping my body melted away. Despite being a tad cantankerous, Dad had always been my hero.

He patted my back and repeated our mantra, the words he'd said since I was old enough to understand. "Remember, you're my brave girl."

I fought back tears of gratitude, smiled up at him

and added my bit. “And you will always have my back.”

“Damn right, Chickie,” he said, releasing me.

I told him about Sofia’s offer to help me in the pro shop.

“I’ll get Gabe on the payroll full time and Sofia will get a bump in her salary. Sounds like a good plan to me.”

I headed for the golf course. No picket-carrying religious nuts on the sidewalk today. Maybe they were taking the day off to make crank calls and deface private property.

The early birds, looking irritated at my tardiness—five whole minutes—waited for me. Sammy wouldn’t let them tee off until I arrived and checked them in. I fielded all their comments about Tristan and deflected the questions, declaring I knew nothing until cause of death was determined, which happened to be the truth. The guys nodded sadly, accepted my answers, and headed for the first hole, The River Styx.

Not so with the Mahjong Mavens who arrived shortly after. They set up their game, talking in hushed tones while shooting furtive glances my way. I noticed one of their regulars, Barbara Tomlinson, was missing. Janice Pomeroy sat in Barbara’s chair.

Apparently Carolyn Talcott drew the short straw. She waited until I’d shooed the last foursome out the door before sauntering over to the counter.

“Hi Carolyn, what can I do for you?” I said, knowing full well what she wanted.

She looked over her shoulder for eavesdroppers before leaning on the counter and whispering. “Herb and I were there last night to witness, you know,

Tristan's sad demise. We overheard your altercation with Annabelle Hoofnagle. What on earth prompted her to make those horrible accusations?"

I chose my words carefully and shrugged like I didn't give a rip. "I really couldn't say. You probably already knew she was dating Tristan. She was terribly upset about his death. Apparently she needed to lash out at someone. I'm guessing I was the target of misplaced aggression. What do you think?"

Flummoxed by our sudden role reversal, she stammered, "Well, um, yes, I suppose you're right." She stepped away from the counter. "Please let us know if we can help in any way."

I assured her I would although I had no intention of doing so. Tristan did not have a relationship with these women. They were fishing for gossip. Plain and simple. Or possibly trying to figure out if I was a murderess. Playing it cool, I frowned at the computer screen while surreptitiously watching Carolyn return to the group. They settled in around the table, heads together, expecting her to dish the dirt. Upon hearing the report, their disappointment was obvious and they returned to their game.

I flashed back to a couple of weeks ago. I was playing junior detective and trying to figure out who killed Mickey Warren. Now, another person with a Fairway to Heaven connection was dead. A chill raced through my body. Maybe I was next.

Thankfully, a full schedule of eager golfers kept my mind busy and fears at bay. Only one incident gave me pause. A couple I'd known since high school, Jeff and Shannon Mallory, had a regular tee time every week at 11:30 a.m. Usually, they came in early and we'd catch up on our fellow classmates. Not today. They arrived at 11:20, their expressions frosty, their demeanor off-putting.

"Hi guys," I chirped. "How are things?"

"Fine," Shannon snapped. "Is play on time?"

"Yes, everyone is moving along," I said, somewhat taken aback at her attitude.

Jeff crossed his arms and stared at me, his eyes narrowed in suspicion. "Tristan's death hasn't caused any problems?"

From my peripheral vision, I saw the Mahjong Mavens freeze in their chairs, heads cocked to one side, avidly eavesdropping.

"We're dealing with it like everyone else. But Mr. Hargraves, the owner, thought it would be best for us to carry on."

"Of course he did," Jeff said. "Business as usual. Might cost him money to close it down."

I paused for a moment to gather my wits and not say anything I might regret later. "I don't run the place. Surely you know I do as I'm told."

"It's no secret you and Tristan had issues," Shannon said. "Poor Annabelle is distraught. She thought she'd found the love of her life."

Struck dumb, I tried to harken back to my high school days. Had Shannon and Annabelle been buddies? Or had Jeff and Shannon been part of the crowd witnessing my embarrassing scene with Annabelle? I decided the best course of action was to be totally upfront.

"I guess you heard about last night. Look, you guys have known me forever. If I have problems with someone, I try to solve them. Tristan and I had our differences, but we always made it work, because it was about work. We didn't have a personal relationship."

Jeff smirked at me. "No worries. The sheriff will make sure everything turns out okay for you."

My anger flared into the red zone. I pinched my lips together to hold back the words ready to burst out. Shannon grabbed Jeff's hand and tugged him toward the door.

Apparently I was today's hot topic on Vista Valley High School's Alumni Dirty Deeds Network.

Chapter Twenty-Five

Shortly after Shannon and Jeff teed off, a grim-faced Riley O'Connor stomped in. The Mavens perked up, not bothering to hide their fascination with all things Libby. I bit back a groan and tried to look pleasant and professional.

Riley leaned across the counter and lowered his voice. "Am I mistaken, or are those women staring at us?"

"You're not mistaken. They were there last night. At Tristan's. Need I say more?"

He shook his head. "We have to talk."

"Right now?"

"Yeah."

I called Sofia to cover for me. No way was I providing further entertainment for the Mavens.

We sought privacy in Riley's car.

"I got a call from the mayor this morning. The guy always has one finger in the wind. He heard about the fuss last night and wanted to know if you and I were seeing each other. I told him we were. He gave me his disapproving frown-y face and said our relationship could be a PR nightmare."

"For him. He's up for election in the fall."

"Exactly," Riley said. "I got a little hot under the collar, told him he had no right to interfere in my personal life."

"Do you still have a job?"

He nodded.

"Look, Riley, I know the guy's a jerk, but we can cool it for a while, until we figure out what's going on."

I slipped my hand in his. His fingers wrapped around mine and squeezed.

"Goes against my grain," he growled.

"I know. Mine too. Does the honorable Mr. Mayor monitor your phone calls?"

Riley's expression lightened. "No way. You can bet I'll be in touch daily."

I leaned over and smooched him on the cheek. "We'll be fine. No worries. I'll keep busy helping Jules deliver booty buns and honey."

"Are the Tomlinsons on your list?"

"Not sure, I'll ask Jules. Why?'

He shrugged. "Earl gets real shifty when I ask him about Mickey Warren. I've subpoenaed his bank records, but it's being slow-walked through the system. Apparently he's a charter member of Vista Valley's good old boy club."

"I know his wife. She's not exactly a close friend, but I'll keep my eyes and ears open."

"Thanks."

I extricated my hand and reached for the door handle. "Guess I'd better get back."

"Wait," Riley said. "There's one more thing you need to know. I wanted you to hear it from me."

Alarmed, I turned to face him. He squirmed, looking everywhere except into my eyes.

"What is it, Riley?"

"I got a call from the coroner's office this morning. Since Tristan's cause of death is unknown, an autopsy has been scheduled. When an attendant went through Kensington's personal effects, they found a bracelet in his pocket. A charm bracelet."

I froze in my seat.

"One of the charms says Libby. Is there any possibility it belongs to you?"

My mouth went dry. I took a shaky breath. "I'm missing a bracelet and yes, one of the charms has my name on it."

"Any idea why Tristan might have it?"

"The night you and I went out to dinner, I was going to wear it. I couldn't find it. I figured I must have worn it to work. Maybe the clasp broke and it fell off. Tris probably found it and planned to give it back to me."

I swallowed hard. I had no reason to feel guilty, but my words sounded incredibly lame.

Riley rubbed his forehead. "Aw, jeez, Libby, this is awkward, but I need to give you a heads-up. Somebody, probably one of my deputies, will interview you about the bracelet. For obvious reasons, it can't be me."

The weight of his words felt like a dagger in my heart. I knew my missing bracelet, coupled with Annabelle's hateful words, were enough to convince people I was the black-hearted villain in this real-life drama.

I gulped and took a couple of deep breaths. "Do I need a lawyer?"

"No, you've got an airtight alibi since we were together when he died. Just be prepared for some personal questions about the nature of your relationship with Tristan."

"We didn't have a relationship. Just work." I

stepped out of the car. Before I closed the door, I said, "The gossip girls are going to have a field day with this one. Guess I'll find out who my true friends are."

"Just consider the source and walk away."

"You don't get it, Riley. I work for these people. I can't walk away."

The mahjong game was breaking up as I re-entered the pro shop. Before they could fire more questions and sidelong glances my way, I beat them to the punch. I stopped next to Carolyn Talcott, who was packing up her game.

"No Barbara Tomlinson today? I see Janice is subbing. Hope Barbara's not sick."

Should have been a simple statement. From her reaction, it was as if I'd asked her for the nuclear codes. She drew herself up.

"She called this morning and said she couldn't make it. Why do you ask?"Carolyn huffed.

I smiled sweetly. "No reason. I'm just used to seeing the four of you here on Wednesdays." I tipped my head toward Janice. "Good thing you have a sub."

Four sets of eyes bored into my back as I walked away. Peace and calm reigned in the pro shop, thanks to my daughter, who had everything under control. I decided not to burden Sofia with the bracelet fiasco until later.

After the Mavens departed, Sofia said, "What's with those old biddies? After you left with Riley, oh my God, they had their heads together, buzzing like Pop's bees. They sent Janice Pomeroy over to pump me for information about Tris. I said she probably knew more than I did since Jonathan Dumas is her daughter's significant other. Plus he and Tris were best buds. She started blinking like crazy and sidled back to the group."

"Good job," I said. "Come back about five. I need to deliver booty buns and Dad's special honey."

She snickered. "Don't get busted. Oh, wait, I forgot. You have a special relationship with law enforcement."

"Yeah, yeah," I flapped a hand at her. "The sand trap on Purgatory Pit needs raking. See you at home."

Minutes later, Dad popped into the pro shop. The tips of his ears were bright red, a dead giveaway to his state of mind. Extreme anger.

"Just talked to Riley. He told me about the mayor. No worries, Chickadee, I called him and made an appointment. I'm heading over there now. Damn fool needs to leave my family alone."

I groaned. "Come on, Dad, I'm a big girl now. Let me handle it. You'll probably made it worse."

"Or better." He marched out the door.

After the clubhouse emptied out, I called Jules and told her about the bracelet. I heard breathing through the phone.

"Two people connected with Fairway to Heaven are dead. You be careful. Hear me?"

"I hear you."

When we clicked off, the eerie mechanical voice and its threats resurfaced in my memory.

Tag, you're it.

Despite the warmth of the day, I shivered.

Chapter Twenty-Six

Several days later, Deputy Colin Shipley perched on the edge of our couch, looking acutely uncomfortable. His sparse facial hair was barely adequate to hide an outbreak of acne.

Note to self: ask Riley if Shipley is old enough to vote.

"Sheriff O'Connor thought it would be better to interview you here rather than your place of work."

I nodded, silently thanking Riley. Hadn't I already provided enough entertainment for the Fairway to Heaven gang? At least I'd be spared another round of embarrassment.

Shipley pulled a small tablet from his shirt pocket, along with a plastic bag. "Well, um, shall we get started?"

"Sure, ask away."

He opened the plastic bag and extracted my bracelet, dangling it from one finger. "Is this your bracelet?"

I walked to the couch. As I approached, he drew back and wrapped his fingers around the bracelet. Did he think I would grab it from him? I barely concealed my snort of indignation.

"Deputy Shipley, I can't identify it if you don't let me look at it."

"Yeah, well, it's my responsibility to preserve

evidence."

"Evidence of what?" I huffed.

"I should have said possible evidence."

"Okey-dokey, then," I snapped. "How about I back away a few steps and then you show it to me. Sound good?"

The guy was oblivious to sarcasm. "Yes, I believe so."

I stepped back. He unclenched his hand and held up my bracelet. Along with the Libby charm, I recognized other familiar charms, among them a baby shoe, a golf club, a honeybee, a golf tee and a miniature golf green complete with flag.

"Yes, it's mine."

"Do you have any idea why it was on Kensington's person at the time of his death?"

I repeated my theory about losing the bracelet and the possibility Tris had found it, planning to return to me.

He tucked the bracelet back in his pocket and scribbled some notes before asking, "What was the nature of your relationship with the deceased?"

"I believe you know we worked together at the golf course."

A flush rose in his cheeks. He swallowed loudly. His prominent Adam's apple frolicked up and down in his scrawny neck. "Sorry, but I have to ask. Did you two have an intimate relationship?"

"Are you serious? Of course not. I'm old enough to be his…" I paused, visions of Annabelle and Tristan dancing through my head. "Well, not his mother, but a much older sister or aunt."

He looked up from his notes. "Were you his

superior at work?"

"It's my job to keep the golf course running smoothly. Tristan was a bit of a slacker. I sometimes had to remind him of his responsibilities."

"So when you reminded him, how did he react?"

I sensed the poor kid was tiptoeing around the crux of the matter and decided to put him out of his misery.

"I didn't yell, bully or threaten Tristan in any way. I'm sure he wasn't happy about our arrangement, but he usually stepped up and did his job after we talked. Bottom line, I have no idea why my bracelet was in his pocket. Are we done?"

I stood, hopefully indicating I had nothing more to say.

He rose from the couch and cleared his throat. "I believe we've covered everything."

Attempting to add a bit of levity, I smiled. "Is this where you tell me not to leave town?"

Stunned, his eyes widened in surprise. "It shouldn't be necessary, but I'll ask the sheriff and get back to you."

"Just kidding, Deputy."

A high-pitched titter. "Oh yeah, totally."

I held out my hand, palm up. "I'd like my bracelet now."

"Sorry, no can do. Remember, it's possible evidence."

"Oh, good God," I muttered and walked him to the door.

After Shipley left, Dad peeked through the swinging door from the kitchen. "How'd it go?"

Prior to the interview, I'd forbidden his presence. He'd reluctantly agreed. I strongly suspected he'd been eavesdropping.

“Fine. The baby deputy was scared of me. Probably a good thing.” I could tell by his expression he had something on his mind.

He pointed at his truck backed halfway down the long driveway. “Let’s go. I called the Kensingtons, asked if we could stop by and offer official condolences as representatives of the golf course.”

“They’re okay with it?”

“More than okay. They have relatives arriving and asked if we had extra booty buns and honey. I’ve got the honey loaded in my truck. We’ll stop by the bakery and pick up the buns. I already gave Suze a heads-up.”

“So this is turning out to be a commercial venture?”

“Not entirely. We’ll still offer our condolences.”

“Meaning I will be the one uttering the appropriate words.”

He beamed at me. “Exactly.”

Tristan’s parents, Harold Tristan Kensington Junior and his wife, Betty, lived in a spacious home adjoining the golf course. By normal standards, it was definitely upper class. By Cavendish standards, a mere starter home. Tris’s sports car was parked in the driveway leading to a three-car garage, squeezed in alongside two upscale vehicles.

Dad started to pull his ratty old truck in behind the other cars.

“Maybe we should park out front in case somebody needs to leave,” I said.

He winked. “Are you dissing my ride, Chicky?”

No matter the situation, Dad could always make me smile.

"Who, me? It got us here, didn't it?"

"Damn straight. Now help me gather up the goodies and we'll make our grand entrance. Ta-da!"

After an inappropriate chuckle, I unloaded the cartons of booty buns while Dad hefted a case of Ed's Special Dark Honey. In my heart of hearts, I hoped the buns and honey would bring a bit of joy to their hearts in this time of grief. Wow, maybe I just invented a new sympathy greeting card.

Then I remembered the purpose of our visit. I thought about Tristan's parents, sobbing in each other's arms. A wave of sadness swept over me. Tris and I weren't best buds, but he died way too young.

Our arms were full, so I scooched sideways and hit the doorbell with my elbow. I fervently hoped it was a normal doorbell, not a Cavendish stereophonic blast. A complicated eight-note chime reverberated through the exterior wall. The last bong was still resounding when the door opened, revealing Harold T. holding a squat glass filled with a brown liquid and ice cubes. Looked like scotch. It took a moment for him to focus.

"Oh, hi Ed and, um…Ed's daughter. Please come in."

"Libby," Dad said. "My daughter's name is Libby."

Harold T. stepped aside so we could enter the foyer. I glanced into the living room and spotted a man who looked like a Kensington and an adolescent who was staring at his cell phone.

"You can take the stuff into the kitchen. Follow me."

He led us into a gleaming kitchen outfitted with an array of stainless steel appliances and glistening granite counter tops. French doors led to a patio overlooking the golf course. Two women sat at a glass top table, sharing a bottle of wine.

"Betty," Harold T. hollered. "Get your checkbook. The honey and buns are here."

I'd seen the invoice for the delivery and, to me, the amount seemed astronomical. Suze said it was justified because it was a rush order. The bill didn't bother Betty in the least. She set her wine glass down. An embossed leather checkbook was extracted from her purse. She scribbled out the amount and handed it to Dad.

His eyes widened a bit. "It's too much."

"It's fine," Betty said. "We appreciate your promptness."

The light bulb in my head flicked on. They thought the reason for our visit was to deliver honey and booty buns.

"We came to offer our condolences. Tristan was a vital part of our Fairway to Heaven family," I said.

I hoped I wasn't pouring it on to thick.

"Oh, right," Harold T. said. "Come into the living room. Have a seat."

Betty made the introductions. "This is Harold's brother, Eric, and his son, Eric Junior."

We shook hands and the two wandered away to another part of the house. Drinks were offered. We declined. Dad and I settled onto the comfy couch. Harold T. and Betty sat in twin recliners across from us. Dad gave me a significant look. Translation: your turn to talk.

I leaned forward. "Mr. and Mrs. Kensington, we're so sorry for your loss. Tristan will be missed."

Harold T. took a big slurp of his drink. Betty

sipped her wine. I slipped my hand behind a cushion and gave my father a vicious pinch on his backside.

After a little yip of pain, he got the message. “Yes, Tristan will be hard to replace.”

Betty took a tissue from her pocket and dabbed at her eyes. “The sheriff came by this morning. It was what we thought, an insulin overdose.”

Dad blinked in surprise. “Insulin overdose?”

“Tristan was diabetic?” I asked.

“Recently diagnosed,” Harold T. said.

“We didn’t know,” I said, stunned.

Harold T.’s expression hardened. He climbed out of his recliner, ice cubes clinking in his empty glass. “I need a refill. Betty will tell you the rest.”

Chapter Twenty-Seven

Betty's gaze followed her husband as he left the room. Tears trickled down her cheeks.

"He feels guilty. They had a falling out. They never had a chance to resolve it. Now, of course, they never will."

Dad squirmed, pursed his lips and rubbed his bristly chin. Family dynamics were not in his wheelhouse. Actually, I had no idea what to say either. The truth of her statement overpowered any words of sympathy I could offer.

I murmured something trite. "It must be terribly hard for both of you. If there's anything at all we can do to help, please let us know."

She nodded. "The diabetes is from my side of the family. I kept telling Tris he needed to watch his diet and get tested more often. His lifestyle made it worse. He liked to party. Harold T. finally put his foot down. Told him to straighten up or move out."

Dad spoke up. "Tristan seemed pretty close to Mickey Warren. Probably hit him hard when Mickey died."

Betty set her glass of wine down and leaned forward in her chair. "I blame Mickey Warren for many of Tris's problems. After Harold T. cut him off financially, Warren lent him money, helped him get the condo." Her voice was a hoarse whisper. She paused and gestured toward the front door. “That expensive car parked in the driveway?”

“Yes?”

“It came from Warren’s agency. He talked Tris into buying it. No way could he afford it. He started missing payments. Mickey told him to borrow money from his dad or he’d take the car back.“

“I bet Harold T. wasn’t too keen on bankrolling that,” Dad said.

“Absolutely not. It caused even more strife between them.” She choked back a sob. “I was totally caught in the middle. He started coming over when he knew his dad was gone.”

“About the insulin overdose,” I said. “I wonder if he got confused. Maybe he thought he missed a dose.”

“He wasn’t good about staying on a schedule. When he was first diagnosed, I hired a private nurse to help him learn about the disease.” She shook her head in disgust. “Annabelle something or other. She helped him all right. Glommed onto him like a leech.”

I blinked in surprise. “Is her name Annabelle Hoofnagle?”

“Mmm hmm. If you ask me, she’s a little gold digger. She figured Tris would make up with his father and the money would start flowing again.”

I thought about the scene she’d made the night of Tristan’s death. It all began to fall into place. She’d just lost her golden ticket and needed someone to blame. I was the obvious choice.

Betty drew herself up. “Can you believe she told Tris she was pregnant? Good God, she must be at least forty. Her eggs are probably dried up. I figured she lied like a rug, trying to get herself a younger guy who might be rich some day."

In spite of the venom Annabelle had spewed my way, I felt the need to defend her. Possibly due to the dried up eggs reference.

"Annabelle and I were in the same class, so I doubt if she's forty. Maybe thirty-nine."

Betty flapped a hand. "What's the difference? She was still too old for Tris. And honestly, he wasn't that into her. He told her if she was pregnant, he needed more proof."

Dad leaned forward. "Did he get it?"

She lifted her hands in a helpless gesture. "I don't know."

Dad stood. "You probably have a lot to do. We should get going."

She walked us to the door. "Thanks for stopping by."

We climbed into Dad's clunker.

"Swing by the bakery. I need more booty buns." I said.

"Why?"

"I'm going to pay Annabelle Snodgrass Hoofnagle a visit."

****

Ninety minutes later, I parked in front of Annabelle's modest ranch-style house, located a couple of blocks east of ours. I was surprised to discover she was practically my neighbor. Apparently she was unaware of the Biblical admonition, love thy neighbor. Either that, or she chose to ignore it.

I'd have been there earlier but had to convince Dad I didn't need a bodyguard. He was concerned Annabelle might attack me using a gun or a butcher knife. All women have butcher knives, he insisted. I assured him I'd be careful and ran for the door.

Annabelle's house was totally without curb appeal, as the realtors say. A battered slime green sedan lurked in the crumbling cement driveway. The picture windows facing the street were tightly shuttered. A large earthen pot of wilting petunias sat next to the porch. My anger at Annabelle was rapidly fading. Clearly, she was down on her luck.

I approached the front door clutching my peace offering. When I lifted a hand to knock, the curtains twitched open a couple of inches. A suspicious eye beneath a scraggly lock of dark hair appeared. I gave her a big, toothy grin and held up the honey and booty buns.

The door opened a crack, revealing a darkened living room and part of Annabelle's face.

"Why are you here, Elizabeth McKenna Carone? I thought I made it clear I wanted nothing to do with you."

Fearing she would slam the door in my face, I slipped my left foot into the crack.

"Annabelle, I feel just awful about our, um, little misunderstanding the other night. I know you're grieving for Tristan."

No response. Time to wave the white flag of peace, munchie-wise.

I held up a jar of Dad's honey, lifting to her eye level. "Look! I brought you a jar of Ed's Special Dark."

The door opened a few more inches.

I waved the white bakery sack at what I hoped was nose level. "It goes real good with Suzy's booty buns. I was hoping we could talk. Can I come in?"

The door opened wider. “Yeah, I guess so.”

I stepped through the door and followed her through the darkened living room into the kitchen. She flipped on the light. Despite the warmth of the day, she was clad in jeans and a flannel shirt. Her dark hair hung in lank clumps across hollowed, pale cheeks. Whatever animus I’d previously harbored toward Annabelle slowly faded away.

Then I remembered my father’s warning and scanned the kitchen. Attached to one wall was a fully loaded magnetic knife strip. Dad was right. All women have butcher knives.

I set the goodies on the table. “Annabelle, I’m really sorry we got off on the wrong foot. You probably don’t need me as a friend, but at least we shouldn’t be enemies. We both cared for Tristan.”

She leaned against the stove and folded her arms across her chest. “You want coffee? I’ve got instant.”

“Sure,” I said, probably a bit too enthusiastically. “Can I fix you a booty bun with honey?”

One corner of her mouth turned up in an almost smile. “Sure, but only if you join me.”

Oh, great.

“Of course,” I chirped, even though I was cringing inside.

Because I didn’t approve of Dad’s hobby, I’d never sampled his extremely popular marijuana-infused honey. I was trying to make a statement, take the moral high ground.

While Annabelle fixed the coffee, I extracted two booty buns and placed them on napkins. After wrenching the lid from the honey jar, I realized a knife would be handy for spreading. Screw that. I poured a liberal amount of honey on Annabelle's bun and a tiny dab on mine.

Annabelle plopped two mugs of brown sludge on the table and eyed the buns. "Looks good, but you need more honey on yours."

She stomped over to the magnetic knife strip.

Oh my God, this was it. I reached for my cell phone, my finger poised over Dad's number. I prayed he wasn't in the middle of a bee emergency.

Annabelle returned to the table with a black-handled spatula knife, the type used to frost a cake. Relieved, I tucked my phone away as she spread more honey onto my booty bun.

She sat and lifted her bun."Cheers."

"Cheers," I replied.

We clinked buns and dug in.

"Yum," Annabelle said, practically inhaling the honey-coated bun.

Though I'm usually not a dainty eater, I nibbled at mine. "Wow, Annabelle, you were really hungry. Have you been eating?"

Her eyes welled up. She shook her head. "Since Tris died, I haven't felt like eating."

She eyed my booty bun. "Are you going to eat that?"

I pushed it over to her. "Be my guest. You need it more than I do."

While she ate, I told her about our visit to the Kensingtons. I was dying to know if she'd seen my bracelet, but decided not to go there. She'd already practically accused me of causing Tris's death. Despite my peace offering, we were still on shaky ground, friendship-wise.

After she'd scarfed down her third booty bun drenched in Ed's Special Dark, I said, "Did you know Tristan died from an insulin overdose?"

"Yeah, I heard. Not that his family cared enough to tell me."

"His mother said Tris wasn't good about taking his insulin. Do you think he got confused and overdosed?'

Her eyes narrowed, and she leaned across the table. "Absolutely not. He had a timer on his watch. When it was time for an injection, it buzzed. I was with him a lot and never saw him miss a dose."

"Betty Kensington said you might be pregnant."

She rolled her eyes. "That old bat never liked me. I'm not pregnant. I thought I was, but it was a false alarm, so to speak."

"What did Tris think about you possibly being pregnant?"

She stiffened. For a brief second, something dangerous flashed in her eyes, similar to the look of madness I'd seen the night of Tristan's death. I scooted my chair back.

"Sorry, I'm being too personal."

Instantly, her expression morphed into one of sheer delight. A smile bloomed on her face. "He was so thrilled. Said he'd always wanted to be a father."

Really? Had her previous crazed look been a figment of my imagination? Hadn't Betty told me Tristan didn't believe her?

She took a shuddering breath. "It comforts me a little, you know?"

I gave her a questioning look.

"He died thinking Tristan Kensington the Fourth was on the way."

I really had no idea how to respond. Time to forge ahead, change the subject.

"Seems like Tris and Jonathan Dumas were close."

She squirmed in her chair. "I guess so. I don't know him that well."

After a brief, uncomfortable silence, I stood. "Once again, Annabelle, I'm so sorry for your loss. I hope we can be civil to each other the next time we meet."

"Yeah, well, I guess I shouldn't have been so hard on you." She rose and extended her arms.

Oh my God, she wanted a hug.

Still leery, I kept some distance between us. We did the type of hug where you stick your butt out, put your hands on each other's back and pat, pat, pat.

I opened the front door. Knowing I could make a run for it if I had to, I said, "They found a bracelet in Tristan's pocket, a charm bracelet I'd lost. It had my name on it. Did he mention it to you?"

Her gaze shifted left, right and up before meeting mine. "No, why would he have your bracelet?"

"No idea."

When I got in the car, I got a text from Dad.

—You okay?—

—Fine. She had a butcher knife, but I fought her off. See ya soon—

After my visit with Annabelle, of one thing I was sure. She was a liar.

Big time.

Chapter Twenty-Eight

I headed for the golf course. Sofia, bless her heart, was filling in for me. When I walked into the pro shop, she was multi-tasking. The phone was tucked between her shoulder and cheek while she stared at the computer screen, her fingers flying over the keyboard.

She hung up the phone. Her forehead was creased with worry lines. "I'm glad you're here. Sammy wants to talk to you. Something's wrong. I'm not sure what it is."

"Does Gabe know?"

"I haven't had a chance to talk to him. It's been crazy busy here. Go find Sammy. I'll hang around 'til you get back."

I headed out, on a mission to find out what was bothering Sammy. Knowing him, it could be something as mundane as finding a candy bar wrapper on one of the greens.

"Mom, hold on a sec."

Sofia waved me back to the counter. She glanced around the pro shop. Two women were checking out golf apparel on the sale rack.

Sofia lowered her voice to a whisper. "How did the interview go? Riley dropped by but wouldn't tell me anything. He said he'd check with you later."

I assured her it was fine and I would do a re-enactment later.

I hopped into a golf cart and zipped over to the work shed where I found Sammy, muttering to himself. His hands were busy adjusting the blades on the special mower he used to keep the greens in pristine condition.

When he saw me, he wiped his hands on a rag and thumped a hand against his chest. "You know I, Sammy Espinoza, always on time every day. Many times early. Right?"

"Absolutely."

"I come in early today, before anyone else is here."

"Uh huh," I said, wondering when he would make his point. I knew from past conversations, Sammy had his own agenda. It was best not to hurry him.

"So come with me. I will show you what I, Sammy Espinoza, found this morning when I arrived."

He marched toward the dumpster, glancing over his shoulder to make sure I followed. He extracted two giant trash bags from the dumpster and upended them. The contents, various-sized poster board signs, each attached to a spike, spilled from the bags.

"Damn *pendejo*," he swore. "Fake minister. Sammy knows it was fake minister who did this."

All the signs contained hateful or threatening messages and were decorated with lurid blood red images of gravestones, skulls and crossbones along with targets one might see at a shooting range. Each target had the word 'death' written in the innermost circle. The messaging was clearly the work of Faraday. It included some of his faves, like, ANOTHER DEATH, ANOTHER DAY. GOD IS PUNISHING YOU. FAIRWAY TO HEAVEN IS A TRIP TO HELL. CHANGE NAME, NOW!

"Were the signs on our property, or out by the

sidewalk?"

"All over the golf course. Looked very bad. Made holes in the greens. I got it cleaned up before golfers arrived."

I patted Sammy's shoulder. "Let's bag this up and let the sheriff have a look at it."

I didn't chastise him for failing to call the authorities. Sammy took great pride in his work. Seeing the vandalism was an affront to his dignity.

We bagged the signs and loaded them onto the golf cart. When I got back to the pro shop, Sofia was alone.

"Pops called," she said. "He's setting up interviews for the new golf pro. He's trying to get the board together, but can't get Earl Tomlinson to respond."

"Maybe they're out of town. His wife wasn't at mahjong this week and she never misses."

Rita's head poked out of the kitchen. "Barbara Tomlinson's not out of town. She's packing. They're selling their house."

I kept forgetting Rita was a veritable font of information about the denizens of Vista Valley. I needed to tap into her database more often.

"Moving?" I called. "Are you sure?"

"Yep, the sign's been up for a while."

Not wanting to shout out private information about our members, I walked over to Rita. "Have you seen Earl around?"

"My second cousin Bernie is a mechanic at Mickey Warren's car dealership. He said Earl hasn't been around for a couple of days."

"Hmm, pretty weird. I wonder why."

"I'll keep my ear to the ground and let you know."

"Thanks, Rita. Sofia looks hungry. What's the soup

today?"

"Clam chowder. I'll dip up a bowl."

I slipped some bills into her apron pocket.

An hour later, Riley came in, walked to the counter, and handed me my bracelet. He winked and smiled. "You scared my boy."

"*Boy* being the operative word," I said. "How old is he? Sixteen? He still has zits."

I struggled with the clasp as I tried to fasten the bracelet, one-handed.

"Allow me."

Riley's thick fingers were surprisingly agile as he fastened the charm bracelet around my left wrist. When it was securely clasped, he slid his hand up my arm. Once again, the warmth of his touch did crazy things to my lady parts. I pulled away.

"Hey, I thought you and I weren't supposed to be seen together."

He grinned. "Your dad had a little talk with the mayor. Everything is copacetic. Do you feel me?"

Did I ever! "Well, if the mayor's on board, who am I to object?"

We were sappily gazing into each other's eyes when Sammy burst through the door.

"Aha, very good! The lawman is now here to examine the evidence. Sammy will walk you through the entire episode. Then, *Señor* Sheriff, you can confront the wrongdoers and throw them into prison forever. Nobody messes with Sammy's beautiful golf course."

Riley's eyes widened. He leaned close and whispered, "Who, exactly, is *Señor* Sheriff supposed to be locking up forever?"

I filled him in on last night's vandalism. He swore under his breath. Sammy joined in with colorful Spanish curses. So nice the boys were bonding.

I pointed at the golf cart parked next to the patio. "The signs are all there, bagged up. Sammy will show you. They're obviously from Faraday's crew. He's invading private property now. The signs were all over the golf course, and according to Sammy, did some damage to the greens."

"Do you have security cameras or a nighttime security person?"

"No."

Riley shook his head in disgust. "Guys like Faraday scope things out. Basically, they're like cockroaches, sneaking around at night and tucked away during daylight hours. "I'll have a talk with him. And I'll have the guys on the night shift keep an eye out. Talk later?"

I nodded.

It was late afternoon and the din from the cocktail lounge spilled over into the pro shop. I stared at the computer, checking tee times for the following day, when Jonathan Dumas strolled in, an unlit cigar clenched between his teeth. Janice Pomeroy's daughter, Serena, clung to his arm, a large handbag slung over one shoulder. When the sale rack caught her attention, she detached herself from Dumas and pawed through the clothes.

Dumas looked at me and chuckled. "The lady likes to shop."

Serena held up a golf shirt. "Can I try this on?"

"Sure." I unlocked the closet-like space we used as a fitting room. She staggered a little as she brushed by me. Alcohol fumes wafted.

Dumas leaned over the counter, one arm braced against the surface. When I skirted around him, his gaze swept over me.

He leaned closer. "How ya doin'?"

"Okay," I said, suddenly tongue-tied. Before I perched on my stool, I pulled it back a few inches.

Something about Dumas was off-putting. He was a big man, but size wasn't the problem. He had no spatial awareness. He invaded my space. Maybe it was a symptom of my claustrophobia, but I liked a bit of distance between others and myself. Especially people I don't know well.

I folded my hands and placed them on the counter. "I saw you the other night when Tristan, um…"

He leaned closer. "Yeah, I was there. Annabelle's a nut job. Tris was trying to break up with her, but didn't have the guts."

His comment seemed harsh coming from someone who professed to be Tris's friend. Once again, I was at a loss for words.

He pointed a finger at my wrist. "Nice bracelet." Squinting, he leaned closer. "Does that charm spell out Libby?"

Was Dumas killing time because he was bored? Why the sudden interest in my bracelet?

"Yes, my name is on one of them."

"Tris found it. He planned to return it to you. I guess he did."

Since I had no intention of sharing the details around the charm bracelet drama, I nodded and kept my mouth shut.

Serena appeared and rummaged through the rack

again.

"Did the shirt work out?" I asked.

"No, didn't fit."

"Let's go, babe. Mom will have a cow if we're late for dinner."

Dumas gave me one last lingering look and a two-fingered salute. "See ya, Libby."

Later, I checked the sales rack. The shirt Serena tried on was missing. I looked in the fitting room. *Nada*. Why would a woman whose mother, according to Abigail Cavendish, had piles of money, steal a golf shirt?

And what was the deal with Dumas and his interest in the charm bracelet? Because of the way my arm was resting on the counter, I was sure the Libby charm was not visible. I rubbed my aching temples.

Questions without answers made me nuts.

Chapter Twenty-Nine

When I got home at seven, Dad met me at the back door. “That Cavendish woman called me. She said your cell phone went to voice mail.”

“Oops.” I checked my cell phone. “Needs charging.”

Dad sighed and shook his head. “Happens at least once a week. What if you have an emergency?”

I was too tired to argue. “You’re right. I’ll try to remember. What did Abigail want?”

“She wants you to come over for what she called a light supper. It’s not about the book. She just wants to chat.”

“Tonight?”

“Yes, Jeeves will be arriving shortly to pick you up in the limo.”

The last comment was delivered without a glimmer of a smile, but I saw a twinkle of amusement in his eyes.

“Now, you’re yanking my chain. There’s no Jeeves.”

He spun on his heel and headed for the living room. “You’ve got twenty minutes to get ready. Be sure to dress appropriately for a light supper.” His shoulders shook with barely suppressed laughter.

“You’re jealous ’cause you don’t get to go.”

He flapped a hand in my direction. “Plug in your

phone."

I slipped into the sundress I'd worn for my date with Riley, ran a brush through my hair and dabbed on a bit of make-up.

The Jeeves person referenced by my dad was a total fabrication. The limo was not. The gentleman who came to the door to fetch me was none other than Felicity Horncastle's husband, Henry. Surprised isn't the word. I had Felicity pegged as a grim spinster. Whereas the no-nonsense Felicity was grim and forbidding, Henry was the polar opposite.

When I opened the door, he whipped off his chauffer's cap and greeted me with a smile. His cheeks were dimpled and rosy, his sparse white hair arranged in an elaborate comb-over. A round little potbelly strained the buttons on his formal black coat. He introduced himself and offered me his arm.

As I stepped through the door, Dad said, "Bye, Cinderella. Remember your midnight curfew and don't lose a glass slipper."

Henry chuckled and led me to the limousine. He opened the back door with a flourish and gestured for me to enter. I was so out of my comfort zone.

"Can I sit up front with you?"

Blinking rapidly, he pondered the question. "Really? Is that what madam wants?"

I could see I'd totally flummoxed him. "Of course, if you don't want me to…"

He gave a slight bow. "I would be delighted for the company."

I climbed into the front seat of the luxury vehicle, and we glided away from the curb. The seat was so comfy, the ride so quiet, I wanted to curl up and have a little snooze. I resisted the urge.

"Have you been with Abigail and Winston long?"

He beamed over at me. "Oh, my yes. Forty years now. I believe you've met my wife, Felicity?"

"Yes, indeed." Good God, I was talking like a character in a British period piece. Get a grip. "Mrs. Horncastle seems very, um, organized."

If I wasn't not mistaken, Henry's bright blue eyes rolled heavenward.

"I must agree. Felicity is extremely organized."

We rolled through the gates and pulled to a stop in the circular drive in front of the house. I started to get out, but thought better of it. I leaned back and folded my hands in my lap. Henry scurried around the front of the car, helped me out and walked me to the portico. Felicity stood in the open doorway, waiting to usher me in.

"Here she is, m'dear. Safely delivered," said Henry.

Felicity gave him a curt nod and scanned my attire with a disapproving gaze. I resisted an eye roll. It's a light supper. I didn't wear my formal gown.

"Mersus Cavendish is expecting you. Follow me."

She took off like a gut-shot gazelle, expecting me to scurry along behind her. Irritated by Felicity's power trip, I waited. I would continue to wait until I turned into a pile of bones.

"Are you coming?" a disembodied voice called.

I'd had a long day and was in no mood to play games. "Will you friggin' slow down? What are you, part greyhound?"

She popped into view, looking not in the least bit apologetic. "I thought you could keep up."

We engaged in a steely-eyed glaring contest. She

was the first to blink, but was far from defeated. She whirled around and proceeded down the hall at a snail's pace, lifting each foot in exaggerated slow motion. I was practically walking on her heels.

I zipped around her. "You know what, Miz Horncastle? I'm tired of your passive-aggressive crap. I'll find my own way, thank you very much."

Her eyes widened. I suspected she'd never been the recipient of such sassiness. She said nothing and inclined her head toward a corridor leading to the left. It looked familiar. I made my way through the kitchen where an elderly woman was hunched over the industrial-sized gas range, vigorously stirring something green. She saw me and pointed toward the patio.

Abigail sat at a small rectangular table covered with a pristine white tablecloth. Apparently the glass-topped umbrella table had been banished.

She rose and gripped my hands in hers. "So glad you could make it, sweetie. How's the book coming along?"

"Pretty good. I've been busier than usual at the golf course because, well, you know what happened. I hope to get back on a regular writing schedule soon."

"No worries, as long as it's done before I croak," she said with a merry giggle.

I was pretty sure the Angel of Death wouldn't dare darken their door, especially if Felicity Horncastle was the greeter.

I smiled. "When the golf season winds down, I'll have more time to write."

She patted my hand, "Excellent. Actually, I told your dear father the purpose of this get together did not concern our book. "Sit, please."

Note to self: Tell dear father about Abigail's comment.

We settled into our chairs. Abigail snapped her fingers. A tall, lank figure popped around the corner carrying a bottle of pricey wine, a white cloth napkin draped over one arm. He appeared to be on the south side of eighty and sliding downhill rapidly. I wondered if Abigail had any domestic workers who were not octogenarians.

"Thank you, Maurice. Please bring the first entrée."

"There are only two place settings. Isn't Willard joining us?" I asked.

Abigail shook her head. "No, Willard doesn't like kale. I certainly hope you do."

Truth be told, kale has never been on the McKenna family's menu. "I'm sure it will be delicious."

The purpose of my visit was not mentioned while we consumed kale pasta, lamb salad with fregola and flaky rolls with butter, along with Abigail's favorite dessert, peanut butter chocolate bars, available at your local grocery store, two for ninety-nine cents. I wondered if Abigail was lonely and needed a dinner companion. When the last bit of chocolate vanished, she got down to business.

She peered through the gathering darkness, as if spies might be hiding in the shrubbery.

"Scoot your chair over here next to me. I have valuable information about Mickey Warren's death. I heard it wasn't an accident," she whispered.

I did as she asked, despite the fact the only people on the premises were hard of hearing. Her eyes sparkled with secret delight.

"I know you're close to the yummy sheriff." She paused and winked. "Perhaps my information will help his investigation."

Did everybody in Vista Valley think I was sleeping with Riley?

"Anyhoo, I won't tell you my source, but the info has to do with the will. Heather and Mickey had a pre-nup, but it only covered divorce. She challenged it and was named the main beneficiary." She took a deep breath. "Now here's the interesting part. She split the money with Mickey's first wife, Patty Warren Taylor."

I struggled to wrap my brain around the information Abigail believed to be so significant. I recalled Rita saying Heather didn't think Patty should receive a single penny. And then, there was the scene at the lawyer's office when Patty and her daughter stormed in.

"I guess Heather decided to be generous," I said.

Abigail shook a finger in my face. "You're not getting it. Those two hated each other. My source thinks they joined forces and you know what that means."

"Actually, I don't."

"They planned it out together, figured out a way to kill him. Heather wanted a divorce. Patty wanted money. She was probably the brains behind the scheme. I hear he was injected with poison."

"Sorry, Abigail, but I seriously doubt one of the wives sneaked onto the golf course and jabbed him in the butt."

She sighed. "You are such an innocent. Have you heard of killers for hire?"

"Well, yeah, but—"

"There's one more thing. I saw them together before Mickey Warren's death."

"Where?"

"I was on my way to visit a friend when I spotted the two of them in Heather's car. It was parked on a side street. I asked Henry to go around the block, and sure enough, they were there, chatting away, thick as thieves. I was in the back seat of the limo. It has tinted windows so they couldn't see me."

"Maybe they decided to bury the hatchet," I said.

"They sure did. Deep in Mickey's butt. And it wasn't a hatchet."

It all seemed incredibly fanciful to me. "How reliable is your source?"

She looked around again and lowered her voice to a whisper. "Very reliable. My friend, Edith, has a granddaughter who's a paralegal for Hochstetter."

So much for lawyer-client privilege.

"The next time you engage in pillow talk with the hunky sheriff, feel free to share my insight."

I assured her I would. Minus the pillow talk.

I pondered her theory as Henry drove me home. The evidence seemed sketchy at best. It flew in the face of everything I'd witnessed and learned. Such a convoluted deception would be difficult to plan and execute.

Yet, in my heart of hearts, I knew far stranger things had happened.

Chapter Thirty

The next day, Dad burst into the clubhouse. I could tell by the set of his jaw, he had an agenda.

"Call Baby Bird to cover for you. We've got things to do."

"Like what?

"I tracked Bruce Hargraves down again. Interrupted his pricey honeymoon. I told him about the vandalism, and he said to hire a nighttime security guy."

"Why am I involved? You can handle it."

"There's more. Three people have applied for Tristan's job. We have to schedule interviews and need a board member to help make the final decision."

"I'm not actually a board member, Dad. I'm just a flunky."

He patted my hand. "Now you are. Consider yourself appointed. Here's the problem. Mickey and Tristan have gone to a better place, hopefully one with a putting green. Big blond busty broad, Stella, is visiting her daughter in Italy. Herb Talcott is an idiot, and I can't get Earl Tomlinson to answer his phone. So I thought maybe you and I should drop by Earl's house and see if we can smoke him out, so to speak."

"You're not the only one looking for him."

I filled him in on Riley's concerns, adding, "What about Janice Pomeroy? She's still around. You'll need someone to take notes."

He flapped a hand. "Fine, fine. We'll stop and see Janice, too. Now give the kid a call."

Twenty minutes later, we parked in front of a two-story brick home with a For Sale sign in the front yard. Located in a nice part of town with oversized lots and beautifully manicured lawns, it wouldn't be on the market long.

We walked across the curved stamped concrete patio leading to the front steps. The front door was a deep shade of red and had a peephole. Dad rapped on the door.

I poked him with my elbow. "We should have brought honey."

He grinned at me. "No worries, Chickadee. If Earl's not here, Barb will talk to me. We were an item back in high school."

I stared at him in shock. "You dated Barbara Tomlinson?"

He puffed out his chest. "Yep, she was Barbara Ann Rogers back in the day. Good looking girl. It was before I met your mom."

"Wow, is there anyone else I should know about? I had no idea you were such a stud muffin back in the day."

"Oh, hush."

The sound of footsteps approaching the front door put an end to our conversation. Silence followed. I figured an eye was at the peephole, checking us out. We must have passed the test because the door swung open, revealing Barbara Tomlinson. Her eyes were red and swollen, her expression slack.

Dad said, "Hi Barb, how are you, sweetie?"

Sweetie?

She patted her hair and forced a smile. "Not so good, Ed."

Dad said, "I need to talk to Earl. He's not answering his phone."

Her chin trembled as she stepped back and motioned us in. The hall was lined with cardboard boxes from a moving company.

"They haven't come for the furniture yet. Let's go in the living room."

She turned and we followed her down the hall and into a spacious living room. Dad and I shifted a stack of clothing to one side and sat on the couch. Extracting a tissue from the pocket of her jeans, she wiped her eyes, blew her nose and plopped down on a loveseat.

"I'd offer you coffee but I just packed the kitchen stuff."

"No problem, Barbara," I said. "We're sorry to interrupt when you're so busy, but we really need to talk to Earl about golf course matters."

Her transformation from sad to furious was instantaneous and startling. Eyes flashing with anger, she stiffened in her chair. Her voice rose to a shriek. "You need to talk to him? If you find him, please tell him I need to talk to him."

Whoa, I had no idea how to respond.

Dad, who lived in a house with two hormonal females, was not similarly afflicted. Factor in the teenage romance and it was a no brainer. He walked over to the loveseat and sat next to her. "My God, Barbara, you don't know where he is?"

"No," she wailed. She waved her hand. "And look at this mess. We just moved here a year ago. My dream house. Now he tells me we have to sell it, and of course, he leaves me to do all the damn work."

Dad spoke in soothing tones. "Did he give you a reason? Is he having financial problems?"

I cringed, thinking Barbara would be totally offended by the question. She wasn't.

"Oh, Ed," she wailed. "I'm not sure what to do. Earl has a gambling problem. He's lost a ton of money. I don't know all the details, but I think he needs money from the house to pay off his debts."

"So," Dad said. "How long has he been gone?"

"Two days. I even went to the casino looking for him, but he wasn't there."

"Have you reported him missing?"

"No," she said. "He's done this before. He usually comes back after a couple of days."

I asked, "Did Mickey Warren know about Earl's, um, problem?"

"I'm not sure. Right before Mickey died, he came over. He and Earl went outside and talked. Earl wouldn't tell me what it was about, but I could tell he was upset."

Dad patted her knee. "Hang in there, kid. Is there anything we can help you with before we go? Want me to go look for Earl?"

She fluttered her eyelashes and gripped his hand. "That is so sweet, Ed. Thank you, but it would be a wild goose chase. I'll let you know the minute he comes back."

Before we left, I said, "Barb, what about your friends at the golf course? I bet they would support you, give you a hand with the packing."

She made a scoffing sound. "No way. You think I

want them snooping around, looking for something more to gossip about?"

"Sorry, I said. "I thought you girls were close."

"Fair weather friends."

She hugged Dad goodbye, a bit longer than necessary. He seemed to enjoy it.

As we walked to the car, I said, "Janice Pomeroy next?"

"No need to go to her house. I'll give her a call."

Hmm, maybe Janice was an ex-girlfriend too. I had no idea Dad was such a hot item in his youth. As I pondered my father's checkered past, my cell phone buzzed.

—Group message from Donny/Ronny to Libby, Ed and Jules: Partaay Time! Please join us posthaste for libations and yummy snacks. Help us launch our new wine, Over the Rainbow Rosé. Libby, Sheriff Hardbody stopped by your place looking for you. Check your damn phone! Please use feminine wiles to entice him to aforementioned party. We promise not to harass, but might drool a bit. See ya soon!—

I checked my calls and text messages. Sure enough, I'd missed both a phone call and text from Riley. I filled Dad in on the message and called Riley.

When he answered, he was breathing hard. I heard yelling in the background.

"Shall I call you back?" I said.

"Nah." He dropped the phone and barked, "Shipley, get this Neanderthal out of here and lock him up."

I heard footsteps and the sound of a door closing. "How ya doing, pretty girl? Stopped by your place earlier.

"Shipley?" I said in disbelief. "The baby detective is dealing with a Neanderthal? Maybe you should hang up and see if he's still alive."

He chuckled. "Hey, you're dissing my boy again. He'll be fine."

"Sorry I didn't get your call. Something important?"

"Do I have to have a reason? Maybe I wanted to feast my eyes on your cute little bod."

I felt a blush rise in my cheeks and glanced over at Dad who was trying to act disinterested.

I told Riley about the Donny/Ronny thing. He said he'd take care of a couple of miscreants and be there shortly.

Dad dropped me off at the golf course. I checked on Sofia who said, "Go home. I'll hang out here until closing. Can I bring Gabe to the party?"

I assured her Gabe was welcome.

"Almost forgot. You know that Dumas guy who's hangs out with Janice Pomeroy's daughter?"

"Yes, what about him?"

"He was here looking for you."

"Did he say what he wanted?"

"No, but he knew you were my mom. That seemed weird."

"Huh," I said. "Anything else?"

"Something about him creeps me out."

Why would Jonathan Dumas come looking for me? Why the sudden interest in the McKenna family relationships? It creeped me out, too.

Chapter Thirty-One

Our formerly quiet street was jammed with a long line of parked cars. A gigantic Party Rentals truck loomed in the boys' driveway. The sound of alcohol-enhanced laughter and music wafted through the early evening air.

I peeked over the hedge. R and D's expansive back yard was decked out with a portable dance floor surrounded by tables and chairs. Food tables were set up next to the house along with a bar, currently manned by Donny. Dad had his spot staked out next to a galvanized tub filled with beer on ice, Suzy by his side.

Ronny spotted me and waved. "Get your buns over here, girl."

I toyed with the idea of changing clothes, but couldn't summon the energy. Sneakers, jeans, and a Fairway to Heaven polo shirt would have to do.

Ronny met me at the gate and wrapped me up in a hug. "Welcome."

"Impressive party. You sure kept it under wraps."

"It wasn't easy. We planned it a month ago, but had to wait for the first shipment of Over the Rainbow Rosé to come in."

With a flourish, he gestured toward the gathering. "Friends are always welcome, but we also wanted to thank our employees. Without them, none of this would be possible."

His eyes moistened and he tugged me toward the bar. “Let’s get you a glass of the new stuff and see how you like it.”

Jules, on the dance floor with boyfriend, Pete, waved and beckoned me over. There was no getting away from Ronny who had a firm grip on my arm.

Donny had a wineglass ready for me. Both of them fixed me with unblinking stares, as I swirled and sipped. I’d planned to heap praise on their new offering, even if I didn’t like it. I didn’t have to lie. It was tasty, not too sweet and not too dry.

In my best wine snob voice, I declared, “Lovely bouquet, perfect blend of fruitiness, acidity and tannin with just a hint of fresh berries.”

Donny’s eyes widened. Ronny’s mouth dropped open. I tried not to snicker.

I didn’t know Dad was behind me until I heard, “You are so full of crap.”

“Full of crap, huh? I plan to write a review, put it on the boys’ website and sign it, ‘a wine connoisseur’.”

“Where’s Riley?” Dad said.

Ronny’s eyes sparkled. “Yes, where is the dear boy?”

“He’ll be here soon. Sofia too, along with Gabe Espinoza.”

I held out my glass for a refill and joined Jules and Pete.

Her eyes sparkled with excitement. “Did your dad tell you? We’ve got more orders.”

I looped an arm around her neck and smooched her cheek. “Great news. Anybody I know?”

“Pete spread the word at work. It seems a lot of people in the financial world enjoy buns and special honey."

Pete grinned at me. "Stress reliever after a long day dealing with irate clients who think we can predict the ups and downs of the stock market."

I gave him a look of mock horror. "You can't?"

Jules snapped her fingers. "Damn, almost forgot to tell you about Janice Pomeroy. The guy who hooked up with her daughter called and placed a big order. Said to charge it to Janice."

"Jonathan Dumas. I wonder if Janice knows."

Jules squirmed a little. "You mind delivering it? I don't deal well with controversy."

"Sure, I thrive on it."

She waved a hand. "Well, looky there. Sheriff Riley O'Connor has arrived. Donny and Ronny are over the moon. Maybe you should go rescue him."

Dad beat me to it. He slipped between R and D, slapped Riley on the back and led him to the beer on ice.

I lowered my voice. "I'm a little worried about selling Dad's special honey. He's not licensed to grow marijuana. And we're part of it. We could all end up in trouble."

She threw an arm around my shoulder and whispered, "Sweetheart, the mayor buys your dad's honey. Stop worrying."

"But…"

"Hush. If you're really freaked out, talk to Riley. I'm pretty sure he won't throw you in the slammer." She gave me a wicked smile. "Although he might consider house arrest since you're such a flight risk. Might be fun for both of you." She gestured at Dad and Riley. "Looks like your dad is giving Riley an earful.

What's that about?"

"No idea."

"They keep looking over here. I bet you're the hot topic."

Riley skirted around the crowd, making a beeline toward me. I smiled and waved. He narrowed his eyes and frowned. Hmm.

"Wow," Jules said. "Somebody looks pissed off. You two have a fight?"

"No. Apparently Dad riled him up about something." I wagged a finger at Jules and said, "Stay," as I intercepted Riley.

She looked disappointed, but made no move to follow.

"We need to talk." He took my hand and led me to the hedge dividing the yards. It was relatively private.

I gulped loudly. "Is this about the honey?"

One eyebrow shot up. "The honey?"

I started to babble. "I know Dad isn't licensed and he could get arrested, and since we're selling it, we could all be charged and…"

With a bark of laughter, he said, "Hold up, darlin'. This isn't about the honey."

An electrical current of relief swept through my body, causing my legs to quiver.

Riley placed his hands on my shoulders to steady me. "You okay?"

Now I felt silly. "I'm fine. You said we needed to talk, and I assumed it was about Ed's Special Dark. My bad."

His hands tightened on my shoulders. "Ed told me about the threatening phone call. Why didn't you tell me?"

"That's what you're ticked off about? The phone call?"

"You could be in danger. I want to help."

"I'm not sure why Dad told you. We've got it covered."

"We might have been able to trace the call."

"Whoever it was probably used a pay phone or a burner. Plus a device to distort his voice."

His face was grim. "Either you trust me or you don't."

"Riley, this isn't about trust. In our family, we take care of each other. We don't look for outside help."

"You're forgetting onc thing. Your dad wanted me to know about the phone call. Translation: He's worried about you and this is his way of asking for help."

He smiled and brushed the back of his fingers against my cheek. "Want to argue about it some more?"

I tried not to smile, but failed. "Is that what we're doing? Arguing?"

He pulled me against his body. I leaned into him and felt the strong, steady beat of his heart. Despite my declaration of independence, I felt safe for the first time in weeks.

When I pulled away, he murmured, "No more secrets. Okay?"

"I'll let you know if I get another call."

"I'll have the night deputy on patrol include your house in his rounds."

"Probably not necessary, but…"

He placed a finger across my lips. "Now is when you say, 'Thank you, Riley.'"

I rolled my eyes and repeated, "Thank you, Riley."

He smiled. "Knew you could do it."

Because I'd promised to be more forthcoming, I added, "Did Dad tell you about Earl Tomlinson?"

"No, and I'm still trying to catch up with him. He hasn't shown up at work."

"His wife can't find him either, and he's making her sell their house."

Staring into middle space, he mulled it over for a minute. "Thanks, guess I need to pay Ms. Tomlinson a visit."

I considered mentioning Abigail's theory about Mickey's ex-wife and current wife joining forces for his demise. It seemed far-fetched, so I decided against it.

Sofia's car chugged into the driveway and lurched to a stop. She and Gabe climbed out. Though I didn't know it at the time, things were about to get very interesting.

Chapter Thirty-Two

"Hey Momser. Riley," Sofia called. She joined us at the hedge, glancing over her shoulder at Gabe who huddled next to her car. "Why aren't you two at the party?"

Riley grinned. "We needed a private moment."

Sofia giggled and offered a fist to bump.

"It's not what you're thinking," I huffed.

She winked at Riley. "Whatever you say, Mother."

I waved at Gabe. "Come join us."

Sofia took my hand and tugged me toward the gate. "Riley, will you excuse us for a sec? I need to talk to Mom."

"No problem."

As he strode away and merged with the crowd, I said, "What's the big secret?"

"There are some things you don't know about Gabe."

"Like what? Is he in trouble?"

"No, and I want to make sure it stays that way."

"Wait a sec. Are you involved?"

Sofia heaved an impatient sigh. "Try not to be judgmental. What I'm about to tell you is for the common good."

"Whose common good, yours or mine?"

"Both."

"I'm listening."

She took a deep breath, blew it out. “It’s hard to know where to begin. I’ll start by saying Gabe is like a computer genius. He finds things out about people. He was upset when Farley on a Harley started bugging us. Then Faraday defaced his family’s property and left nasty little signs all over the golf course. That was the last straw. Gabe started looking into Faraday and The Last Bus Stop to Heaven. What he found is pretty interesting.”

Now I was intrigued. “Is Gabe a hacker? You obviously didn’t want talk about it in front of Riley.”

She shrugged. “Maybe. Do you want to know what he found out or not?”

“I do.”

“Promise you won’t do your Spanish Inquisition thing. I mean it, Mom.”

I pinched my lips together, mostly to keep from laughing. “Well damn, I left my implements of torture at work.”

“And please, no where, why, how or what. Got it?”

“Okay, okay, I promise.”

“Alrighty, then.” She led me over to Gabe. “Mom’s cool. Go ahead.”

“Hi Gabe,” I said. “I’d like to know what you found out.”

He looked up from studying his shoes and briefly met my gaze. “Hi, Miz McKenna.”

“Call me Libby, and no worries, whatever you have to tell me goes no further unless you want it to.”

He glanced over at Sofia who gave him an encouraging smile. “Tell her, Gabe.”

“For starters, he’s not who he says he is. His name isn’t Farley Faraday and he’s not an ordained minister.

His real name is Lester Buxton. He was in prison for almost beating a guy to death. Something about a drug deal gone bad."

Sofia shot me a warning glance. I bit my tongue to keep from asking, How do you know this? Instead, I gave him an encouraging nod. "Anything else?"

"He got out a couple of years ago and was off the grid for a while. Last year, he reappeared as Reverend Farley Faraday. His wife's maiden name was Faith Hatzenbeler. She inherited a shit load…" He clapped a hand over his mouth. "Sorry, Libby. She inherited a bunch of money from her dad who created software for video gamers. I'm talking big bucks."

Sofia added, "By inherited, Gabe means the father died and Faith was the only beneficiary."

Gabe continued, "She probably hooked up with him while he was incarcerated. I guess some women are attracted to convicts. It's probably her money they used to buy the church. Should be easy enough to check, if you want me to."

I tried to form a question my daughter wouldn't react to by screaming, "Objection!"

"I wonder how he came up with the new identity."

"Oh, please, Mom," Sofia said. "Do you know how easy it is to get a new identity? All you need is money and Faith has plenty."

I stayed quiet for a few moments, trying to decide the best course of action without scaring the heck out of Gabe.

Finally, I said, "I'd like to talk to the sheriff about this. I won't mention your name. Their department probably has a computer tech who can access prison records. Okay with you?"

He looked over at Sofia and lifted his hands. "What do you think?"

She slipped her arm through his. "It should be fine. Riley is a good guy. Besides, my mom has special privileges."

They both had a good laugh over her zinger at my expense.

I added a weak chuckle. "I'm heading back. You guys coming?"

Sofia said, "We'll be over later, after you do your thing with you know who."

Well aware of my assignment, I gave her a thumbs-up and went back to the party. Pushing my way through the crowd, I stopped when a pair of beefy arms encircled my waist.

"Come dance with me, pretty girl."

The words were murmured into my ear in a familiar voice. I turned and brushed against a bristly chin attached to my favorite lawman. The music had transitioned from salsa to hard rock, and then to one of my favorites, an oldie but goodie by the Hollies. I may have lost my virginity while listening to this song. Water under the bridge.

Riley led me onto the dance floor and folded me into his arms. I was tired of fighting it, so I leaned into his body and enjoyed the moment.

When the song ended, I was weak in the knees, and it didn't bother me a bit.

He gazed down at me. "Where you been all my life, girl?"

"Right here, in Vista Valley, waiting for the right guy."

I took his hand and pulled him away from the

crowd. "There's something I need to tell you. But first, you have to promise not to scare the crap out of the informant."

The corners of his mouth quirked up in a smile. "Call this is a stab in the dark, but I'm guessing your secret informant is either Sofia or kid she's with. Am I getting warm?"

"It's about Farley on a Harley."

His face darkened. He raised his right hand. "Unless it involves the intent to injure or cause bodily harm to an innocent victim, I promise I will not use the power of my badge to harass, intimidate or incarcerate said person. Good enough?"

"It'll do."

We retreated to our former rendezvous spot next to the hedge. I told him what Gabe had found out. He peppered me with questions, I held up a hand. "Whoa. We're talking about a kid who probably did some illegal hacking. Okay?"

"I want to talk to him."

"Remember your pledge."

He pointed at my house. "You go in first. Tell him he's not in trouble. I want to nail Faraday as much as he does. Besides, this kid sounds like he has potential and I'd like to meet him."

I studied his face, looking for any sign of duplicity. Seeing none, I headed for the house, all the while hoping I was making the right decision.

Chapter Thirty-Three

After doing my best to convince Gabe he wasn't in trouble, he reluctantly agreed to stick around. When Riley stomped into the house, Gabe's eyes widened, but he didn't bolt. Progress.

Kitchen or living room? I opted for informality and herded everyone into the breakfast nook, Gabe and Sofia on one side, Riley and me on the other. Despite the cozy quarters, Gabe perched sideways on the bench seat, muscles tensed, feet planted firmly on the floor, ready to make a run for it.

Riley quickly put him at ease. He extended his right hand across the table. "Hey, buddy, I don't think we've met. Forget the sheriff part. Just call me Riley."

Gabe introduced himself. "I talked to you the night Faraday defaced our property. We have a big family, so you probably don't remember me."

They chatted a while. Sofia and I kept quiet which was hard for both of us. Gabe began to relax.

Riley noticed it, too. "Libby told me you've got information about Faraday's background. Tell me what you found. You don't have to say how you found it."

The words tumbled out as Gabe repeated the story, even slipping in a few more details, like where Faraday—Lester Buxton—was born and raised.

Impressed, Riley slapped the table, scaring poor Gabe out of his wits. "Kid, when you're ready to leave the dark side, let me know. I could use your help. I've got a computer tech. But he doesn't know diddlysquat. You would have access to some databases that maybe, um…" He hesitated and glanced over at me.

I narrowed my eyes at him. He got the message.

"Let's just say, you could help us out and enhance your knowledge of the legal system."

"Hey!" I punched him in the arm. "Are you trying to steal one of my valued employees?"

"Are you kidding? I'm trying to stay on your good side."

Sofia snickered. Gabe grinned.

"We can work around his job at the golf course. What do you think, Gabe?" said Riley.

Gabe nodded. "Sounds good to me."

Sofia leaned across the table and gazed at Riley with an intensity I knew well. "Do you plan to pay him for his time?"

Riley grinned. "What are you? His agent?"

She took a huge preparatory breath, ready to leap to Gabe's defense. Riley lifted a hand to stop the onslaught of words.

"He'll be paid from our discretionary fund."

"The computer tech who doesn't know diddlysquat, is his name Shipley?" I asked.

"You putting my boy down again?"

"Just answer the question."

"Yep, it's Shipley."

I gave him a smug grin. "Ready to go back to the party?"

He slid out of the bench seat. "Let's hit it."

"You guys coming?" I asked Sofia.

"We'll be there soon."

Before we could leave, Dad and Suzy pushed through the back door and entered the kitchen. Dad grinned like a lunatic. Suzy wobbled on her stilettos. When Dad spotted me, he sobered quickly.

"Chickadee," he said. "I forgot to tell you something extremely important."

Judging from past experience, I figured it was bee-related. Maybe his queen was languishing in the hive, unwilling to pop out thousands of potential baby worker bees. Maybe he had a swarm to capture. Maybe he'd run out of his Special Dark and was declaring a national emergency.

"Tristan's mother called," he said. "Bottom line, Tris has been cremated. They opted out of a formal ceremony. Instead, they want to scatter the cremains in a sand bunker at dawn."

"When?"

"Tomorrow."

He peered around me and spotted Gabe and Sofia. "Oh, good, Gabe is here." Dragging Suzy behind him, he marched over to breakfast nook. "Son, I'd appreciate it if you'd let your dad know about tomorrow. Okay?"

Gabe's mouth opened and closed. No words came out.

"Dad," I cautioned. "Sammy won't like the idea of cremains in one of his bunkers."

Gabe, still speechless, nodded vigorously.

Dad lifted his hands in a helpless gesture and tried to look innocent. "I told them tomorrow would be fine. They plan to add signage at a later date."

"Signage?" I shrieked. "What will it say? 'Here Lies What's Left of Tristan Kensington III?' Wow, Dad, maybe we should add our own sign saying, 'Free

Drop, if You Don't Want to Disturb Tristan's Cremains.'"

"Aw, come on, Chickie. How could I say no?"

I glared at him. "It's easy. Repeat after me: I'll get back to you after I run it by the board of directors."

"Too late." He winked at Suzy. "How did I get such an uptight daughter?"

"I'm guessing they want the ceremony at one of three holes," I said. "Sixteen-Eternal Rest, Seventeen-Pearly Gates, or Eighteen-The Hereafter."

"Bingo, smarty pants. Eternal Rest."

"Are we involved?"

"Yes, she wants all of us there. You, Baby Bird, and me."

"I'll pass. I don't do cremains," Sofia said.

"I already said we'd be there. Buck up, Buttercup. It's just a few minutes of your life and it will mean a lot to the Kensingtons."

Even though I sincerely doubted the truth of his statement, I said, "We'll be there."

Sofia glared at me.

Gabe, looking a little pale, stood. "Guess I'd better go talk to Pop."

"I'll go with you," Sofia said.

"Bright and early tomorrow, Baby Bird. I'll wake you up."

Sofia, still in a snit, reluctantly agreed to attend the dawn sprinkling of Tristan's ashes.

Gabe tried to comfort her. "Pretend it's sand from the beach."

"With random bits of bone," Suzy added.

"You're a big help," I huffed.

Dad wrapped an arm around Suzy's shoulders.

"She's just trying to defuse a tense situation."

"Well, it's not working." I wandered back to the breakfast nook and slid in beside Riley who'd been silently watching the McKenna family drama unfold. I could tell he was trying not to laugh.

"Welcome to Crazy Town," I muttered.

"No worries. Most families live in Crazy Town."

"Do you want to join us tomorrow, Riley? You can be an honorary ash sprinkler," Dad said.

"Dad," I scolded. "Not funny. We're talking about Tristan."

"I'll pass, but thanks for the invite."

Suzy tugged on Dad's arm. "Let's go back to the party. You guys coming?"

Riley clapped his hands around my waist and scooted me out of the breakfast nook. "You bet we are. Ed, I know dawn comes early tomorrow. I won't keep your daughter out too late."

"Keep her out as late as you want. It might improve her attitude." Dad winked and grinned.

Chapter Thirty-Four

Awakened at 4:30 a.m. the next morning, attitude improvement was not on the agenda. Sofia and I had a serious case of the grumpies. We clutched our travel mugs of coffee and piled into Dad's truck. The sun peeked over the horizon, bathing the foothills in a fiery glow.

Dad was his usual cheerful morning self. "Beautiful day for an ash sprinkling."

Sofia's response was an incoherent snarl.

I tried to act grown up. "Do the Kensingtons need anything from the clubhouse? Maybe chairs?"

"No, they just want us to show up." He peered around me at Sofia. "How did it go with Sammy last night?"

"He pitched a fit. Gabe got him to calm down. Told him he'd rake the sand trap when the Kensingtons leave and nobody would know the difference."

"At least until the sign goes up." I shook my head. "Bad idea."

"I agree," Dad said. "I'll talk to the family when this thing is over. I'm sure the men's club will pay for a plaque and his picture to put in the pro shop."

I patted his arm. "Glad you see it my way."

"Your way? *Phhtt!*"

The Kensingtons' car was in the parking lot. Apparently they'd already trooped out to Eternal Rest.

An enormous black SUV pulled in and parked as we climbed out of the truck. Jonathan Dumas was behind the wheel. Janice's daughter, Serena slumped over in the passenger seat. Dumas exited and closed the door gently.

Dumas wasn't my favorite person, but I opted for a modicum of civility. "Are you here for Tristan's, um, scattering?"

The minute I said the word, I wanted to take it back. Scattering sounded horribly inappropriate, and my cheeks warmed up.

Dumas failed to notice my awkwardness. "Yeah, it's kind of weird, but I guess it's what the family wants."

I gestured toward his car. "Is Serena coming?"

He grimaced. "She's a little hung over."

"Okay, see you at the Eternal Rest bunker."

As I joined Dad and Sofia, a slime-green battered sedan chugged into the parking lot.

Sofia gasped. "Mom, it's that awful Annabelle woman, the one who yelled at you the night Tristan died. It's a good thing Dad and I are here. We won't let her attack you."

"Thanks, but Annabelle and I are okay. I stopped by her house with your grandfather's special honey."

She heaved a sigh of relief. "Good. I'm not up for a physical altercation this early in the a.m."

I laughed and gave her a little shove. "Go with Pops. I'll talk to Annabelle and be there shortly."

Dumas was trying—unsuccessfully—to rouse Serena as I walked over to Annabelle.

"Hi, are you here for Tristan's ceremony?"

Annabelle, clad entirely in black, climbed out of

her car. She gave me a visual onceover worthy of pageant mom checking out her daughter's competition gown. Maybe I should have dressed in more somber attire instead of khakis and white polo shirt.

"Yes," she said. "Whether his parents like it or not, Tristan and I were a couple. It's my duty to show up." Her eyes flashed with anger. "Jon told me about it."

"So the family doesn't know you're coming?"

She scowled. "It's a free country, Elizabeth McKenna Carone," she said, and scurried away to join Dumas.

It appeared Annabelle's good will toward me had vanished along with Ed's Special Dark.

I caught up with Dad and Sofia walking down the Number Sixteen fairway toward the sand trap. Sixteen's moniker, Eternal Rest, wasn't just a reference to the last nine holes known as Heaven. Actually, it wasn't heavenly and should probably be part of Hell. Diabolically formed, the green was slightly convex, causing most balls landing there to roll into the bunker. I'd heard more than one golfer complain bitterly about the design. The comment usually ended with, 'Every time I hit the green, my ball comes to eternal rest in the damn bunker. Might as well just throw it in and get it over with.'

Sammy handled their complaints by lifting his hands in a helpless gesture. '*Si*, it is an evil hole. Unfortunately, Sammy cannot fix it.'

The Kensington family, all clad in golf duds, clustered next to the bunker. Betty Kensington, clutching a basket, approached us.

"Thank you for coming."

She thrust the basket toward us. It contained small

cellophane packets tied at the top with curly black ribbon. Each bag contained a grainy substance.

"Please take a memorial packet of cremains. Each person will relate a memory about Tristan and sprinkle the ashes into the bunker."

Dad and I plucked a packet from the basket. Betty offered the basket to Sofia. Her complexion blanched into a ghastly shade of yellow. She was swaying slightly.

I gripped her arm. "Sofia isn't feeling well. She needs to sit down." My plan was to walk her over to the bench next to the number seventeen tee box.

But when I uttered the word *sit*, Sofia's knees buckled and she plopped down on her butt. I leaned over and whispered, "Stay put. You'll feel better in a few minutes."

She shot an evil look at her grandfather, "I told Pops I don't do cremains."

Dad, pretending to ignore the drama, gazed wistfully at his baggie of cremains, probably planning his eulogy. It would include phrases like 'Tristan was a valued employee and he will be missed.' Therefore, I would have to come up with something a bit more personal.

The color was beginning to return to Sofia's face when Annabelle and Jonathan arrived. Betty Kensington's eyes widened with alarm when she spotted Annabelle. She clutched the basket to her bosom and hurried over to the Kensington family group. She counted the remaining packets and whispered something in Harold T.'s ear.

Sofia noticed, too. "Tell Tristan's mom to give Annabelle my memorial packet. With pleasure."

If Annabelle noticed her less-than-warm welcome, she took great pains to cover it up. Gripping Jon's arm, she gazed up at him, chattering a mile a minute.

I approached Betty and reached for the basket. "May I help?"

She flushed. "Jon was invited. I wasn't expecting that woman."

"It will be fine, Betty," I said, wresting the basket from her white-knuckled grip. "We'll make it work."

As the sun climbed higher in the sky, we gathered around the bunker and bid farewell to Tristan Kensington III. Sofia managed to get to her feet. She leaned against my body, her gaze averted from the sprinkling.

I'd just finished my brief eulogy when she whispered, "Mom, Sammy alert."

Sammy, in a golf cart with one passenger aboard, barreled down the sixteenth fairway.

I bumped against Dad to get his attention and pointed at Sammy. He peeled away from the group and trotted toward the speeding golf cart.

My head swiveled back and forth between Tristan's final resting place and Dad's interception of Sammy. Dad danced back and forth, arms outstretched, attempting to block the golf cart's forward progress. Sammy gesticulated wildly, pointing at the sixteenth bunker. An eclectic mixture of English and Spanish floated on the early morning breeze. I wasn't close enough to make out the words, but the message was clear.

Sammy was not a happy man.

Sammy's passenger scrambled off the cart and charted an unsteady course toward the gathering. It was

Serena, clutching her handbag. I wondered if the missing golf shirt was inside. Jonathan glanced over his shoulder, stiffened and looked again. A classic double-take.

He held up a finger. "Back in a sec."

The proceedings ground to a halt as all heads turned toward the fairway. Dad managed to take control of the golf cart. Dumas intercepted Serena and walked her over to me.

"Serena needs a bathroom."

"No problem," I linked my arm in hers and headed for the golf cart where Dad and Sammy were still arguing.

Sofia trailed after me. "Can I come?"

I lowered my voice. "Oh, for God's sake, Sofia. You're the only McKenna left. If you feel woozy, sit down. I'll be back soon."

I squeezed Serena into the golf cart between Sammy and Dad who now manned the steering wheel. "Serena needs to go potty. I'm coming with her." Then climbed onto the back bumper. "Pedal to the metal, Dad."

Sammy still muttered in Spanish as we zipped down the cart path toward the clubhouse.

I leaned close. "Give it a rest, Sammy. Gabe will add more sand and rake it after the family leaves. Let them have their moment. They just lost their son," I whispered.

He faced me. "Hokay, Sammy will try not to think about Tristan's dead body in sand trap. But why don't they bury him in the graveyard?"

Light bulb moment. Sammy's objection wasn't wholly based on protecting his beloved golf course.

Different cultures. Different ways of dealing with death.

I patted his shoulder. "The Kensingtons believe it's what Tristan would have wanted. We have to respect that."

He nodded slowly. "I tell Gabe, get ready with sand."

Dad unlocked the clubhouse, and I guided Serena into the women's locker room. She offloaded her handbag on the vanity next to the sink and made a beeline around the corner to a toilet stall. The handbag was gaping open, practically begging me to peek inside.

And we were missing a golf shirt from the pro shop.

Judging from the sounds emanating from Serena's stall, her sudden reappearance seemed unlikely. Feeling guilty, I took a deep breath and gingerly opened the purse, halfway expecting a shrieking alarm or a mousetrap to snap onto my fingers. Clearly, I was not cut out for snooping.

The contents of Serena's bag looked like every woman's purse. Wallet stuffed with credit cards. Three shades of lipstick. A compact. A hairbrush. A packet of tissues. A plastic container with an assortment of pills. A bag of tampons. No golf shirt.

A flash of white beneath the jumble caught my attention. Heart thumping in my chest, I paused and listened. Apparently Serena was still doing her thing. I used my thumb and forefinger to extract a legal sized envelope. It was from the law offices of Hochstetter, Schmidt and Barker, addressed to Janice Pomeroy.

My hands trembled as I extracted a single sheet of paper from the envelope and scanned it quickly.

Dear Ms. Pomeroy,

As per your instructions, your last will and testament has been revised, naming your daughter, Serena Marie Thompson, as the sole heir. All we need is your signature. Please call and make an appointment at your earliest convenience.

Sincerely yours,

Russell Hochstetter

Startled by the sound of the toilet flushing, I slipped the letter back into the envelope and returned it to its original position. When Serena appeared I stood before the mirror, fluffing my hair and trying to look innocent.

"Feel better?"

"A little," she said, with a forced smile. "Guess I'd better make an appearance at the scattering of the ashes."

Whoa, someone else used the word scattering. I was beginning to warm up to Serena Marie Thompson.

I used the golf cart to deliver her to the sixteenth bunker, all the while thinking. Why does Serena have mail addressed to Janice? Is the fact that Janice changed her will significant?

And finally, what should I do with the information?

Chapter Thirty-Five

My mind swirled with confusion as I led Serena from the clubhouse. Sammy and Dad were nowhere in sight. Serena stopped at the edge of the patio and looked around.

"Do we have to walk all the way out there?" she whined.

I resisted an eye roll and pointed at the line of parked golf carts. "I'll go grab a key and be with you in a sec."

As I trotted back inside the clubhouse, my cell phone pinged with a text from Dad.

—We have a problem. Get out here. Fast.—

—On my way.—

"Hang on, Serena," I warned as I steered the golf cart off the gravel path and bounced across two fairways leading to the Eternal Rest bunker. Serena yipped a little in surprise, but latched onto the seat braces with both hands. Thankfully, she was so busy hanging on she stopped whining.

As we approached the bunker, it appeared the ashes of the dearly departed had been duly deposited. The Kensingtons and their guests walked briskly toward the parking lot. The only people remaining were Dad, Sofia, Jonathan Dumas, and Annabelle.

Serena spotted Annabelle. "What's she doing here?"

I attempted to be tactful, not my strong suit. "I believe she and Tristan were a couple."

"Oh, gag me with a spoon. A couple? She's a predatory female. You know the type."

I gave a noncommittal nod.

"She was helping Tris with his insulin. So maybe he had a little fun with her, but it was nothing serious."

"Okay."

She grabbed my arm. "Look at her! She's rubbing herself all over Jon like a lovelorn pussycat. I wouldn't put it past him to give her a whirl. Know what I mean?" she whispered.

I nodded again.

"What do you think I should do?"

I stifled a groan. "Trust me, I'm not an expert on relationships. Maybe you should talk to Jon."

She thought for a moment and then clapped her hands. "I know! Men cannot be trusted. Men are the pits. I'll become a lesbian."

"Um, Serena, I don't think you can switch sides that easy, but whatever floats your boat."

Dad waved his arms, signaling *hurry the hell up.*

I pulled the golf cart up next to Annabelle and Jon. "Gotta run, Serena. Best of luck."

She flounced out of the cart with nary a thank you and inserted herself between Jon and Annabelle. Guess she decided not to become a lesbian after all.

I joined Dad and Sofia. "What's up?"

"Barb Tomlinson called me, crying, totally hysterical. Earl finally got in touch. She wants to talk to us."

"Now?"

"Yeah, the movers are at her house. She wants to

meet us at Dinky's Diner. Said she'll get a booth and wait for us." He grinned in anticipation.

Dinky's Diner was a Vista Valley fave for breakfast aficionados, and Dad loved the lumberjack special. Dark clouds of suspicion floated through my overloaded brain. How did Barbara Tomlinson know Dinky's was Dad's favorite place to break his fast? Was Dad her secret crush? Was Dad cheating on Suze?

Get a grip. Stop thinking like Serena.

When I asked Sofia if she was okay opening the pro shop, she blew an exasperated sigh. "Yes, Mother, totally," she snapped.

It was still early when we walked into Dinky's, but the curmudgeon crew was out in full force. Dad was compelled to meet and greet each and every one. Therefore, it took a while to wend our way to Barbara's booth, well away from the crowd.

For a woman in the throes of an emotional crisis, she looked quite fetching. Her makeup was tastefully applied, her hair styled in a smooth bob. Dressed in dark pants and a pale pink sweater, she rose from the booth in a cloud of pricey perfume and gave Dad an overly long hug. Hmm. We scooched into the dinette.

"Ed, thank you so much for coming." After a short but significant pause, she added, "You too, Libby."

The waitress took our orders, lumberjack special for Dad, veggie omelet for me, dry toast for Barbara.

Dad reached across the table and patted her hand. "Now, how can we help you, Barb? Did Earl come home?"

She extracted a tissue from her handbag, dabbed at her eyes and drew a hitching breath. "No, but he called and told me everything. Oh, Ed, we're in such a mess. I don't know what to do."

"Does it involve Mickey Warren?" I asked.

"Yes. Earl borrowed money from the car dealership. That was the term he used. *Borrowed.* I call it stealing. It was a large sum of money, thousands of dollars. Mickey found out, told Earl he had to pay him back with interest, or he'd call the authorities and have him arrested. Obviously, Earl didn't have the money. Since the real estate market is hot, Mickey ordered him to sell the house. This all happened about two weeks before Mickey died." She choked back a sob. "Here's the awful part. When we had an offer on the house and a tentative closing date, Mickey forced Earl to write a postdated check for the amount he owed. Then the offer fell through and Mickey died."

"What happened to the check?"

"Earl's been trying to contact Mickey's wife, but she won't return his calls."

Dad groaned and shook his head. "What's the date on the check?"

Her shoulders drooped and she swiped at her eyes. "The first of next week. When she cashes it, the check will bounce. I'll be the laughing stock of Vista Valley, not to mention destitute."

"Earl needs to get his butt back here and straighten this out."

"He's scared," Barbara said. "He thinks he'll be a murder suspect when people find out about the embezzlement."

My thoughts exactly. I glanced over at my father. Had he been sucked into this marital and financial mess out of the goodness of his heart?

Of course he had.

"Barbara, I want to talk to Earl. Tell him to call me and we'll try to figure this out together."

I was tempted to kick him under the table.

When we left the restaurant, I said, "Take me home. I need my ride."

"Why?"

"I have to pay someone a visit."

****

I was the focus of Riley's steely gaze as he stared at me from across his wide, uncluttered desk. After my recital of the facts regarding the Tomlinson's tale of woe, an ominous silence followed. Even though I felt guilty about my blab-a-thon, I'd omitted a few pertinent facts, like Dad's search for Earl.

"Why do I have a feeling there's more to the story?"

I squirmed a little. "Not really."

"Does Ed know you're here?"

"I'm sure he figured it out."

He heaved a sigh that came from the soles of his well-worn cowboy boots. "Anything else?"

They say confession is good for the soul, so I told him about Abigail's wacky theory. Let's call it the two-wife theory, where the current and ex-Mrs. Warrens got together to plan Mickey's demise. Oh yeah, I also told him that Betty Kensington said Mickey was squeezing Tristan for money. And about Annabelle, the nurse hired to help Tristan deal with his insulin.

He threw up his hands. "Good God, woman, why am I just hearing about this now?"

Normally, my anger builds slowly, but I'd had quite a morning. I jumped out of my chair, braced my hands against his desk and glared. "Maybe you forgot."

"Huh?'

"Shortly after Mickey's death, you approached me. You asked me to keep an ear to the ground, to let you know if I heard anything suspicious. Well, guess what? This is me reporting something suspicious."

"Damn, girl, I think you're right." He stepped around the desk and held out his arms. "Sorry, darlin'. Forgive me?"

Still pissed off, I hesitated but not for long. I stepped into his embrace and wrapped my arms around his neck. "I'll think about it."

One could say I caved pretty fast. Our snuggle-fest was interrupted by a knock on the door. It opened a few inches. Before I could step out of Riley's embrace, I caught a glimpse of a long, narrow face topped with mile-high gelled hair.

I pushed Riley away, "Baby detective alert."

"What's up, Shipley?" Riley bellowed.

He slid through the door and closed it behind him. "That kid, Gabe?"

"What about him?" Riley barked.

"He came in last night. He's really good. When you get a minute, I'll let you know what we dug up about the Faradays."

"Shipley."

"Sir?"

"I believe you know it was Libby who came to us about the Faradays, and she is responsible for Gabe helping us out. So speak!"

He gave me a sickly grin. "Faraday is not his real name."

"We already know that. Anything else?"

"We found out his wife, Faith something or other,

was a regular visitor at the prison. They got married while he was still incarcerated." He paused and blushed. "Apparently they have a conjugal visit facility there."

"How convenient," Riley said. "Anything more?"

"When he got out, Buxton changed his name to Faraday and started a religious podcast. People liked his message and sent him money. When the Episcopal Church here closed down, they bought it for $250,000 and changed the name to The Last Bus Stop to Salvation."

"Good work, Shipley," Riley said. "I'll have a little chat with Faraday."

As he exited the room, my cell phone beeped with a message from Jules.

—I'm at the golf course with the delivery for Janice Pomeroy. Where the heck are you?—

I blew a kiss at Riley. "Gotta run."

"Hey, girl detective, call me if you come up with more suspects."He grinned.

"Will do," I promised and dashed out the door.

Chapter Thirty-Six

Jules leaned on the counter, dishing the dirt with Sofia when I arrived. A large Bunz and Honey basket was on the floor next to her. She lifted a hand, palm forward.

"High five, girlfriend. You're looking at the top-of-the-line, super-sized basket of goodies. We may be able to retire soon."

I smiled and slapped her hand. "Think I'd better hang on to my job a little longer. At least until I get my baby girl through college."

I leaned over, plucked the bill from the basket, and gasped. "Good Lord, I hope Janice doesn't faint when she sees what Serena and her boyfriend ordered."

Sofia peered at the bill. "Hope her check doesn't bounce."

"No worries," Jules said. "She can afford it. I added original artwork as a special bonus."

Along with the astronomical amount owed, Jules sketched a queen bee, complete with crown and scepter, sitting on a throne atop a beehive.

"Should help ease the pain," I said. "I'll deliver it after I get off work."

"Want me to do it?" Sofia said.

I thought about Jonathan Dumas peppering her with questions and drunken Serena with her half-baked theories. "No, I'll take care of it. Actually, you've been covering for me a lot, working long hours. Take off. Go have some fun."

I expected an argument, but didn't get one. Her eyes brightened.

"My car's at home and Pops is off on some secret mission. I'll find Gabe and see if he can take me home."

As she dashed out the door, Jules and I exchanged a look.

"I was going to offer her a ride. Can't imagine why she'd choose a hunky Latino hottie over her mom's best friend."

Her phone pinged with an incoming text message. She frowned at the screen. "Micah needs his soccer shoes for practice. Damn kid forgot 'em again. Let me know how it goes with Janice. And I want to hear how the book's coming along."

She blew me a kiss and left.

I knew Dad's secret mission was beating the bushes for Earl Tomlinson because he wanted to impress Barbara. Thinking those thoughts bothered me, so I was happily distracted by Rita.

She sashayed over to fill me in on her latest theory. Cupping her hands around her mouth, she whispered, "Do you think anything's fishy about Tristan's death?"

"What do you mean?"

"What do you think I mean? Maybe somebody killed him." She snorted in exasperation.

"The coroner's report said it was an insulin overdose. Besides, who would want to kill Tristan?"

She looked around. "Keep your voice down," she whispered, despite the fact we were alone in the pro shop. "Maybe Annabelle Hoofnagle."

When she said Hoofnagle, she drew out the f so it came out sounding like, "Hoofffffffnagle."

"Annabelle adored Tristan. She would be the last person to kill him."

"I heard she had access to insulin."

"She was a private nurse, Rita. Tristan's mom hired her to help him learn how to inject his insulin."

"I know that. I heard Annabelle was pregnant. Maybe she and Tris had an argument, and she shot him up with an overdose."

"I hate to rain on your parade, but Annabelle isn't pregnant."

"Why are you defending her? I hear she's been pretty nasty to you."

I shrugged. "It's an interesting theory, but you can't go around accusing people of murder because you don't like them."

She leaned closer and tapped her forehead. "I've got a sixth sense about these things. Something inside my noggin tells me she's not as innocent as you think. I'll keep you posted." Huffy at my disbelief in her theory, she retreated to the kitchen.

"You watch too many true crime shows," I called after her.

It was half past seven when I chased the last few laggards from the pro shop and locked the door. When I reached the parking lot, Riley pulled up next to me. He lowered his sunglasses and waggled his eyebrows suggestively.

"Hey there, sweet cheeks, can I take you to dinner?"

I hefted the Bunz and Honey basket. "Gotta a make a delivery. How about tomorrow?"

He looked disappointed, but nodded. “Your dad home? I hear he’s been out looking for Earl Tomlinson.”

So much for Dad’s secret mission. Despite his aw-shucks, Texas cowboy demeanor, Riley O’Connor possessed a razor-sharp intellect.

I hesitated, searching for the right words. “Dad and Barbara Tomlinson were a couple back in high school. He feels obligated to help her. Maybe you’ve noticed, once he’s on a mission, there’s no stopping him.”

“Uh-huh,” Riley said, his laser beam gaze pinning me to the asphalt pavement. “I’ll grab a pizza and swing by your place. Have a little chat with Ed if he’s there. When you get home, we’ll figure out dinner for another time.”

He zipped up the window and drove off.

Did Riley plan to interrogate Dad? I dithered about whether or not to text my father, but decided to let him deal with it. He was a big boy. If he wanted to be a hero, he could take the consequences.

Earl was in my thoughts as I drove to the Pomeroy’s. Did he have it in him to be a killer? He had plenty of motivation. Mickey was squeezing him for money, forcing him to write a post-dated check. Earl would lose his house and likely, his wife. He’d always been Mickey’s sidekick, his yes-man. Perhaps beneath his bland, innocuous surface, rage and impotence reached the boiling point and he committed murder. People have killed for less.

Janice Pomeroy’s house was located adjacent to the last stretch of Hole Number Eight, A Woman Scorned. From the tee box, the fairway was straight as an arrow for over a hundred yards. After a dramatic dogleg to the left, another straight stretch led to the green.

There were no houses on the first section where Mickey Warren's body was found. Lined with shrubs on the right and a heavily wooded area, slicers and hookers lost many a ball. Once around the bend, the fairway was bordered with a variety of upscale homes. Some faced the golf course. Others, like Abigail's and Janice's, had expansive patios and backyards, suitable for sipping adult beverages and watching golfers pass by.

I parked in the driveway and lugged the gigantic basket of goodies onto the porch leading to the recessed front door. Using the brass knocker, I announced my presence. When I got no response, I searched for the doorbell and found it hiding behind a hanging pot of ivy. What was it with rich people and their doorbells?

My plan was to get in and out fast because I really had to pee. I cursed myself for not going before I left work, but as usual, I was in a hurry and put it off. I also wanted to see what was going on at home.

The front door flew open, revealing Serena clutching a glass of wine. When she spotted the goodies and me, she beamed with delight and ushered me into the foyer.

"Mom," she called. "Libby's here. She's the one who was so nice to me this morning at Tristan's thing."

Gee, I hadn't realized Serena and I were now besties. Maybe she'd let me use her bathroom.

I tilted my head toward the gift basket. "Where would you like this?"

"Follow me." Holding her wine glass aloft and slightly unsteady on her feet, she went down three stairs leading to the cavernous sunken living room. "Be careful. I always forget about these damn stairs." She paused and giggled. "Can't count the number of times I've fallen on my butt."

Serena led me outside where Janice was sitting on the patio reading a book. When she spotted the gift basket, one eyebrow shot up in surprise.

"Hello, Libby. What have we here?"

I stifled a groan. Janice knew nothing about the pricey order.

"Oh, didn't Jon tell you? He thought you'd enjoy local products, Bunz and Special Honey."

"Shall I give the bill to Jon?" I asked, trying to make the best of an awkward situation.

Serena squirmed and lifted her hands in a helpless gesture. "He's not here right now."

I followed Janice and Serena back into the house and set the basket on the floor. No way would I haul this humongous thing back home. "I can stop by tomorrow when Jon's here. He can pay me then."

"No," Janice said. She plucked the bill from the basket. She perused the amount, lips compressed in a thin, white line. "I'll write you a check."

Serena gazed longingly at Ed's Special Dark as Janice led me to a desk located in a small alcove next to the kitchen. She extracted a checkbook from the top drawer.

Feeling guilty, I said, "Listen, Janice. If you didn't know about this order, you should let Jon pay for it."

"No." She hunched over the desk. Her hand shook as she extracted a check. "I'll take care of it."

Not wanting to hover, I stepped away from the desk and bumped against a black leather case propped against the wall. I reached down to replace it. It was embossed with the letters AlphaCorp Pharmaceuticals. Business cards for Jonathan Dumas, pharmaceutical representative, were tucked into the attached cardholder.

Janice scribbled out the check and handed it to me. By this time, I was doing my pee-pee dance.

"Would you mind if I use your bathroom?" I asked, flushing with embarrassment.

"No problem." She smiled faintly and led me down the hall.

We paused in front of a closed door. She cocked her head at the sound of water running.

"Looks like Serena's in this one. You can use mine."

She pointed at an open door leading to the master bedroom. I thanked her and hurried to the attached bathroom. Janice was nowhere in sight when I finished my business. I gazed around the expansive bedroom. Floor-to-ceiling windows fitted with white plantation shutters offered a splendid view of the golf course. The wall facing the bed featured a freestanding brick fireplace, complete with hearth and a white mantel lined with framed photos.

Curiosity got the best of me. I charted my exit course so I could peruse the family photos. They appeared to be a pictorial history of Janice's life. It commenced on the left with a framed black and white photo of a chubby toddler standing between stern-looking parents. The last photo on the far right was a shot of Janice and Serena, heads together, smiling into the camera. It was the photo smack-dab in the middle that caught my attention.

A beaming Janice clung to the arm of a familiar-looking dark-haired boy. Both were clad in formal attire, their heads topped with crowns. They stood beneath a banner identifying them as Vista Valley High School's Junior Prom King and Queen.

I left the bedroom, thanked Janice for the order and scampered out to my car.

My mind swirled. I was fairly sure I'd just seen a photo of Janice with a young Mickey Warren. Were they a couple? Was Serena their daughter? Is that why she looked familiar? I needed to pick Dad's brain, jog his memory of high school days.

I needed answers.

Chapter Thirty-Seven

A block away from the Pomeroys' house, I parked next to the curb and texted Sofia to call me.

I stared at the cell phone like I could force a prompt reply. Actually, I didn't expect to get one. Sofia often left her cell phone in her bedroom or forgot to charge it. The apple doesn't fall far from the tree.

I was pleasantly surprised when my phone jangled with "Stairway to Heaven".

"Momser? What's going on?"

"Are you home?

"No,"

"Okay," I groused. "I guess this is a multiple choice question. Are you: a, at a bar? B, working out? Or c, with Gabe?

"C."

"Excellent answer."

"Why are you being weird?"

"Is Gabe doing his thing at Riley's office tonight?"

"Not tonight," she said. "Why?"

"I have a favor to ask and it's not exactly legal."

Sofia snort laughed into the phone. "Stop, you're shocking me."

I ignored her sarcasm and forged ahead. "Would it be possible for Gabe to check out AlphaCorp Pharmaceuticals and Jonathan Dumas's employment history with them?"

I heard muffled conversation as she passed my question to Gabe. "No worries, Momser. He says it's a piece of cake."

"Thanks. Have you been home?"

"Yeah, Pops was there with Earl Tomlinson. When Riley drove in, I left. Testosterone overload."

I chuckled. "I'll go home and add estrogen to the mix. See what the boys are up to."

"Good luck. Bye."

It was twilight when I got home. I found the "boys" in the back yard, sitting around the recessed fire pit. No beer was being imbibed. Earl Tomlinson was hunched in his chair. Normally immaculately groomed, he had a three-day growth of scruffy gray whiskers. His hair hung in greasy clumps. Colorful food stains on his shirt proclaimed his fondness for meals served with mustard and catsup.

Dad's arms folded across his chest, legs extended, cap tilted back, head cocked to one side as he listened to Earl's rambling monologue. Riley leaned forward, elbows propped on his knees. I pulled up a chair and silently joined the group. Clawdius was in Dad's lap, his eyes at half-mast. When he spotted me he hunched his back, hissed, and stalked away.

Earl ran a hand through his greasy locks. "So that's it. I screwed up, and you're right, I had a good reason to kill Mickey, but I didn't." His voice broke. "He was my friend. Friends cut you a break, don't they? I told him I'd pay him back. Mick saw my little problem as a moneymaking opportunity and decided to squeeze the hell out of me. And now, the damn check is missing."

Riley stood. "Let's go for a ride, Earl. We'll pay a visit to the widow Warren and see what we can do about the postdated check."

Earl's eyes rolled in panic. "Are you going to arrest me for embezzlement?"

"Not if you work out a repayment plan and have it notarized. I'll keep a copy in my office and you'll check in with me every week."

Earl pushed out of his chair, slightly unsteady on his feet. "I swear I didn't kill Mickey. Do you believe me?"

Riley clapped a hand on Earl's shoulder. "Earl, my man, somehow I don't think you have it in you to sneak up on Mickey Warren and jab him in the butt with a hypodermic needle. I could be wrong, though."

"You're not wrong." Earl's voice was shrill with alarm. "Ask my wife. She'll tell you I was with her."

"She's pretty ticked off at you, Earl," Dad said. "Do you have a Plan B?"

Earl's face was a mask of misery. "No."

Riley gripped his arm. "Tell ya what, buddy. We'll talk it over and figure out how to get your lovely wife back on board. I've had a great deal of experience dealing with pissed-off women."

Before they walked away, Riley leaned close to me. "I hope you're not one of them," he whispered.

"Not at the moment," I said. "Who knows what tomorrow will bring?"

"Duly warned." He marched Earl toward his car.

Dad remained quiet, gazing at the flickering flames in the fire pit.

"Where did you find Earl?"

"Sleazy biker bar by the fairgrounds. He was crying in his beer."

I told him about my delivery to Janice Pomeroy

and the photo I'd spotted. "Were Janice and Mickey Warren a couple in high school?"

"Yep."

"You never mentioned it before."

He frowned at me. "Why would I?"

"Did Mickey get her pregnant?"

"Probably. It was all hush-hush back then. Janice's family was hard up moneywise, and also super religious. They sent her off somewhere. She came back for her senior year, definitely not pregnant. The rumor was Mickey's dad made them break up. I never saw them together again."

"How sad," I murmured, feeling a wave of pity for sixteen-year-old Janice, pregnant, destitute, and abandoned. "I think Serena is Mickey's daughter."

"Huh," Dad said, still staring into the flames. "Why the sudden interest in ancient history?"

"I'm just trying to fit the puzzle pieces together. I wonder if Serena knows Mickey was her father?"

Dad shrugged. "I guess you could ask her."

"Nah," I said. "Too personal."

Dad placed a small log onto the fire. It flared up and crackled.

"Nice out here," I said, relaxation seeping through my body. My eyelids drooped. It was much too early to go to bed. I had work to do.

I pushed out of my chair. "I'll be inside. I need to write another chapter."

"Oh, yeah, she called."

All the residual light had faded to darkness. Therefore, he didn't see me roll my eyes. "Abigail?"

"Man, she's a talker. I bet she's lonesome. Shall I take her some Ed's Special Dark?"

“Does she want me to call her back?” I said through gritted teeth.

“Of course. Why else would she call?”

Clawdius was lurking under the apricot tree as I walked by. With a throaty yowl, he sprang and wrapped his front paws around my bare left ankle, claws digging in.

“Ow!” I yelled. “Dammit Dad, call off your attack cat.”

Dad’s shrill whistle pierced the night air. Clawdius retracted his claws, reversed course and trotted away, tail waving in triumph.

I rubbed my ankle and sprinted toward the back door.

Abigail wasted no time making her point. “Did you tell the sheriff about my theory?”

“Are we talking about Mickey Warren and the two-wife theory?”

“Yes, the two-wife theory. What an excellent name. Did he look into it?”

“I believe he’s planning to visit Heather Warren soon. I’m sure he’ll check it out.”

I purposely didn’t tell her the reason for his visit was to ask about Earl’s post-dated check.

“And, you’ll let me know what he finds out?”

“I will if I can. You know how law enforcement people are. They keep things pretty quiet. Anything else I can do for you, Abigail?”

“Did I see you at Janice Pomeroy’s house this afternoon? It sure looked like you.”

Wow, she must have those binoculars ready to go at all times.

“Yes, I delivered an order to her. Suzy’s Bunz and

Dad's Special Honey. If I'd known you were looking, I'd have waved."

A long silence ensued. Finally, she said, "Poor Tristan. I heard they scattered his ashes in a sand bunker."

"Yes, I was there."

"You know, he was a regular visitor at Janice's house. Almost every night, he was on the patio with what's-his-name, Janice's long-lost daughter's man friend."

"Jonathan Dumas," I said.

"Yes, Jonathan. Were they just buddies or was it something else?"

"Well, um," I stammered, not quite sure how to respond. "Tristan had lots of girlfriends. I think he and Jon were just friends."

"Maybe," she said. "I wonder how long mousy little Janice will foot the bill for those two."

"Maybe she likes having her daughter there."

"I heard they have very expensive tastes and they bully her into paying."

Despite curiosity about her source, I didn't want to encourage her, especially when it involved golf course members. Time to change the subject. "Guess what, Abigail? As soon as we're done with our phone call, I'm starting Chapter Fifteen."

After a trill of laughter, she said, "Goody, goody! Can't wait to read it. Well, my dear, I won't keep you any longer. Ta-ta."

I had scarcely settled into the breakfast nook with my laptop when the landline rang. It was probably a honey order for Dad who was presently gazing into the fire. He would, of course, expect me to deal with it.

Muttering under my breath, I answered it.

"Libby? It's Serena. We need to meet."

"When?"

"Now."

Chapter Thirty-Eight

Following Serena's slurred directions, I parked a block away from the Pomeroy house. Each time headlights appeared in the rearview mirror, I slumped down in the driver's seat, out of view. Private security patrolled this neighborhood. How would I explain my presence? I'm waiting for a girlfriend didn't seem like the right response, especially after Serena's lesbian reference. Yikes. I hoped that particular idea had flown from her alcohol-saturated brain.

A few minutes later, I saw Serena. Swaying slightly, she navigated the sidewalk as if it contained landmines. I zipped the passenger window down. She braced herself against the car, peered through the open window, and gave me a drunken smile.

"Thanks for coming, Libby. You're my only friend." She slid into the car. "You know where the Gas 'N More is?"

I nodded.

"It's open all night. Go there. We'll sit in the parking lot and talk."

I bit my tongue and did what she asked.

After I pulled into a semi-dark parking place, I asked, "What's with the cloak-and-dagger thing?"

She frowned at me. "The what?"

"The late night meeting. The pickup a block from your house. Why?"

She reached over and grabbed my hand. “I’m sorry, Libby. I had to wait until Jon fell asleep before I left the house. By the way, if anyone asks, I went for a walk. I do that sometimes late at night.”

“Jon sounds kind of controlling.” I pulled my hand free.

She hiccupped. “You have no idea.”

“You’ve got your mom now. Why do you need Jon if he’s not treating you well?’

“It’s complicated. I’m his little cash cow.” She stifled a sob. “That’s what he calls me, his little cash cow.”

I stared at her in confusion. “It sounds like he needs you for money. Have you talked to Janice about it?”

“I can’t.”

“Why?”

“Like I said, it’s complicated.”

I stifled a yawn. It was late. I was tired and my alarm was set for six a.m. I felt pity for my new best friend, but we were getting nowhere.

“Serena, concentrate and listen to me.”

Her head bobbed up and down.

“You called, said you wanted to talk. So far, I’ve heard Jon is greedy and controlling. Now what is it you wanted to tell me?”

She hung her head. “It’s about Tristan. Like Jon always says, sometimes I talk too much.”

And drink too much.

“What about Tristan?” I prompted.

Getting her to focus was like trying to swat a fly in midair.

She slumped in her seat and buried her face in her

hands. “I had a little too much to drink one night and let something slip.”

“About…?

“Something bad happened to Mickey Warren.” She started to sob. “If I’d kept my mouth shut, Tristan wouldn’t be buried in a sand trap; he’d still be alive.”

My grip tightened on the steering wheel. “What exactly did you tell Tristan?”

She lifted her head and shook it violently. “You’re tight with the sheriff. If Jon knew I was talking to you, he’d be so mad.”

From what she’d told me, I assumed she’d shared that something bad happened to Mickey Warren with Tristan. Now Tristan was dead, and she blamed herself. Was she implying Tristan’s death was not an accident?

She pinched her lips together, presumably to prevent more information leaking out. I searched for a way to unlock them.

“Did Janice tell you Mickey Warren is your father?”

Her glance darted away from mine. She nodded.

“You look like him.”

“I never met him,” she said. “But I’ve seen pictures.”

I needed to pry more information from her dizzy, alcoholic brain. I had only one ace in the hole and hoped I wasn’t fibbing.

“If you want to tell me something more, I promise I won’t tell the sheriff.”

Her eyes widened and then narrowed. “You’re trying to trick me into saying something I shouldn’t.”

I bit my lip to keep from snapping at her like an enraged turtle. God, give me patience. I heaved an enormous sigh.

"Okay, Serena, here's the deal. I'm tired. I picked you up when I'd rather be sleeping. If you need help, now is the time to tell me. I'll do my best."

"No, I've said enough. You can drop me off where you picked me up."

On the drive back, I pitched a few more questions at her. Her only response was when I asked if Jon was physically abusive. She squeezed her hands together and wouldn't look at me.

"Not really. Sometimes I think he wants to hit me. Remember what I told you earlier? I'm his little cash cow. I feel like it's the only thing keeping him from punching me in the face. It's more emotional abuse. He keeps telling me how stupid I am."

"I don't think you're stupid. Maybe you drink a little too much, but you can get help if you want it. Talk to your mom."

Her head swiveled toward me. "You really don't know her very well, do you?"

"Not well," I said. "She seems like a good person, just a bit timid."

She shook her head. "You don't know her at all."

When we approached her neighborhood, I didn't like the idea of her walking unaccompanied to her house. If she fell and hit her head, I'd never forgive myself. I drove down her street and stopped two houses away from hers.

"I'll wait here until I see you go into the house."

"Worried about me?"

I hated to admit it, but I was growing fond of my little drunken friend. "Yes, I'm worried about you. If Jon threatens you, call me."

I scribbled my cell phone number onto a gas receipt and handed it to her. She thanked me and hauled herself out of the car. When she turned onto the brick walkway leading to her house, she waved. I returned the gesture and put the car in gear. As Serena approached the front door, it opened slightly. She froze in her tracks for a moment before entering the house. I couldn't see who opened the door.

Looked like Serena was busted. I hoped she would stick to her story about taking a late night stroll.

I fretted all the way home. I'd promised Serena I wouldn't talk to Riley and now regretted it. My promise accomplished nothing. She'd crawled into her shell and turned mute. From her disjointed conversation, I gathered she knew something about Mickey Warren's death and accidentally shared it with Tristan. I was bursting with the need to talk it out with a rational, sane, not-drunk person. Nobody to talk to at home. Dad and Sofia were both in bed, where I should be. Thankfully, Jules was a night owl.

She answered on the first ring and listened without interruption as I related the details of my bizarre meeting with Serena.

A long pause.

"Are you there?"

"Yeah, still trying to process. It sounds like Serena's on a huge guilt trip. Add alcohol and Ed's Special Dark to the mix, and you've got one screwed-up woman. Do you believe her?"

"Yes, I believe her. She knows what happened to Mickey Warren."

"*In vino veritas*," she said.

"Excuse me?"

"Sorry, I was forced to take Latin in high school. *In vino veritas* means in wine, there is truth. So you were right to believe her. Maybe you should talk to her again, earlier in the day when she's not three sheets to the wind."

I sighed. "Not sure there is such a time, but I'll try. Thanks, Jules."

"What's going on with the hunk?"

"Which one, Striker the pirate, or Riley the sheriff?"

She laughed. "Riley."

"He's trying to help Earl Tomlinson get straightened out and off the hook."

I made her promise not to share the info and filled her in on the backstory.

"Wow. You have quite a lot bouncing around in your busy brain. I know what you need."

"What?"

She proceeded to tell me in graphic detail. Let's just say it involved Riley O'Connor and *moi*. I was laughing when I clicked off.

Thank God for good friends!

Chapter Thirty-Nine

The next day at work, I looked up Janice Pomeroy's information and called her house. I wasn't surprised when the call went unanswered. In the era of cell phones and caller ID, reaching a person via landline is rare.

"Hi, this is Libby McKenna. Serena, if you're there, please give me a call."

When my cell phone rang, I glanced at the display. Riley. He wasted no time with small talk. "Mickey Warren's body was found on A Woman Scorned. Right?"

"Yes, hole number eight. It's called A Woman Scorned because it doesn't have a ladies' tee box. Why?"

"I'd like to check it out again. Do you have time to run me out there? Or shall I wait until play is over?"

"I'll make time and now is fine."

"I'm five minutes away."

Rita said she'd cover for me if I made it snappy. She added she'd warm up some chili and corn bread.

I grabbed a golf cart and met Riley in the parking lot. "Climb in and hang on."

He tipped his hat and grinned. "Yes, ma'am."

"What happened with Earl?" I asked as we sped down the cart path.

"We went to see Heather Warren. She made Earl

grovel but finally agreed to give the check back."

"Before or after she found out it would bounce?"

"After, of course. That was a piece of cake compared to what happened when Earl got home."

"Barbara was pretty ticked off."

"Ticked off? More like pissed-off wolverine. My plan was to drop Earl off at his house and leave. He insisted I come inside. It's a good thing I did. He was barely through the door when his wife grabbed a humongous bowl of artificial fruit and started firing missiles at him. Oranges, bananas, grape clusters, apples. Earl just stood there, letting them bounce off him. When the fruit was gone, she gave a god-awful screech and tried to bash him over the head with the bowl. Since Earl wasn't defending himself, I had to stop her."

"Hell hath no fury."

"Like a woman scorned." He gave me a measured look. "Don't I know it?"

Seemed like the quote resonated with Riley, but I let it slide.

"Barbara wasn't scorned for another woman. She was devastated about losing the house of her dreams."

"I hung around a while until she calmed down. I told them there might be a way to work it out with the mortgage company. Earl still has a job, even though he has a ton of money to pay back."

I gave him a playful punch in the shoulder. "You're a good man, Riley O'Connor."

He waggled his eyebrows at me. "You have no idea how good I can be."

Jules's explicit words from last night flashed through my mind. A flush warmed my cheeks. "I guess that remains to be seen."

"Yes, indeedy."

Thankfully, we arrived at the tee box for A Woman Scorned. Two couples teed off. I parked the cart well away, alongside the wooded area.

"After they hit their drives, we'll go to the spot where Mickey was found. While we wait, any conclusions about Abigail's two-wife theory? She's convinced they joined forces to get rid of Mickey."

"I told Heather Warren I wanted to talk to her again. She immediately bristled up and said she'd come in with her lawyer. I haven't had a chance to talk to the ex yet. Too busy dodging fake fruit."

When the foursome disappeared around the bend, I drove down the cart path and stopped adjacent to the murder scene. Seized with an involuntary shiver, I recalled the image of Mickey Warren sprawled on the fairway. His vivid red shirt. The lush green grass. His face, distorted in death. As if sensing my unease, a sudden gust of wind rattled the branches of the trees lining the fairway.

Riley scrambled out of the cart. "Come with me. I need another opinion."

I shook off the grisly memory and followed Riley into the copse of trees. Fully leafed out for summer with their branches intertwined, the trees formed a formidable barrier for any golfer in search of an errant ball. We scrambled through the underbrush and stopped where we still had a view of the fairway.

"As you know, I had my guys out here looking for anything unusual. We concluded the murderer was hiding here, waiting for Mick. Your greenskeeper, Sammy, said Warren had a wicked slice off the tee and came out here to retrieve his golf balls. We found nothing. *Nada*."

"Because Sammy picked them up when they were loading Mickey into the ambulance. Didn't he tell you?"

Riley's gaze swung over to me. "What?"

"He said Mickey always hit into this very spot. To prove his point, he beat the bushes until he found Mickey's golf balls."

Riley frowned, lifted his hat, and scratched his head. "Either he didn't tell me, or I got lost in the Spanglish."

I grinned at him. "It happens."

Riley took my hand and led me back to the golf cart. "If the golf balls were in the woods after he died, maybe Warren didn't have time to retrieve them."

"Which means the person who killed him could have been on the fairway."

Riley nodded. "Pretty hard to sneak up on someone in broad daylight."

"It was probably somebody he knew. A lot of people despised Mickey. He liked to brag about his wealth. As you know from the Earl Tomlinson disaster, Mickey was all about getting more money."

"Since he was jabbed in the ass, it means Warren trusted the killer enough to turn his back."

"Or didn't think he or she was a threat. I'm leaning toward a female killer."

"You are, huh? Females being the more vicious of the species?"

"Females being more unlikely to forgive. Mickey was a known womanizer. Love 'em, leave 'em, and on to the next. The I Hate Mickey Warren club had a large membership."

"Long list, huh?"

"In case you're wondering, I'm not a member."

We boarded the golf cart and headed for the pro shop. Riley downed his chili and corn bread with gusto. Before he left, he leaned on the counter. "In case you're interested, I'm busting Farley on a Harley later. Want to ride along?"

My mouth fell open in surprise." You're kidding! What's the charge?"

"Farley Faraday aka Lester Buxton, has a wife and three minor children in Kellogg, Idaho. He never bothered to divorce said wife and hasn't supported his family in years. A deputy from Kellogg followed the trail and tracked him down. Buxton will be a guest in our facility tonight. Tomorrow, he and I are going on a road trip. I'm meeting the Idaho deputy in Spokane and making the transfer. Looks like the Farley billboards will have to come down."

"You're making my heart sing. I wonder if Faith knows."

"We'll find out tonight. He has an evening service at seven. My deputy and I plan to show up while people are arriving. Maximum embarrassment. Win, win. I'll swing by your place at six-thirty. You can follow us there."

I offered him a fist to bump. "Good work, Sheriff. I'll be ready."

I spent the rest of the day with a goofy smile plastered on my face. Date with hot sheriff. Front row seat at arrest of one of my least favorite people, probably the perpetrator of the creepy, anonymous phone call.

What more could a girl ask?

Chapter Forty

I followed Riley and his deputy—not Shipley—to The Last Bus Stop to Salvation located in the west end of town, not far from my house. It was an attractive all-brick edifice with a soaring steeple surrounded by an expanse of well-manicured lawn. Mature deciduous trees formed a living border around the property. The paved driveway led to a parking lot filled with four-wheel drive pick-up trucks, motorcycles, minivans and a scattering of sedans. I trailed behind Riley and his burly back up as they walked toward the front entrance. Both men wore side arms. An eerie silence fell over the throng of churchgoers. We were the recipients of quizzical looks and sidelong glances.

It was a stifling hot day for late June. I licked the salt from my lips and swiped the beads of sweat from my forehead. The oven-like heat would remain until the sun dipped below the foothills surrounding Vista Valley. No leaves fluttered in the trees. Even the birds were too hot to sing. The scent of freshly mowed grass tickled my nose. I stifled a sneeze.

Once inside the narthex, the crowd milled around and parted like the Red Sea as Riley scanned the room for Faraday. His gaze zeroed in on the closed double doors leading to the sanctuary.

I felt a tap on my shoulder and whirled around. A heavily tattooed biker wearing baggy jeans, a T-shirt with the sleeves cut off, and a blue bandana tied around his greasy ponytail checked me out. He smelled of gasoline and motor oil. His bloodshot gaze flicked up and down my body, lingering at chest level and all points south.

"I'm Ernie. Looking for a church home, sweet cheeks? Let me be the first to welcome you. Come with me and I'll introduce you to Reverend Faraday. He's in the sanctuary getting ready for the service."

Yes! He didn't know I was with Riley. The idea of being the first to surprise Faraday was too good to pass up.

"Why, thank you, Ernie. I'd love to meet the reverend," I declared in a ringing voice.

Riley swiveled toward me. He frowned and shook his head. I smiled and winked. Ernie clamped a grimy hand around my upper arm and marched me toward the entrance to the sanctuary. The doors were locked but Ernie wasn't deterred. He rattled the door.

"Hey, Farley! I got a new one for ya. Open up," he yelled.

A press of people crowded behind me as they moved toward the sanctuary. I peeked over my shoulder. Riley was pushing his way through the crowd. He caught my eye and pinched his lips together in disapproval. I considered blowing him a kiss.

The doors swung open revealing Farley, clad in a voluminous white robe tied at the waist with a braided sash. The garment was adorned with a bizarre assortment of red and black symbols. Sun, moon and stars. A gloved hand. An upside down swastika. What?

When Faraday spotted me, it took a moment for my image to register in his brain. His eyes widened in surprise. He gathered his wits quickly.

"What are you doing here?" he snarled.

I smiled sweetly. "Hello to you too, Reverend. Remember your motto? You kick Satan to the curb every damn day. I'm here to make sure it happens."

I'd barely uttered the words when Faraday's face purpled in rage, Ernie began babbling an apology, and Riley stepped in front of me.

"Okay, you've had your fun. My turn."

He nodded to the deputy who handed him a document with the words Warrant for Arrest printed at the top in bold black letters.

"Farley Faraday also known as Lester Buxton, I have a warrant for your arrest." His words were loud and reverberated through the crowd.

The flush in Faraday's cheeks faded. "You can't arrest me. I'm a man of the cloth. This is my sanctuary. This is my flock. They won't allow it."

An angry buzz rippled through the crowd.

"What's the charge?" a man yelled.

I peeked around Riley. Faith stood next to Faraday. She wore the same gown, albeit a much smaller size.

Riley kept his gaze on Faraday. "This man is not an ordained minister. He's an ex-con named Lester Buxton who abandoned his wife in Idaho without benefit of divorce. He fathered three children with her and doesn't support them financially or any other way. Any more questions?"

A hush fell over the crowd, but not for long. Faith howled like a wounded banshee and began beating on Faraday with her tiny fists.

"You son of a bitch! You bastard! You bigamist!"

The colorful expletives bursting from Faith's lips

would make a sailor blush. The barrage of curse words continued to flow. I held my breath and glanced at the ceiling. One of Dad's favorite sayings was never swear in church, or the ceiling will cave in.

The ceiling was intact even as Faith continued furiously attacking her pseudo husband. The crowd pressed closer, getting into the action.

"You tell him, Faith!"

"Give it to him, girl!"

So much for Faraday's devoted flock. They itched for action, and Faith was up for it. Riley and his deputy stepped in. Riley secured Faraday's hairy wrists with zip ties while his deputy tucked Faith under one arm.

"Okay, little lady. I think you made your point."

Faraday's flock followed us to the parking lot and cheered when he was loaded into the back seat.

As I headed for my car, Riley caught up with me. He wrapped an arm around my neck and pulled me tight against his body. After my encounter with Ernie, Riley smelled positively scrumptious. Fresh soap. Earthy aftershave. The corn bread he'd had for lunch. Yum.

He put his lips next to my ear. "You don't like to follow orders and I'm okay with that. But I don't like it when you put yourself in danger."

I looked up at him and fluttered my eyelashes. Yeah, I really did, in spite of the fact I'm not a natural flirt. "I don't recall you giving me orders. Maybe I wasn't paying attention."

He spoke through gritted teeth. "Okay, they weren't exactly orders. And I get it. You wanted to see Faraday's reaction when he saw you. Just don't do it again. Okay?"

I planted a big smooch on his cheek. “No promises, Sheriff.”

After a heavy sigh, he said, “You’re a stubborn woman.”

“You’re right.”

He patted my back and released me. “I’ll be gone all day tomorrow. Stay out of trouble.”

“I’ll try.”

As the patrol car drove away with Faraday caged in the back seat, I breathed a sigh of relief. One of the many things plaguing me had been solved. In my heart of hearts, I hoped Riley would find a connection between Faraday-Buxton and Mickey Warren, therefore killing two birds with one stone, so to speak.

Too good to be true? Probably.

Chapter Forty-One

Euphoria over Faraday's arrest vanished in the middle of the night, when The Dream shattered my peaceful slumber.

The slimy walls of the cave moved inward. I'd be trapped there until my skeletal remains were discovered in the next century. Panic-stricken and gasping for air, I fought my way to consciousness. Once fully awake, I gulped water and listened to the pounding of my heart.

I walked to the window and peered into the backyard. A brisk, westerly breeze had blown in from the Cascade Mountains, providing blessed relief from the sweltering heat. The cool night air, scented with freshly cut grass and honeysuckle, gently caressed my face. I breathed in and out. Listened to the chorus of crickets. Looked for the brightest star. Whispered to my mother.

Yet, when I returned to bed, sleep eluded me. I tried a technique that sometimes worked, a mental review of the last forty-eight hours. Usually, its banality and boredom lulled me back to sleep. Not this time.

Guilt has a way of worming its way into your subconscious. Maybe it manifested itself in The Dream. Two days ago, I'd promised Serena her secrets were safe with me, that I wouldn't pass them on to Riley. I now regretted my words. The list of suspects for Mickey Warren's murder had dwindled dramatically.

Earl Tomlinson was in the clear. Abigail's two-wife theory, though possible, was a stretch. It would require a partnership of two women who despised each other. Unless Faraday was the guilty party—highly unlikely—the best lead resided in Serena's tipsy soul.

Once I realized what was nibbling at the back of my mind, my eyelids grew heavy. I'd straighten it out tomorrow.

Serena beat me to the punch. I'd assumed, wrongly, she was a late riser. Maybe noonish. Therefore, I planned to call her at one. The pro shop phone rang at 9:10 a.m.

"Libby? It's Serena. I called your cell and left about a million messages."

She sounded whiney and irritated. I reached in my pocket. No cell phone. I'd left it home again. Apparently I'd ignored my own handwritten sticky note posted next to the car keys reminding me to TAKE PHONE!

"Sorry, Serena. I'm glad you called. I was hoping we could get together."

Mollified, she lost the attitude. "What time do you get off work? I'll pick you up and we can hit the Pine Village. They have a great happy hour. If we get there before seven, it's half off for drinks, even the fancy ones. It will be our girls' night out."

Whoa. Serena, no doubt under the influence, planned to pick me up? In a car? Serena in the driver's seat? I attempted to regroup quickly since I had an agenda. Apparently I'd remained silent a moment too long.

"No drinking and driving. I'll order a ride share. Okay?"

With a huge sigh of relief, I agreed.

At six-thirty, I locked up and headed for the parking lot. The window of a blue compact SUV zipped down and Serena waved. I joined her in the back seat.

She pointed at the man behind the steering wheel. "That's Fred, our Sober Driver."

I smiled. "Works for me."

Serena was clad in pressed jeans and a white sweater, her normally unruly hair pulled back into a sleek ponytail. She appeared to be sober. I couldn't tell for sure because her eyes were hidden behind a pair of dark sunglasses.

I patted her hand. "You look nice."

As Fred pulled slowly out of the parking lot, her cell phone rang. She glanced at the screen. "It's my mom."

The conversation was one-sided, Serena responding with a series of okays before clicking off.

"Fred, we need to go back to the house."

He nodded and reversed course.

Alarmed, I said, "Is something wrong?"

"Not really. Mom wants to thank you for the gift basket. Do you mind?"

How could I refuse? Sweet little Janice had forked over a bundle for Ed's Special Dark and Suzy's Booty Buns. As one of our best customers, it would be rude to blow her off. Not to mention I was pretty sure she was being bilked and bullied by Serena and Dumas.

I flapped a hand. "Of course I don't mind. Call her back; see if she wants to join us."

"Nah, she's not a happy hour person."

I poked her with an elbow. "You never know. Deep inside, your mom might be a total party animal."

My attempt at humor fell flat. Serena's lips were sealed. I figured she was ticked off because after seven, we'd have to pay full price for our drinks.

Sober Driver Fred parked in front of the Pomeroy house and killed the engine. The windows facing the street were tightly shuttered, giving the vast brick home a closed-up, unwelcoming appearance. Was that the case when I'd delivered the gift basket? No, I clearly remembered the late afternoon sun bouncing off sparkling clean windows and a Boston fern visible inside.

I followed Serena into the living room. Janice was nowhere in sight. Serena hesitated for a moment as if unsure what to do next.

I peered through the dimly lit room. "Is Jon here?"

"No, he's out with friends."

My flutter of nerves subsided. "Okay, let's go talk to your mom. Where is she?"

"Out on the patio like usual."

Serena extended a hand and clasped mine. Hers was trembling slightly and clammy with sweat.

Warning bells clanged. I freed my hand.

"Are you okay?"

"Yeah, I'm fine. Just fine."

Her demeanor did not match her words. I needed to get her alone. Pry out the guilty secrets making her crazy.

Serena led me across an expansive flagstone patio overlooking the fairway of A Woman Scorned. The outdoor furniture was arranged around a firepit. Janice sat on a comfy upholstered couch. I spotted the empty gift basket next to the couch. The goodies were gone. Only a twisted pile of shredded blue cellophane remained.

When we approached, Janice rose and reached for my hands. Her grip was surprisingly strong. Though her eyes were still downcast, she greeted me warmly.

"Libby, thank you so much for befriending Serena. The last few months have been hard for her. So many changes. Right, Serena?"

Serena nodded like a bobble head doll and wouldn't meet my gaze. I looked across the fairway at Abigail's house. Feeling uneasy, I hoped she was she on her patio, binoculars trained on Pomeroy's back yard. I saw no one.

I chose my words carefully. "You're welcome, Janice. Serena and I are going out for a drink. You're welcome to join us."

"Nice of you to offer, dear, but no, thank you." She waved me into a chair. "Sit, please. We need to chat."

We do? My anxiety grew as I perched on the edge of the chair.

Janice pointed to a glass pitcher on a side table. "Serena, pour Libby some iced tea."

I shook my head. "No caffeine for me this late in the day."

"It's a special blend. Mint. Chamomile. No caffeine. You'll like it."

Janice being bossy surprised me. Not wanting to offend a good customer, I nodded. Obediently, Serena picked up the pitcher, sloshed some iced tea into a tall glass, and thrust it into my hand.

"Cheers." Janice clinked her glass against mine.

I noticed Serena was abstaining. "Saving yourself for happy hour?"

"I don't like tea," she muttered and sat next to her

mother.

My plan was to slurp down the iced tea, chat with Janice and beat feet to the front door. With this in mind, I took a couple of swigs and set the glass on the patio table.

"Very good," I said. "Refreshing."

Janice and Serena remained mute. With no chat forthcoming, I didn't plan to stick around.

I stood. "Ready to go, Serena?"

A tidal wave of dizziness washed over me.

Chapter Forty-Two

Serena had an aura. She was now Serena times two. I staggered backward and gripped the arm of the chair to keep myself upright.

Janice rose and gazed into my eyes. Random thoughts floated through my mind. Had I ever seen her eyes? No, I would have remembered. Almost devoid of color, they were the palest shade of blue possible, with pupils like slash marks.

"Are you okay, dear? Maybe you should sit down. Then we'll have our chat."

Though every fiber of my being screamed *Run*, my legs would not obey. My knees buckled and I plopped onto the chair.

Janice's gaze never left me. The change in her was alarming. The sweet, timid person referenced earlier had morphed into a stranger. The Janice I knew always tried to fade into the background. Now her back was rigid, her gaze unblinking. The hair on the back of my neck prickled.

"Serena sneaked out of the house. You picked her up. She shared information with you."

"Mom, I told you, I don't remember saying anything," Serena wailed.

My tongue felt thick. "Serena may not remember, but I do. We rode around, chatted about stupid stuff and I dropped her off. That's it. I'm leaving now."

"I don't think so," Janice said.

A little voice inside my head screamed to get the hell out of here! Once again, my body would not obey. I was a prisoner in the Pomeroy Nut Farm.

Janice gave me a grim smile, her hands folded primly in her lap. "When Serena drinks too much, she talks too much. She told you about Tristan."

I searched my foggy mind for the right response. "She felt bad about his death. Nothing more."

"She should feel bad. She caused it."

"I did not! Tris borrowed money from Mickey. He said he wasn't sorry Mickey died because now he didn't have to pay it back. Then I said it worked out good for everybody because my mom was glad he was dead, too."

"He figured it out, Serena. Tristan wasn't a fool," Janice snapped.

My heart banged against my ribs like a caged bird seeking freedom. I struggled to my feet, took a couple of wobbly steps. Janice scooped up the gift basket and threw it at me. It bounced off my head. The shredded cellophane stuck to my sweaty face, temporarily blinding me. Off balance, I fell back into the chair.

Red-hot anger scoured the fear from my body. I swiped at my eyes.

"You drugged my ice tea. What the hell is going on?" I screamed.

Serena buried her face in her hands.

Janice smiled. When I looked in her eyes, I saw madness. Probably why she always gazed at the floor.

Despite brain fog and trembling knees, I stood, swaying like young sapling in a stiff wind. "This is crazy! I'm stuck in the house with you lunatics and

Serena didn't tell me one damn thing."

Janice wagged a finger at me. "Serena told you nothing? Doubtful. You have a relationship with the sheriff. It's just a matter of time before you connect the dots. Maybe you already have. Either way, you're a danger to us, so you won't be leaving."

Two spots of color rose in her cheeks. Rage flashed in her spooky eyes.

"I've been waiting for years to punish Mickey Warren. I was just a kid when he got me pregnant. He abandoned me. Wouldn't speak to me. My parents shamed me. Sent me away. Made me give up the baby. Trust me, the world is a better place without Mickey Warren. When Serena and Jon came, they needed money. Did you know people will do anything for money? And with Jon a pharmaceutical rep, he had the goods."

"You and Jon planned it! Not me!"

To my detriment, I was now aware of the whole sordid story. The odds of my escaping were slim to none. Still, I refused to go down without a fight. In spite of my impaired state and slurred words, I attempted to cop an attitude.

"Your plan sucks. You think you can get rid of me? Guess again. You'll have a mountain of trouble parked on your doorstep. The sheriff. My family. My co-workers. Friends. If you have any brains at all, you'll let me go and get the hell out of town."

"They have plan, Libby. Jon is going to make it look like an accident. He'll put your body in your car and—" Serena piped up.

"Shut up, Serena."

Ah, a glimmer of hope. At least I had one person

on my side. Even though she was the weakest link. Throwing caution to the wind, I willed my feet to move and charted an unsteady course toward the front door.

"Libby!" Serena called.

"Let her go," Janice said.

Let her go? Had she changed her mind?

Staggering, almost falling, head spinning and stomach flip-flopping, I made it through the kitchen and into the living room and ran into Jon. He blocked my way, fists clenched. He stepped closer, but froze when the doorbell rang.

I tried to scoot around him. He grabbed my arm and shoved me toward the couch. I stumbled backward, arms flailing. As it usually does, gravity won. As I plummeted to the floor, my forehead banged against the corner of a glass coffee table. Blood poured from the gash, blinding me. Groaning in pain, I tried to stand. To speak. I could do neither.

I swiped at the blood on my face and curled up in defensive mode. Snippets of conversation wafted through the room.

"Don't answer the door." Janice.

"You're both crazy!" Serena, screaming.

"I'll take care of it." Jon.

The last thing I heard before everything turned gray and fuzzy was Sofia's voice.

Chapter Forty-Three

Stunned by the blow to my head, I faded in and out of consciousness. My hands were bound behind my back. I was hoisted up.

"She's getting blood on my white carpet. Put her in the broom closet. I'll tell her daughter she went next door to talk to Stella Roy about some golf issue."

Even in my altered state, I marveled at her ineptitude. I knew my daughter. They didn't. Sofia wouldn't buy their version of the truth.

Jon slung me across his shoulder, staggered across the living room and into the kitchen. Grunting with effort, he opened the closet door and tossed me. Suddenly airborne, I braced for the landing.

My head bounced against the back of the closet. I slithered down the wall into a world of pain. Blood still dripped from the gash in my forehead. My skull felt like a bruised cantaloupe. Add to the mix a rumbling stomach and vertigo, complete with flashing disco lights. The door slammed shut. Stifling darkness closed in. I tried to control my rising panic. Unbidden, I was bombarded with terrifying images. Trapped forever. Walls moving in.

No way out.

Breathe in. Hold it. Breathe out. Focus on the strip of light at the bottom of the door. You're okay.

Despite the stern self-talk, my heart pounded

violently against my ribs. I bit my lip to stifle the scream of terror rising in my chest.

At some level, I was aware of footsteps and hushed voices. Random thoughts floated through my altered mind. How long would I be in the closet? Surely they'd wait for total darkness. By then, I'd be catatonic with fear, unable to defend myself. "Mom, it's me, Sofia!"

The scream I'd been holding back gathered strength and burst free. "Sofia, I'm here!"

"Where's my mom, you assholes? I know she's here! I heard her!"

Janice shouted orders. Jon spewed curses. Serena wept. And then the sickening sound of a blow followed by Sofia's howl of pain. Despite the agony shooting through my body, I inched my way across the closet and banged my feet against the door.

"Hurt my daughter again and I'll friggin' kill you."

The door flew open. Jon held a struggling Sofia in his arms. Her wrists were bound together by a strip of duct tape. Jon looked down at me and smirked.

"Yeah, I'm really scared."

He flung Sofia. Light streamed in through the open door. She took one look at my bloody face and passed out. Jon closed and locked the door.

I scooted next to her, wanting so badly to rock her in my arms, hug her, promise to keep her safe. I had to settle for pressing my body against hers.

"Sofia, love, I'm okay. It's just a little scratch. Please wake up. We need a plan if we're going to get out of here alive," I whispered.

She moaned and leaned into me, seemingly aware of my comfort.

Janice and Jon didn't bother to lower their voices

as they planned our demise.

"You've got the girl's cell phone and car keys, right? Move her car into the garage and close the door. Shoot a text message to her dad. Tell him she's spending the night with a friend." Janice.

"When it's completely dark, I give them both a little shot of night-night juice and load 'em into the kid's car."

Footsteps receded.

"But what if—?"

"No worries. Once the car goes over the cliff, there won't be enough left of them to test for cause of death." Jon.

His words slammed into me like runaway eighteen-wheeler barreling down the freeway toward an unsuspecting mini van. After the initial shock subsided, I realized I should be grateful to Jonathan Dumas. Claustrophobia was now the least of my worries. If I survived, I'd be sure to thank him.

The heady mixture of outrage and fury, along with a strong desire to live, chased the paralyzing fear from my body. We needed a plan. Sofia needed to wake up. I banged my shoulder against hers, none too gently.

"Sofia, for the love of God, if you want to live, wake up and help me!"

She stirred, her body stiffened and she struggled to sit up. "Sorry, Mom." She groaned. "Your face. It was all bloody. Are you hurt bad?"

"I'm okay."

She took a deep shuddering breath. "I'm okay, too."

"How did you find me?"

"You forgot your cell phone. Riley sent you a bunch of texts. Said he won't be back until tomorrow. I was heading out the door when Abigail Cavendish called. She saw you in the Pomeroy's backyard and wants you to stop by. Your car was still at the golf course, so I figured somebody picked you up."

A flicker of hope sparked to life. "So Abigail knows I'm here?"

"Yeah. Should we yell for help?"

"She's clear across the golf course, and Winston is deaf as a post."

I filled her in on the Pomeroy Plan for Death by Car Crash. After a moment of shocked silence, she leaned close.

"Guess what, Mom. We're not going down without a fight. So what's the plan?"

"Don't actually have one. We're in a broom closet. Maybe there's something in here we can use for a weapon."

"And do what?" Sofia asked. "Sweep them to death?"

"If you have a better idea, I'm listening," I replied, a bit miffed.

"Don't get bent out of shape. We'll figure something out. First off, we need to get our hands free."

Panic rose in my chest again. "As soon as it's dark, they're coming for us."

Sofia's voice was calm and reassuring. "Lucky for us it's the longest day of the year. The summer solstice."

I gulped back my fear. "I swear, if we get out of this alive, I'll dance naked in the moonlight every year on June twenty-first."

Despite our perilous situation, Sofia snickered. "Let's scoot around on our butts and see if we can find something useful."

"As quickly as possible. Tick, tick, tick."

Using our legs, we scrunched our way around the closet. Other than the broom and dustpan that fell from a hook onto my head, the search was fruitless.

"Jeez." Sofia snorted. "What kind of a weirdo only has a broom in her broom closet? Where's the mop and bucket? The vacuum cleaner and attachments? Cleaning supplies?"

I scooted back toward the door. Terrible images flashed through my mind. Sofia and I, helpless. Plummeting off a cliff to certain death.

Sofia broke the silence. "Are you wearing your charm bracelet?"

"Yes. Why?"

"There might be a something on it I can use to saw through your duct tape. My hands are taped together in front, not in back like yours."

Delicate butterfly wings of hope fluttered in my chest. "The golf tee charm might work. It has a sharp point. And remember the new charm you gave me at Christmas? It's a miniature golf green with a pole and flag. The flag is perpendicular to the green and has an edge to it. I always snag it on my clothes."

Sofia's voice quivered with excitement. "Okay, we have a plan."

I refused to think about the obvious. Even if we managed to free our hands, our only weapons were a broom and dustpan.

First things first.

Chapter Forty-Four

How hard could it be to position Sofia behind my back, her fingers gripping my charm bracelet, searching for the right tool?

Damn hard!

Might have been easier if we weren't in a pitch-dark broom closet. Squirming and sweating, we began maneuvering our bodies, using only our feet and sense of touch. I bit my tongue as Sofia barked out orders.

"Scoot around. No, the other way. Ouch, you sat on my fingers. Move up a little. No, not that far."

Once in position, I sucked in my gut, rolled forward, and stretched my arms back as far as humanly possible. "Can you reach the bracelet?"

Her bound hands slid down my arms. The charm bracelet jingled as she unclasped it.

"Got it."

"Try poking holes in it with the tee before you use the flag charm."

She sighed in exasperation. "Please, Mom, let me handle it. If I stab you with the tee until you bleed, I might faint again."

"It's dark. You won't be able to see the blood. By the way, do you know what they call fainting without awakening?"

"Mmm, no."

"Death. So stab away."

"Good point."

It was my turn to snicker. "Good point? Clever pun."

"Please shut up."

I gritted my teeth as she used the tiny tee to poke multiple holes with into the duct tape binding my wrists. I tried not to wince when the sharp point stabbed into the tender skin inside my wrist. "Hurry, hurry," I urged.

We froze at the sound of approaching footsteps.

"Maybe it's Serena," Sofia whispered.

"How ya doing, girls? Everything okey dokey in the broom closet?" Jon.

"Keep going. I'll do the talking," I whispered. "Snug as two bugs in a rug."

Sofia switched to the flag charm and began sawing at the duct tape. Blood trickled from the puncture wounds in my wrist.

"Enjoy your last hours together, ladies. I'll be back soon."

"Hey, Jon. I know you killed Mickey Warren, but why Tristan?"

"You think I killed Mickey? No way. Janice did the deed. Said she'd been waiting a long time for the opportunity." He barked in amusement.

After seeing the madness in Janice's eyes, the news did not come as a shock.

"Wanna hear something funny? Warren totally underestimated her. Janice knew his routine. When she showed up on the fairway, he said, 'How ya doing, Jannie? Out for a morning stroll?' I'm sure you know the rest. She chatted him up and followed him into the woods. When he bent over to pick up his golf balls, she jammed the needle into his butt. She said his look of surprise was priceless. He staggered out to the fairway and collapsed. Janice stayed inside the tree line and walked home."

"But why Tristan?"

"Serena and her big mouth. She told Tristan she felt guilty and never wanted Mickey to die. God only knows what else she told him. She was so damn drunk, she doesn't remember. Tris figured it out. He was hard up for money, kept dropping hints. No way were we going to let him cut in."

"So the insulin overdose wasn't an accident."

"He knew I had access to pharmaceuticals. I sold him insulin at a reduced price. I tinkered with the dosage and waited. Sooner or later, I knew he'd use the right one. Or in Tristan's case, the wrong one. The fact that he had your charm bracelet in his pocket was frosting on the cake. He planned to return it to you but guess what? He died before that could happen. Pretty cool, huh? Made you look guilty."

His cold-blooded confession sent a chill through my body. I pressed my lips together to suppress my outrage.

"Any more questions, Libby? How's your cute little daughter doing? Still passed out?"

Sofia drew a breath. Before she could speak, I snapped, "Yes, thanks to you."

"How convenient. You're the only one I'll need to tranquilize. Later, girls."

The floorboards creaked as he walked off. I still had unanswered questions, but I really wanted him to leave. We had work to do, escape plans to make.

"Asshole," Sofia muttered, still sawing away.

"Progress?"

"I've got it loosened. I'm going to use my teeth and try to rip it apart."

Still gripping my wrists, she grunted in effort. Thankfully, she was young and flexible. Her teeth scraped against my abraded skin. I clenched my teeth to keep from crying out.

"Sorry, Mom," she said.

Agonizing pain shot downward from my shoulders, but it didn't matter. My hands were free!

I shook my arms to restore the circulation and groped around until I could wrap my arms around Sofia. "You did it!"

She shook and tried to stifle her sobs. "I tasted blood. I made you bleed."

I gave her a little shake. "Big picture time. We'll get your hands free. Then we'll have a fighting chance to get out of here alive."

Her head bobbed up and down against my body in agreement. She pressed the charm bracelet into my hand.

Sofia's hands had been hastily bound together. I was able to loosen a corner of the overlapping tape with the sharp point of the tee. I gripped the corner and yanked. The sharp edge of the flag finished the job.

We struggled to our feet, did a little celebratory dance and tried to figure out what to do next.

When they came for us, we were ready. Sofia gripped the broom with both hands.

As footsteps approached our prison, I cautioned, "Remember what I said."

"Yes, Mother, I know. Go for the crotch."

"And then?"

"Run like hell."

The door flew open. Jon held a hypodermic needle in his right hand. Janice hovered in the background. No Serena.

Screeching like enraged wolverines, we burst from the closet. Sofia jabbed the business end of the broom handle into Jon's family jewels. Gripping the metal dustpan in two hands, I swung. It smacked into the side of his head with a satisfying clang.

Moaning in pain, he doubled over. I kicked the hypodermic needle across the room.

"Go, go!" I urged Sofia.

Her face was ashen, her gaze fixed on my face. Apparently, she'd forgotten the Run like Hell directive.

"Oh, my God, your face, Mom," she cried. "It's all bloody."

Jon, growling like a feral animal, began crawling after us.

I grabbed Sofia and dragged her toward the front door. "Now is not the time for hysterics. Get a grip."

Janice trotted after us, her eyes rolling in panic. She wrapped a bony hand around Sofia's arm. "Stop! I can explain."

It only took one little shove. She plopped down on her butt. I leaned close. "Let me explain. This is what happens when you try to separate a mother and daughter. "

Still towing a wobbly Sofia behind me, I opened the door and plowed into Abigail Cavendish. Her chauffeur, Henry Horncastle, stood next to her, holding a large black handgun.

Abigail looked me over, stepped backward and gasped. "Oh dear girl, you're covered in blood. I just knew you were in a pickle. I saw your daughter climb over the hedge and sneak in the back door."

Her words seemed to shimmer and float through the air before bouncing around my throbbing skull. A wave of dizziness swept over me. I tried to formulate an answer, but the words wouldn't come. Still gripping Sofia's hand, I staggered down the sidewalk, fixated on my goal, Abigail's limousine parked at the curb. With every step, it seemed to be farther away. My knees shook uncontrollably.

Sofia slid my arm around her shoulders and braced my body against hers. "We're okay, Mom. We're okay."

Darkness closing in. Vision fading to a pinpoint.

"Gotta make it to the car, baby girl. Then we'll be safe," I murmured before the light blinked out.

Chapter Forty-Five

One Week Later

Party kings Ronny and Donny had done it again. A giant banner was, of course, mandatory. This one read: LIBBY MONTGOMERY! SOFIA CARONE! OUR HEROES!

Granted, it was over the top. Nevertheless, Sofia and I agreed to enjoy every single moment, especially after our near-death experience. We had but one request: invite only those who were truly significant in our lives. It was a fruitless request. Therefore, half the town of Vista Valley showed up, including the mayor.

A large group of Fairway to Heaven golfers joined us. Jules brought her kids and boyfriend Pete. Gabe kept a watchful eye on Sofia. The entire Espinoza family was in attendance and had come bearing homemade tamales. Suzy's enormous tray of booty buns served with Ed's Special Dark vanished quickly. Abigail and Winston Cavendish mingled with the crowd, seemingly delighted to be among the riff-raff.

I'd insisted they invite Henry Horncastle, who'd been willing to come to our aid. In the spirit of generosity, we included his formidable wife Felicity. After ingesting a goodly amount of Ed's Special Dark, she was salsa dancing with Sammy Espinoza. Truly an unforgettable sight.

A raucous crowd spilled over into our backyard. Attack cat Clawdius was highly offended by their presence and ascended to the apricot tree where he glared down at the partygoers.

Riley and I sat at a table beneath the shade of a giant elm. A brisk breeze stirred the leaves, providing nature's air conditioning. Brilliantly plumed hummingbirds fought duals at the feeder hanging from a nearby limb.

Riley slid an arm around my shoulders. "Feeling okay?"

Since The Incident, the men in my life, namely my dad and Riley, had morphed into super-protective mode. Though I appreciated their concern, their constant hovering grated on my nerves.

Sofia set me straight.

"Here's the deal, Mom. They're consumed with guilt because they weren't around to knock the door down and rescue us. So be a good sport and let them hover."

With that in mind, I forced a grateful smile. "I'm fine, Riley. Just fine."

I knew what was coming. He gave me a squeeze. "Just checking since you were concussed."

Concussed was Riley and Dad's new favorite word. As in, 'Be careful when you drive. You've been concussed.' Or, 'Are you sure you should go back to work so soon after being concussed?'

It took every ounce of willpower not to roll my eyes and snarl something inappropriate. I gritted my teeth.

"The doctor said I'm good to go."

Apparently when Dumas tossed me head first into

the broom closet, the impact of my skull colliding with the wall rearranged my brain jelly. In addition to being concussed, the gash in my head required some stitching.

The lacerations on my wrists had scabbed over. The scars would be a permanent reminder of our imprisonment and my daughter's ingenuity. Fortunately, Sofia was physically unscathed. The medics treated her for shock, her reaction at seeing my blood-streaked face. All in all, mother and daughter were doing well.

I pushed away my irritation about overprotective males and snuggled into Riley's comfortable girth. "Any news on Dumas?"

His jaw tightened. He shook his head. "Vanished like a phantom in the night. He left his cell phone behind. Stole a neighbor's car and then dumped it in Ellensburg. Best guess is he's heading for Canada. Apparently he has a butt load of cash because there's no trace of him using credit cards."

The question keeping me awake at night remained unspoken. The look of hatred in Dumas's eyes had taken up permanent residence in my mind. I'd ruined his get-rich-quick scheme. Maybe he'd return to Vista Valley to even the score, go after Sofia. A shiver scampered down my spine.

Ever mindful, Riley picked up on my anxiety. He slid one hand along my cheek, tilting my face toward his.

"Look at me, Libby. If he comes back here, we'll nail him. Okay?"

I shook off my fear. "And if you don't, Dad and I will."

He chuckled. "That's my girl."

"What's happening with Serena?"

"She cooperated fully, said she got swept up in the whole scheme and couldn't figure out how to extricate herself. Looks like the judge will order her to a treatment facility followed by probation."

"Probably fair. At least Janice is locked up. She's a stone killer."

Riley looked away.

"What?"

"She got herself a high-priced lawyer He's asking for a mental evaluation."

"Mental evaluation?" I jumped up and glared down at him. "Here's my evaluation. She's batshit crazy. That doesn't mean she should walk free. Janice jabbed the needle into Mickey Warren's butt. Janice aided and abetted Dumas when he killed Tristan with an insulin overdose. For God's sake, Riley, it was Janice who came up with the plan to put us in a car and push it off a cliff."

Riley stood, slung an arm around my shoulders. Though he tried to hold it back, the corners of his mouth quirked upward in a smile. "I love your attitude. You'll make a hell of a witness for the prosecution. Janice won't walk free."

"Promise?"

"Yes, I promise."

A loud whistle pierced the air. Only one person I knew could produce a sound of that magnitude. My father. "All right, folks, it's time for the program. Our very own Sheriff Riley O'Connor will present the awards. Libby and Sofia, get your cute little buns over here," said Ronny.

"Program? Awards? I thought this was a backyard

party," I said.

Sofia and I were ushered onto a makeshift stage with Riley. Our friends and neighbors gathered around.

Riley held up a hand for silence. "Less than a year ago, I arrived in Vista Valley, a total stranger. When Mickey Warren's body was found on the golf course, I knew I needed help from an insider, someone who daily came in contact with dozens of her fellow citizens. That's when I asked Libby McKenna to be my eyes and ears at the golf course." He paused and glanced over at me. "Plus, look at her. She's hot!"

The crowd erupted into wolf whistles and laughter. Sofia lapsed into a fit of giggles. My cheeks warmed up.

When the noise subsided, Riley placed his right arm around me, his left around Sofia. He swallowed hard. "I didn't realize I was putting mother and daughter in harm's way. If you haven't heard the details about their ordeal, their bravery, and their determination to survive, I'd be happy to share it with you." He dipped into his shirt pocket and pulled out two gold badges. "Therefore, I'm happy to present honorary deputy sheriff badges to Elizabeth McKenna and her daughter, Sofia Carone."

Riley pinned on our badges amidst cheers and whoops from the crowd.

"And now," Riley said, maneuvering me front and center. "How about a few words from Libby?"

Public speaking was not my forte. I gave Riley a playful punch in the arm. "I may have to arrest you for that."

He offered me his wrists. "Anytime, baby, anytime."

After the laughter died down, I looked through the crowd until I spotted my dad. "I've done a lot of thinking the last few days. I'm incredibly lucky to be alive, to have a supportive family and caring friends. To our family, Fairway to Heaven is more than a golf course. It's our livelihood, our pride, and joy. You all know the motto, right?"

The crowd chanted, "You have to go through hell to get to heaven."

I nodded. "I guess you could say it's a metaphor for what Sofia and I experienced. Mickey Warren's body was found on A Woman Scorned. Trying to figure out who wanted him dead was as twisty as a Serpent's Tail. When Sofia and I were held captive at the Pomeroy house, believe me it was Purgatory Pit."

Vivid images of our ordeal flashed through my mind. I stopped and wiped my eyes. My hand trembled. Riley leaned close.

"Keep going. You're doing fine," he whispered.

I took a shaky breath and reached for Sofia's hand. "But we made it through Hell, Sofia and I. We made it to the back nine, Heaven. You all know Heaven has nine holes. Which one do you think we chose?"

Shouts of The Hereafter, Happy Hunting Grounds and Angel Crossing floated through the evening air. Dad raised his hand, opened and closed it three times. Hole number fifteen, Promised Land. I smiled and gave him a thumbs-up.

"That's right, Dad. When Sofia and I escaped from Purgatory Pit, we knew we reached the Promised Land."

I hugged my daughter. Tears streamed down her face. Dad joined us on the stage.

A loving family. Loyal friends. Priceless.

I gazed at the brilliant night sky, looking for the brightest star. When I found it, I repeated Sofia's words as we fled the Pomeroy house. "We're okay, Mom. We're okay."

A word about the author...

Marilee Brothers is a former teacher, coach, counselor, and the author of twelve books. Marilee and her husband are the parents of three grown sons and live in central Washington State.

After writing six young adult books, Marilee is once again writing for the adult market. She loves hearing from people who have read her books. Feel free to contact her at:

http://www.marileebrothers.com.
www.facebook.com/marilee.author
https://twitter.com/MarileeB
http://bookblatherblog.blogspot.com

The last website features aspiring and published authors as well as some tidbits of Marilee's own.

~*~

If you enjoyed this story, leaving a review at your favorite book retailer or reader website would be much appreciated. Thank you!

www.ingramcontent.com/pod-product-compliance
Lightning Source LLC
Chambersburg PA
CBHW051536260626
47170CB00003B/965
* 9 7 8 1 5 0 9 2 3 3 4 7 2 *